Beyond
the
Tomorrow
Mountains

Beyond
the
Tomorrow
Mountains

Sylvia Louise Engdahl

ILLUSTRATED BY RICHARD CUFFARI

Atheneum 1974 New York

Author's Note

This book, although wholly independent in its action, is a continuation of the story begun in THIS STAR SHALL ABIDE. *Readers who would like to know more about Noren's world—and about how he, as a villager, sought out its secrets, winning thereby the right to share the privileges and burdens of those working toward fulfillment of the Prophecy—may turn to that volume for a more complete explanation.*

To readers without knowledge of the Founding, it should be said that Noren's people are not descended from people of Earth; the solar system from which they came was not our own, and the faiths of their forefathers were unlike ours.

". . . The land was barren, and brought forth neither food nor pure water, nor was there any metal; and no men lived upon it until the Founding. And on the day of the Founding men came out of the sky from the Mother Star, which is our source. But the land alone could not give us life. So the Scholars came to bless it, that it might be quickened: they built the City; and they called down from the sky Power and Machines; and they made the High Law lest we forget our origin, grow neglectful of our bounden duties, and thereby perish. Knowledge shall be kept safe within the City; it shall be held in trust until the Mother Star itself becomes visible to us. For though the Star is now beyond our seeing, it will not always be so. . . .

"There shall come a time of great exultation, when the doors of the universe shall be thrown open and every man shall rejoice. And at that time, when the Mother Star appears in the sky, the ancient knowledge shall be free to all people, and shall be spread forth over the whole earth. And Cities shall rise beyond the Tomorrow Mountains, and shall have Power, and Machines; and the Scholars will no longer be their guardians. For the Mother Star is our source and our destiny, the wellspring of our heritage; and the spirit of this Star shall abide forever in our hearts, and in those of our children, and our children's children, even unto countless generations. It is our guide and protector, without which we could not survive; it is our life's bulwark. And so long as we believe in it, no force can destroy us, though the heavens themselves be consumed! Through the time of waiting we will follow the Law; but its mysteries will be made plain when the Star appears, and the sons of men will find their own wisdom and choose their own Law."

—from the Book of the Prophecy

I

THE ROOM WAS HIGH IN ONE OF THE CITY'S TOWERS. ITS window viewed a vast panorama of grain fields dappling gray-purple wilderness, and of more wilderness beyond: a vista rimmed by the jagged yellow ridges of the Tomorrow Mountains. Noren was not looking at the view, however. His back to it, he sat nervously on the edge of a low couch, eying the closed-circuit video built into the opposite wall and thinking of the heavy responsibility that soon would fall to him. He was too young and unskilled to conduct an interview so crucial as the one to come; he had been told that frankly—still it was deemed best that he be entrusted with it. He'd accepted the job gladly, despite his inexperience. Only now, with the time at hand, had he begun to feel other misgivings.

The screen before him showed the ceremony taking place outside the City, on the wide stone platform before the Gates. It was a public recantation. The robes of the Scholars were brilliant blue against the white pavement, a sharp

3

contrast to the green uniforms of the Technicians and the mud-stained gray garment of the prisoner whom they guarded. The crowd in the plaza was not visible, being behind the camera, but the audio picked up hostile murmurs. The sentencing was over and the people were beginning to jeer again, though they would throw no actual dirt in the Scholars' presence; it would not be seemly, for Scholars were High Priests and were revered.

The prisoner, Brek, knelt before the Scholars, his hands bound behind him. His hair had been cropped short, a sign of penitence and shame, but there was neither penitence nor shame in his bearing; he held his head high. Through the ordeals of the ceremony, his spirit had not faltered. The spectators might think that he'd been broken, but it was not true. On the contrary, Brek had just passed the final test of indomitability.

Noren's heart warmed with sympathy and admiration. It took courage to do what Brek was doing. He was a heretic; he had maintained that it was wrong for the Scholars to keep their knowledge secret and that the sacred Prophecy in which the villagers and Technicians believed was a fraud, a foolish story invented to forestall rebellion against the priest caste's supremacy. He'd refused to recant despite his assumption that refusal was punishable by death. Yet now he was recanting after all, voluntarily denying most of his former convictions, though it meant exposing himself not only to the contempt of believers, but to the abuse and scorn of fellow-rebels who would think that he had sold out.

Noren understood how hard an act that was; he had recanted himself less than a year before.

Loud music burst forth, drowning the noise of the crowd, as the attending Scholars, in solemn procession, left the platform. Noren switched off the screen; Brek had been surrounded by a protective cordon of Technicians and was no longer in sight. A few minutes later the door of the room

4

slid open and the Scholar Stefred, Chief Inquisitor, stood in the archway, still clad in his ceremonial robe. Unfastened, it flapped open to reveal plain beige clothing like Noren's own. "Brek's on his way up here," he said. "I'll leave you alone with him; you can help him more than I can at this point. Set his mind at ease, Noren."

Noren nodded. "I'll try. He must have caught the symbolism of what was happening to him out there; he took it well."

"Very well indeed, and it was a greater triumph for him than for you; he lacks your natural self-confidence. But as you know, the next step's difficult, and Brek has suffered more than you did. You had nothing in your past life to feel guilty about."

"Neither does he."

"No, but he thinks he does, and I couldn't let him know otherwise. In the early stages of his inquisition I had to play on it." Stefred sighed, troubled. "I was ruthless with Brek. I manipulated him more cruelly than I do most heretics; that's necessary in the case of a Technician. I wouldn't have done it if I hadn't been sure of him, and even surer of you. How you handle the next few days will determine whether it leaves lasting scars."

Alone once more, Noren paced back and forth with growing apprehension. He hoped fervently that Stefred's confidence would prove justified, for he owed Brek a great deal. The two had met only briefly, some time back, when as a villager Noren had never imagined friendship with a Technician; Technicians, who lived in the enclosed City and were permitted to handle machines, were of a higher caste than villagers and were viewed by most of them with awe, though Noren himself had felt bitter envy. Yet Brek had defied both custom and religious law in an attempt to save him from the heretic's supposed fate: punishment, perhaps torture, at the hands of the Chief Inquisitor. In those days

5

neither of them had shared the prevailing trust in the Scholars' goodness.

Once actually in Stefred's hands, one learned to trust, but the trust developed gradually. Terror had to come first. At the outset Stefred concealed his true sympathies, not only to test the prisoner's resolution but because he knew that no committed heretic who doubted his own ability to withstand terror would be able to make an objective decision about voluntary recantation. During the inquisition, before learning the secret facts about the Prophecy, a heretic must feel real fear: worse fear than of the rumored death sentence to which he was resigned. With Noren there'd been no need to generate that fear; as a villager to whom the forbidden City was awesomely mysterious and who had never before seen a Scholar at close range, he had been sufficiently terrified by his mere surroundings. For a Technician it was different. Noren knew what had been done to make Brek afraid, and he did not like to think about it; it was a grim piece of deception. Not that any lies had been told—but Brek's imagination must have tormented him in more ways than one during the solitary confinement he'd experienced.

Again the door opened, and this time it was Brek who appeared. His wrist manacles had been removed, but he still wore the gray penitent's garb; he'd had no opportunity to remove it or to wash the mud from his face and arms. Though at one time Noren would have raged at the idea of a person's being subjected to such degradation, he knew that what Brek had undergone had not been degrading. Stefred never degraded anyone. Heretics who agreed to recant under pressure were not exposed to the abuse of the crowd. Those permitted to face such abuse did not suffer from it; one mark of a man ready to share the Scholars' secrets was his ability to endure outward humiliation without loss of inner dignity.

6

Brek's difficulties weren't over, to be sure—nor, for that matter, were Noren's. The consequences of heresy were grave. They changed the course of one's whole life, and the interval since Noren's own recantation was still relatively short. During that interval he had acquired both privileges and burdens; to these he must now introduce Brek. *Set his mind at ease,* Stefred had said . . . yet, Noren reflected ruefully, he himself felt no peace of mind. There were certain things he dared not let himself contemplate, and it would be hard to keep them out of the coming discussion. In the past half hour uncertainty had stricken him. Was it right to keep such things out, to conceal from Brek his recent fear that the Prophecy's fulfillment was less sure than one believed when, in recanting, one affirmed it?

The escort of Technicians withdrew. Brek stepped forward into the room, his drawn face lighting with startled recognition. "I didn't know whether they'd let me see you," he said, his voice low but steady. "I wanted to, Noren, though I don't suppose you can ever forgive me."

"No, I can't," said Noren, determined to keep worry from his smile. "There's nothing to forgive."

"But you were condemned because of me! You were living a normal life back in your village until I tricked you into a public admission of heresy."

"You did the job assigned to you, as you were bound to under the High Law. And then after the village council convicted me, you helped me to escape from jail; you gave me your Technician's uniform and stayed behind in my place! You claimed you weren't risking anything, but I know better now."

"I wasn't arrested for that," protested Brek. "Oh, I was accused of it later, but not until I'd balked at setting a trap for somebody else."

Noren sat down on the couch, offering a place to Brek, who after slight hesitation joined him. "You've gotten to

7

know Stefred, and you've learned that he was sincere when he told you that it's better for a heretic to be trapped than to be caught accidentally when there are no Technicians around to protect him from his fellow villagers," Noren said. The High Law required anyone convicted of heresy to be turned over to the Scholars unharmed; but without Technicians to enforce this, there was real peril, for people who blasphemed against the Prophecy—or worse, against the Mother Star itself—were deeply despised by villagers and were occasionally murdered.

"I know Stefred tries to suppress heresy without hurting anybody," Brek agreed. "I know he doesn't torture or kill those who won't recant. But I didn't know it *then*."

"So the second time, you defied him openly and were brought to trial for it?"

"Yes. Originally I was charged only with disobeying orders, but when the Council of Technicians asked me why I'd done it—well, I told them. From then on it was a full-scale heresy trial, though not much like the farce you went through with that self-righteous village council. Afterward, during the inquisition, the emphasis was on what I believe, not how I'd acted."

"Was it rough?" Noren inquired, knowing that it had been, and that talking about it would help to heal the wounds.

"No rougher than I deserved," Brek answered grimly. "It seemed ironic the way the punishment fit the crime: not heresy, which is no real crime at all, but the part I'd played in your conviction. You see, there was a time when they let me think they'd broken you."

"Stefred told me," said Noren. The stress of a heretic's inquisition was not intended as punishment, and Brek must be made to realize that. "I'd convinced you that I'd never recant, no matter what they did; you honestly believed that I could hold out despite the rumors that nobody ever has.

8

So they showed you films of my recantation—edited films, the worst parts—without any comment at all, and then they locked you up to think it over."

In agony, Brek confessed, "I almost cracked up, Noren. I hadn't even known that you'd been recaptured! I'd been clinging to the hope that you'd escaped, that I hadn't really brought you any harm. But after those films, I could only think that heretics must be subjected to something more terrible than either of us imagined. I knew you wouldn't have given in to save your life, or even to spare yourself pain, at least not beforehand—"

"Neither would you," Noren interrupted. "That's why it was done: to prove that you wouldn't."

"To Stefred?"

"No. He was already sure; if he hadn't been, he'd never have risked using that kind of pressure. His aim was to prove it to *you*."

"But Noren," Brek admitted unhappily, "I wasn't sure at all! I was shaking so hard I could hardly stand when I was taken to see him again; I didn't know how I'd answer until I heard my own voice."

"That's the point. Stefred knew you weren't going to crack—but you didn't, not till the moment came. And you needed to know. You wouldn't have felt right about recanting if you hadn't been shown that you could have held out if you'd chosen to."

Brek nodded slowly. "That's true. He never did try to force me to do anything against my will! I got the feeling that he respected me for defying him, even for disobeying his orders in the first place; I just wish I'd done it sooner." Bowing his head, he added miserably, "Nothing can change the fact that you'd be free now if I had."

Noren regarded him, concerned. This must be settled quickly, for his main task was to bring Brek face to face with a more difficult dilemma. "Brek," he asked seriously, "are you sorry you became a heretic? Do you regret speaking out against the Prophecy and the High Law when you were tried?"

"Of course not. They wanted me to say I was during the ceremony, but I drew the line there and was pronounced impenitent, though I was warned that that'll affect what becomes of me." He faced Noren with returning pride. "I don't care! I recanted because they proved that the High Law is necessary to keep people alive on this planet until the Prophecy can be fulfilled, but I'm not sorry for having challenged it."

"That isn't what I mean," Noren said. "I refused to fake penitence, too, and as a matter of fact that's what Stefred hoped we'd do; the official script we were offered was designed to give us the satisfaction of rejecting it. But are you sorry all this happened, that you've been told secrets that will keep you confined here in the Inner City for the rest of your life?"

"No," Brek declared. "It—it's worth whatever comes, I guess, to know the truth."

"Then don't you suppose it's worth it for me? Truth was what I cared most about, what I set out to find, and I couldn't have found it back in the village."

Brek stared at him. "I haven't looked at it that way. I thought only of your being imprisoned." He glanced around the room, with its comfortable though austere furnishings and its breathtaking view, for the first time aware of the strangeness of a prisoner's being left unguarded in such a place. "What's it like, Noren? I've been told nothing."

Noren hesitated. He remembered only too well how it felt to be told nothing: to kneel on the hot shimmering pavement and hear the grim sentence, *Perpetual confinement, subject to such disciplines as we shall impose,* and to know that despite the Scholars' kindness, that sentence was no more a lie than any of the earlier and more frightening warnings. "It's hard to accept at first," he said frankly, "but

10

not much like what you're expecting. You'll be surprised." This was not the time to mention that some of the surprises would be pleasant, since for someone in Brek's position the wished-for things were the hardest to accept of all.

"Stefred said I'd be equal to it," Brek reflected.

"He tells everyone that. He means it, too, because no one gets this far who isn't. People who don't qualify rarely get past the inquisition phase."

"Qualify? That's an odd way to put it."

"You didn't know you were being tested?"

"Well—well, yes, at some points. It was pretty clear that they wouldn't have let me in on any secrets if I'd been willing to recant under threat, or if I'd accepted the bribe they offered."

"It's more complicated than that. There are still secrets to learn, Brek; so far you've not heard the most important one. They think I'm the best person to enlighten you." Noren smiled, trying to seem reassuring, though he still found it incredible that he should tutor Brek: Brek, who was nearly two years older than he, who'd been born a Technician, trained in electronics instead of farming, and whom he had once addressed as "sir"!

"You enlightened me to start with," Brek told him. "I might never have known I was a heretic if it hadn't been for what you said at your trial."

"That's why you were sent to observe it," said Noren levelly.

"You mean Stefred *knew* how I'd react? But then why—" He broke off, appalled. "Noren, was I led into a trap, as you were? Was the whole thing planned?"

"Yes. From the beginning." Pausing again, Noren wondered what tactics to pursue. There were no hard-and-fast rules, but he must proceed carefully, he knew; he must cushion the shock. Brek must figure out as much as he could for himself.

Brek's eyes were anguished. "I'd come to trust them."

11

"Why?" Noren asked. "You've known all along that Scholars watch anyone suspected of having heretical ideas."

"They don't like the way things are any better than we do, though," Brek asserted. "They don't want to keep machines away from the villagers, and they don't want to hide their knowledge; they're doing it only because they have no choice. And as for being venerated as High Priests—well, they hate it."

"All of them? Or just Stefred?"

"Stefred's the only one I've ever really talked to, I suppose. But in the dreams—"

"In the dreams you shared the First Scholar's recorded memories and you knew what he believed, what the other Founders believed; you knew that they never sought power. Yet they lived long ago. What's to prove that all their successors are like them? What's to say some aren't out for personal gain, as you claimed at your trial?"

"Why, I—" Brek stopped, frowning. "*You* weren't at *my* trial."

"I've heard the transcript of it." Slowly, aware that having broached the key issue, he must say something more direct, Noren added, "I've also dreamed those dreams a second time, Brek, and they're—different. There are things in the recordings that only Scholars are permitted to know."

"Then how do you know them?"

Noren drew breath, his heart pounding. The most painful part of his job could be put off no longer. "I am a Scholar now, Brek," he admitted steadily. "I don't wear the robe, but I'm entitled to."

Stunned, Brek recoiled from him, then rose and walked away. "I've been naive," he declared dully. "Before revealing the truth they offered me further training in exchange for unqualified submission, and I turned them down . . . would they have gone *that* far if they'd wanted me enough?" With a bitter laugh he added, "You've a sharper mind than

12

I have; you'll be useful to them. I don't wonder you could set your own price."

Fury spread in a hot wave through Noren, but he kept his face impassive. Brek couldn't be blamed. It occurred to him that Stefred would have foreseen this, that his own levelheadedness was no doubt being evaluated; the challenges of the training period were at times no less demanding than the qualifying ones. And if he failed to meet this one, it was Brek who would be hurt.

"My recantation was as sincere as yours," he said quietly, "and I knew no more of what was in store for me than you did. You see, the biggest secret—the one that was edited out of the dreams—concerns the scheme of succession. The status of Scholar is neither sold nor inherited; it is earned. No man or woman attains it whose trustworthiness is unproven. If you doubt that, remember that you could not have knelt to Stefred and the others, even ceremonially, if there'd been any question in your mind about their honesty."

Brek turned and for a long moment appraised Noren in silence, noticing the lines of weariness in his face, marks that made him seem older than his years. "There's no question about yours," he said finally. "I don't understand everything yet, but one thing's clear: somehow they recognized that, even in a former heretic, and bestowed rank and power where it was deserved." Approaching the couch where Noren still sat motionless, he continued, "I never knelt to Stefred in private, at least not after my arrest; while I hated him I ignored the conventions, and then later I sensed that he disliked them as much as I. Before the crowd I did it simply in honor of what he stood for. But I kneel to you, sir, as I now have new cause to beg your forgiveness." He dropped to his knees as was customary in addressing a Scholar, not subserviently but with dignity, his eyes meeting Noren's without flinching.

13

"No!" exclaimed Noren hastily, sliding to the floor himself and gripping Brek's outstretched hands. "Not to me, and never again to Stefred. And you don't call me 'sir,' either. Those customs don't apply; we're equals."

"Stefred's acknowledged me his equal in all the ways that matter. If Scholars must pass some special test of worthiness, that makes them all the more entitled to the courtesy due their rank. Do you think I'd want such status myself?"

"You have it whether you want it or not," said Noren gently, "since you too have earned it."

Brek drew back with incredulous dismay. "Scholar rank? But that's awful; it can't possibly work like that! I wouldn't have recanted if I'd known there'd be any such reward."

"Nor would the rest of us; that's one reason we weren't told."

"The rest of us . . . there are others?"

"All the others, even Stefred, when he was young! He wasn't born a Scholar; no one is. Scholars' children are given up for adoption. All candidates prove themselves in the same way."

Outraged, Brek persisted, "You mean the whole system's a sham—those chosen must demonstrate their outlook toward this setup, with all its evils, by humbly submitting to a ceremony of recantation?"

"No," Noren assured him. "Not by recantation, but by unrepented heresy."

*

It was past noon, and there was barely time left for Brek to bathe and dress before the refectory closed. That was just as well, Noren thought; there would be fewer people to confront than had greeted him during his own first meal as a Scholar. One was not permitted to retreat from one's new status; however great the strain, one was plunged immediately into the regular routine of Inner City life, and the adjustment was trying. It was supposed to be. Villagers

14

and Outer City Technicians assumed that Scholars knew no hardship; the sooner a heretic learned that this was not the case, the sooner he could overcome his natural resistance to membership in a "privileged" caste. All the same, the traditional requirement that he appear in the Hall of Scholars' refectory shortly after recantation, maintaining his poise while receiving with bewildered embarrassment the congratulations of men and women hitherto viewed as a class apart, imposed arduous demands.

Brek bore up well, though his face was set and he spoke little as he and Noren made the rounds of the occupied tables. "The first few days are rough," Noren told him when they were settled with their food at a small table in a corner. "But once you get started on your training, you won't have time to worry about anything else. And you'll like it. Stefred says you're well-fitted to become a scientist; you always wanted to do such work, didn't you, even before you learned what the Scholars' main job is?"

"Not at the price of outranking people who have no chance to learn."

"We don't. Anyone on this planet is eligible to earn Scholar status; scientific aptitude has nothing to do with it. Some of us study other fields, or choose work that doesn't require study. The old lady who filled our trays, for instance —she was a basket-weaver in her village, and a grandmother; the council that convicted her of heresy thought she was a witch. Most women like that turn out to have no real heretical convictions, and they become Inner City Technicians without being required to recant, but not this one. She had her doubts about the justice of the High Law, and Stefred couldn't shake her. So he took her the whole way: the dreams, recantation in its most difficult form, everything. She works in the refectory kitchen now, but she ranks the same as a fully trained scientist and her vote has equal weight."

15

"Maybe so," Brek protested, "still, I'm never going to feel right about the system."

"Naturally you're not," agreed Noren. "Don't you see, Brek? A person who doesn't think anything's the matter with it isn't fit to hold power! The caste system necessary to human survival here is evil. The system whereby Scholars control all machines and all knowledge is evil, even though the villagers run their own affairs and enforce the High Law themselves through their elected councils. We who were heretics knew it was, and said so; we got ourselves tried and convicted and we refused to recant, believing we'd die for it. No one who's not that strongly opposed to such evils can qualify."

"But in the end we did recant."

"We're impenitent, though. We still have the same values, the same goals; we recanted only when we found that the other Scholars share them." Noren spoke firmly, doing his best not to rouse the conflicting feelings he'd suppressed during nearly a year of concentration on study. He had allowed the thrill of absorbing knowledge he'd always craved to engross him, but some of that knowledge had been disturbing. Some of it had raised questions that had not occurred to him at the time of his recantation, questions he did not want to think of, much less discuss with Brek.

They had both recanted because of the secret that was revealed to them through controlled dreams, the secret of the Founding: of how their ancestors had actually come from the sky as the Book of the Prophecy said, having traveled through space from the Six Worlds of their home solar system; and of how when their sun became a nova and destroyed those worlds, the First Scholar and others who'd escaped with him had come to the planet, dismantled their starships and sealed the life-support equipment that enabled their race to survive in a literally poisonous land safe within the City to keep that equipment from being lost. The planet

16

lacked the resources necessary to sustain life; native vegetation was inedible, unprocessed water undrinkable, and even the soil required periodic treatment. Worse, there were no metals suitable for fabrication of the essential machines. The people who staffed the original research station hadn't planned to settle permanently on such a planet. If they'd known about the nova, their spirit would have been crushed; they'd had strong ties with their mother worlds and they couldn't have borne the idea that they were the only ones left alive out of the entire human race. What was more, they'd have realized that their descendants had no chance of survival without the metallic elements needed to manufacture more equipment. Once they'd given up hope, they would have stopped bothering to avoid unpurified water, suffered chromosome damage, and produced offspring with subhuman intelligence.

The First Scholar had not allowed that to happen. Instead, to explain why the former research-station staff was shut out of the newly built City and why no more supply ships arrived, he had pretended to be insane. He'd set himself up as an apparent dictator, knowing that people would hate him and eventually kill him for it, and had kept silent about his reason for depriving them of all that must be safeguarded for posterity. Even when he lay dying—when he recorded his idea for the religion through which an abiding hope was to be sustained—his wish had been that the truth about him should never be known to any but those judged fit for stewardship; he had not wanted to be idolized as prophet and martyr.

"What went on before the ceremony this morning was— arranged, wasn't it?" Brek asked. "I relived the dream where the First Scholar was killed; I stood in the same spot outside the Gates while people threw mud at me, just as they'd thrown stones and knives at *him*. At first I was so stunned I thought I'd lose control of myself, and then it

17

dawned on me that Stefred meant me to feel—well, honored."

"Of course. He honored you by recognizing that you look at things the way Scholars do, that you'd understand the symbolism, as well as the fact that if people like the ones in the crowd were given no outlet for their hatreds there'd eventually be bloodshed. But he meant you to feel something more, Brek."

Noren glanced around the smooth windowless walls of the refectory—ancient walls that had been constructed on one of the Six Worlds, since the Hall of Scholars, like all the Inner City's towers, was in reality a converted starship—and then raised his eyes to the prismatic glass sunburst, symbol of the Mother Star, that was fixed to the center of the ceiling. "We agreed to go through that ceremony," he continued slowly, "because we'd learned not only that the prophesied appearance of the Mother Star is based on fact, but that changes are honestly expected to occur when the Star does appear. The Prophecy is what keeps people hoping. It's the only means of telling them that the world won't always be as it is now. In time, when the light of the nova reaches this planet and the real Mother Star becomes visible, the Prophecy's promises must come true; yet they can't be fulfilled if we don't manage to synthesize usable metal by then."

Brek frowned. "Is there any question about it? The starships that escaped the nova got here generations ago, and Scholars have been working ever since to create metallic elements through nuclear fusion. Haven't they been making progress?"

"Brek," Noren said sadly, "you can't say *they* any more; you've got to say *we*. We're working under terrible handicaps—even worse handicaps than you could guess from the dreams—and if those of us who've proven ourselves fit for the job don't do it, the Prophecy will become as false and

18

empty as we thought it was when we laughed at what sounded like a silly legend."

The words seemed stiff. Was it really possible, mused Noren, that he was not giving Brek the whole truth? Was he hiding not merely fear, but fact? He was repeating what he himself had once been told; he'd been utterly convinced of its validity; yet deep inside, he sensed that dreadful doubts were stirring. Pushing them back, he went on, "When we re-enact the dream, we take on all the responsibility it implies. That's what we're meant to feel, not so much during the ceremony as afterward, when it seems that we've been duped into selling out."

Thoughtfully Brek said, "I'm willing to do any work I'm given, just as I was willing to do what had to be done to uphold people's respect for the Prophecy and the High Law. But becoming a Scholar is something else again. It means giving the impression that I'm in favor of the way things are."

"You've already done that; you made your decision when you consented to the ceremony. What's the difference now?" Noren averted his face as he spoke, for he knew perfectly well what the difference was; night after night he had lain awake for hours on end, unable to come to terms with it. He wondered if he was hoping that Brek would tell him that no real difference existed.

"The difference," declared Brek bluntly, "is that during my recantation I was hated, but most people don't hate Scholars nowadays. They worship them."

Their eyes met, and there was no need to say anything further; neither of them was wearing the blue robe of priesthood, and that was not merely because the occasion wasn't formal enough to warrant it. "It's rightfully yours," Noren had said when he'd given Brek the clean clothes set aside for him, "but you need not put it on unless you choose to. The robe's a symbol; among us it represents full commitment. Scholar status was conferred on us without our knowledge or consent, but we are free to decide how we'll use that status, and whether we'll reveal it to anyone besides our fellow Scholars. So far I'm committed only to scientific training."

He had agreed to train for the research work that must be done if synthesization of metal was to be achieved, because Stefred had convinced him that he'd betray his own principles if he refused to contribute actively toward the Prophecy's fulfillment. It had been a difficult step to take, since like Brek he'd longed desperately for the training and had been incensed at the idea of receiving such an incredibly high privilege as the result of having conceded that the world could not be transformed overnight; still, reason had told him that it was the only course. The work was an obligation, not a reward, and the fact that he would enjoy it did not make it any less vital. But to assume the role of High Priest—to share responsibility for the control of the City's contents, or to appear in public, when he was old enough not to be recognized as a former villager, and receive people's homage—of that he wasn't at all sure. Yet somebody had to do it. Stefred hated it, and for that matter, so had the First Scholar. And the First Scholar had been wise enough to arrange things so that nobody who wanted that kind of power would ever have it.

The First Scholar had been wise in many ways, but his greatest accomplishment had been the creation of a scheme under which power could be held only by those who, under pressure, had proven themselves incorruptible. Never in the history of the Six Worlds had there been such a scheme; authoritarian systems, benevolent or otherwise, had always selected leaders from among their supporters instead of their opponents. The First Scholar had loathed the forced stratification of society he'd established; while he'd been aware that without it, the human race would be unable to preserve the essential life-support equipment during the generations when the growing population must live and farm by Stone Age methods, his plans had centered on the day when the system could be abolished. He had had the wisdom to know that it would never be abolished if people who approved of it wound up on top.

So through the years, the secret truths had been passed to those who approved *least:* those who had offered their lives in opposition to the supposed tyranny. To be sure, some heretics failed to qualify; they were motivated by desire to seize power for themselves or they weakened during the stress of the inquisition and its aftermath; but these people suffered no harm. Though they could not be released, they had the status of Technicians and did work of their own choosing.

And the Scholars themselves could not be released, neither from the physical confines of the Inner City nor from the unsought burden of representing a system which, while indispensable to mankind's survival in the alien environment, was abhorrent to them. It was they, not the villagers, who lived in bondage.

"It's not easy," Noren declared as he and Brek left the Hall of Scholars and walked through the Inner City's enclosed courtyard toward one of the other towers, where Brek was to lodge with him.

"Stefred warned me in the beginning that a day would come when the consequences of my choice would seem so terrible that I'd beg to be let off," Brek admitted. "I thought he was threatening to kill me, and I scoffed. Later I thought he'd been referring to the nightmarish parts of the dreams, or to the ceremony, or to imprisonment. But this—"

"This is worse than anything we envisioned," agreed Noren. "We dedicated ourselves to resisting the Scholars' authority, and now we've become what we most despised."

On leaving the lift at the level of Noren's cubicle, they

21

paused by the passageway window. The afternoon had gone swiftly; it was dusk, and the ring of large domed structures—the Outer City—that encircled the clustered towers looked dark and forbidding, an even more impenetrable barrier from within than it had once seemed from without. "Noren," Brek ventured, "in your village . . . there was a girl, Talyra, wasn't there? A girl you'd planned to marry?"

Noren lowered his eyes; it still hurt to think about that, and he did not want to speak of it. "Scholars aren't barred from marriage," he said. "We can even marry Technicians."

"But not villagers."

"No," Noren replied shortly. He did not add that when certain conditions were met, villagers already married or betrothed to heretics could become Technicians, and that he'd dismissed the matter because he'd felt that in the City Talyra would be fearful and unhappy.

For a few moments they were silent. Far away across the fields stood the sharp silhouette of the Tomorrow Mountains, now pale below three crescent moons. *"'And Cities shall rise beyond the Tomorrow Mountains, and shall have Power, and Machines, and the Scholars will no longer be their guardians,'"* Brek quoted softly. "How soon, I wonder? It's not all going to happen on the day the Star appears! If we're to be ready by then, the Prophecy must begin to come true long before."

Noren, upset by Brek's uninformed confidence, did not answer. Then, behind them, a voice said, "Maybe it will be sooner than you think, at least in a small way."

Turning to greet the Scholar Grenald, the oldest and most distinguished of his tutors, Noren demanded, "What do you mean? Could it start in our lifetime after all?" The Time of the Prophecy—fixed by the distance in light-years to the Six Worlds' exploded sun and chosen by the First Scholar not only for its symbolic value, but because sur-

22

vival without more metal could scarcely continue long past the time the light of the nova would arrive—was still several generations in the future.

Though Grenald smiled, the worry in his tone belied the hopefulness of his words. He looked at Noren intently, pleadingly, as if he somehow expected confirmation from a mere trainee. "It could," he said. "You're aware that it will start as soon as the research succeeds—"

"Of course," agreed Noren hastily. The old man had been engaged for years in a series of experiments that was soon to culminate, and its outcome would give an idea of how much more research was needed; some Scholars felt that the results might point the way to an impending break-through. "We could be close, Grenald," Noren declared. But as he spoke undeniable fear surged up in his mind, for he knew that if they were not close, they might not be on the right path.

And if that was the case, the Prophecy might never come true . . . yet he and Brek, like others before them, had publicly denied their heresy solely on the grounds that it would.

*

That night Noren dreamed he was the First Scholar again. It was not a controlled dream induced by the Dream Machine that fed recorded thoughts into one's brain; but since experiencing those in which he'd shared the First Scholar's thoughts, their content had recurred often in his natural dreams, particularly when he was tired or troubled. The controlled dreams of the revelation hadn't been enjoyable; they had been nightmares. Though after the first Noren had submitted to them willingly, his hunger for the truth being stronger than his fear, the emotions they'd roused still frightened him.

So over and over, when he slept, he watched the nova explode into a blinding sphere of intolerable fire that filled the starship's viewport; and usually he awakened then,

23

drenched with sweat and hoping that he had not cried out aloud. But this time he dreamed on, images from his personal past mingling with those from the controlled dreams. He was the First Scholar, weighed down with the grief of what had been and what he knew must come, yet he walked through a village the First Scholar had never seen: the village where he, Noren, had been born. He saw the place—the rough stone houses, the sanded roads marred by sledge tracks and the hoofs of plodding work-beasts, the desolate gray shrubby areas surrounding quickened fields—through a Scholar's eyes, and it seemed even more dreary than when he'd been growing up there. He had the First Scholar's memory of the Six Worlds, of a civilization that had built interstellar ships! He was a stranger in the world where he found himself. . . .

Yet even in the dream he was aware that it had always been that way. He'd been a misfit since childhood, for most villagers were not unhappy; they did not crave the sort of knowledge he had craved, or care about truth as he had always cared. They were content with the life they had. The Technicians who brought Machines to clear the land and to quicken it never interfered with anyone's personal freedom, and who but the impious would envy their right to handle those Machines? Who but a presumptuous fool would be concerned over why even greater wonders were reserved for the City alone?

"You are a fool, a lazy dreamer," Noren's brothers said to him as, dreaming, he found himself back in the house of his family. They were right, he suspected; he had no aptitude for crafts or trading and he was ill-suited to be a farmer, though for Talyra's sake he was prepared to try. He must try something, for he had absorbed the meager offerings of the village school and was a grown man by his people's standards, although on the Six Worlds he would have been thought too young to work, much less to marry.

24

Such wasn't the case in this land of more primitive custom; his impending marriage was the one thing to which he looked forward with pleasure. . . .

But even Talyra could not understand the urge that drove him to question the Prophecy. And so he turned his face to the City, the impenetrable stronghold of all knowledge, compelled by some inner longing that outweighed his belief that to enter it would mean death. In the way of dreams, his view was abruptly transposed. He feared not the City, but a future that might imperil it. While dreaming, he knew that if there were no City everyone would die, and that if none dared challenge its mysteries, there would be no Scholars to keep it functioning. The ground he trod was permeated with a substance damaging to life that had evolved elsewhere; because the mutations it caused reduced mental capacity to a subhuman level, no biological adaptation would ever be possible. Machines must continue to inactivate the substance so that imported grain could be raised. The City was needed to guard all machines: not only those used in the fields, but the more complex ones for rainmaking, for purifying additional water, for irradiating grain seed—and for generating the nuclear power upon which the other machines depended. And of course, the City must safeguard the computers. In those computers' memories was stored the accumulated knowledge of the Six Worlds, and if that were ever lost, there would be no second beginning. There would be no chance of achieving what must be achieved if the new world was to become a place where men could thrive. . . .

"And the land shall remain fruitful, and the people shall multiply across the face of the earth, and at no time shall the spirit of the Mother Star die in the hearts of men." He, Noren, stood again at the table in his father's farmhouse and said the words automatically, as he'd done before every meal, disbelieving them, yet maintaining the pose be-

25

cause that was the way life was. Besides, had not his mother believed them? His dream-self recalled how she'd died believing, died slowly and in pain because the Technicians had not arrived in time to save her from the poisonous briars. . . .

But it was a native poison for which there was no cure; as the First Scholar, he too was dying of it. The scene of the dream shifted once more, and he lay within the City, realizing that such poison had been on the knife that had struck him down. He'd faced the mob at the Gates knowing what would happen, and knowing also that he could nullify his people's hatred in no other way. He had not known, however, how much pain there would be, or how long it would take to die. *There shall come a time of great exultation . . . and at that time, when the Mother Star appears in the sky, the ancient knowledge shall be free to all people, and shall be spread forth over the whole earth. And Cities shall rise beyond the Tomorrow Mountains, and shall have Power, and Machines, and the Scholars will no longer be their guardians. For the Mother Star is our source and our destiny, the wellspring of our heritage; and the spirit of this Star shall abide forever in our hearts, and in those of our children, and our children's children, even unto countless generations. . . .* They were comforting words! True words! His friends could stop the pain, but if he allowed that, he could not record the words that were so important. Yet how had he found them? He'd tried for years to frame such words, and had failed, for he was no poet; he was only a scientist.

"And so long as we believe in it, no force can destroy us, though the heavens themselves be consumed. . . ." It was Talyra who was saying them now, although that could not be, for had not she whom he loved died aboard the starship, died because the Six Worlds were gone and humanity was gone and she lacked the courage to live in a universe

26

that seemed so empty? When he, the First Scholar, had looked down upon his wife's lifeless form, the face had been Talyra's face. . . . Still Talyra stood before him, alive, believing, and her sorrow was not for herself but for him. "May the spirit of the Mother Star go with you, Noren. . . ."

As the voice faded Noren awoke, dazed and shaken, lying still while he sorted the dream from the reality he had so recently begun to understand. "The First Scholar did not write the Prophecy," Stefred had told him. "The idea was his, but the words are not in the recording; you supplied them yourself." And also, much later, "The last dream was particularly dangerous for you, since as a child you watched your mother die by the same poison. I hesitated, Noren. All the rules of psychiatry said I should not let you proceed. Yet what was I to do? You had proven yourself fit to become a Scholar; was I to disqualify you on account of a tragic coincidence that had already caused you more than enough hurt?"

That Stefred himself could be hesitant and unsure was something Noren hadn't realized till then; Scholars, as guardians of all mysteries, were, in the villagers' eyes, omniscient, and though he'd once thought them tyrants, he had not suspected that they were ever doubtful about anything. After coming to trust Stefred, he had assumed that the man's wisdom was limited only in regard to the basic problem of creating metal. Gradually, however, he'd begun to discover that this was not the case. In the first place, no single Scholar knew everything that had been known on the Six Worlds. The amount of knowledge was so vast that it was necessary to specialize, and Stefred, as a specialist in psychiatry, had little training in other fields. Furthermore, in every field there were areas not thoroughly understood by the experts. The existence of such gaps amazed Noren. Truth was far more complicated than he'd supposed it to be when he had demanded free access to it; the further he got into his training, the more evident that became. On mornings like this one the thought was frightening. . . .

His surroundings seemed somehow unfamiliar; as he came fully awake, Noren saw that it was because the room's study viewer was folded back into the wall. When it was out, there was scarcely space to turn around, so to accommodate Brek he'd put it away for the first time since entering training. That was probably why he'd dreamed as he had: in talking things over with Brek, he had allowed his worries to surface as he had not done on previous days, when study had absorbed his entire mind.

All his life he'd sought opportunity to study; and, Noren reflected, this aspect of being a Scholar had surpassed his greatest hopes. He had natural talent for it—especially for mathematics, on which he had so far concentrated as the first step toward specialization in nuclear physics—and though he'd been told he was progressing much faster than average, the days were not long enough for all he wanted to learn. Much of his time was occupied with more sophisticated training techniques than the reading of study tapes; still he always kept a tape on hand to use in spare moments. Brek, on the upper bunk that had until now been unoccupied, was still asleep. Noren rose and restored the study viewer to its normal position before even putting on his clothes. It made the cramped room more comfortable, for any link to the Six Worlds' huge store of knowledge was, to him, a marvel that compensated for all the difficulties and confusions of his strange new life.

But as he settled himself silently before the viewer, the mood of his dream failed to pass. Talyra's face loomed between him and the information he was perusing; Talyra's voice echoed in his ears. Irritably, he blamed Brek for having raised the subject. Brek had been persistent, unwilling to let it drop; they had talked on after bidding Grenald

28

goodnight. "She was the one who got you clothes after you left the jail, wasn't she?" Brek had said. "After watching her at the trial, I guessed she would, though I saw why you couldn't trust me enough to say so."

"I'm the one who should be asking your forgiveness," Noren had muttered, recalling his unfounded suspicion that a trap might be laid for Talyra also. "Yes, she gave me clothes and money, too, in spite of believing that to aid an escaped heretic was sinful."

Talyra was very devout; they'd quarreled bitterly when he had first told her of his heresy. She had broken their betrothal then, declaring that she would marry no man who did not revere the Mother Star, and when at his trial he had denied the Star's very existence, she had been genuinely horrified. But she had grieved for him, knowing that he would not back down to save himself, and had gone counter to all she'd been taught in order to help him. "Talyra believed every word of the Prophecy," he'd remarked to Brek, "and she was *right!* I just wish I could tell her that."

Brek had looked at him, frowning. "Without telling her why? You were both right, but she would still think you'd been wrong to question! And anyway, she may well have heard that you recanted."

"She didn't hear," Noren had said grimly. "She saw. She was there, and she must have thought what you thought when you were shown the films." In anguish he remembered the pain that had filled her eyes when the public sentence was passed upon him. The harshest consequence of heresy was that one could not comfort one's loved ones.

To be sure, a reunion might be arranged at the price of permanent Inner City residence for Talyra, but Noren had told Stefred that he would prefer separation. Talyra had her own life to live; after his arrest she had accepted the

Scholars' appointment to the training center where she was preparing for the semi-religious and highly respected vocation of a village nurse. Though that appointment had been made partly so that her disappearance from home could be explained if she chose to share his confinement—a fact of which she herself was unaware—he couldn't ask her to make the sacrifices entrance to the Inner City would entail. It was better that she should suppose him broken and condemned to prison.

Noren dropped his head in his arms, too disconsolate to turn back to the normally fascinating study viewer. All thought of seeing Talyra again was foolish in any case, for the decision was not his; a village woman in her situation could be brought into the City only if she herself took the initiative by requesting audience to plead the cause of the man she loved. Stefred had seemed to think Talyra might do that, but Noren knew she would never question the rightness of the High Priests' decision.

There was a knock at the door; hurriedly Noren opened it and stepped into the corridor, greeting in a low voice the man who stood there. He did not want Brek disturbed, not when the ordeals of the previous day had been so great and when other demanding things lay ahead.

The man, a casual acquaintance, had merely stopped by with a message. "Stefred wants to see you," he told Noren. "Right away."

"Right away? That's funny; yesterday he said not till I'd gotten Brek initiated into our routines. We had the whole schedule planned."

"I wouldn't know about that, but he spoke to me at breakfast and asked me to send you over to his office. It sounded urgent; maybe it's something to do with tonight's meeting."

"What meeting?"

"You haven't heard? I suppose not, if you haven't been

30

downstairs yet, but there's a notice posted. We're to assemble right after Orison—all Scholars, even the uncommitted —in one general session. And from the look of the executive council people, I'd say something important's come up."

II

NOREN WAS ALWAYS GLAD OF A CHANCE TO TALK WITH STEF-
red, who, as head of recruiting and training, maintained close
friendships with all the people he had guided through the
steps leading to Scholar status. He had little free time; still
Noren had dropped by to see him occasionally, and had
often felt the better for it, although he was invariably offered not consolation, but challenge. And of course, they
had had several discussions within the past few days about
Brek.

On his way up in the Hall of Scholars' lift, Noren recalled
what had taken place during the last of those discussions.   .
Stefred had been quieter than usual, and there had been
something in his manner reminiscent of their early inter-
views, before any of the secrets had been revealed. "You're
hiding something," Noren had accused finally. "If I'm to
help Brek, I've got to know all the facts."

"I've told you all that are pertinent," Stefred had replied
slowly. "But there are—other issues, Noren, and I don't

want you sidetracked right now. If things work out as I expect, you may soon be placed under rather more pressure than is usual for a trainee of your age. Once again I may have to gamble on your ability to withstand it."

"Won't I have a choice?" Noren had demanded.

"Of course. But knowing you as I do, I'm pretty sure you'll choose involvement—and you won't understand what you're getting into until it's too late." Soberly Stefred had added, "Think that over. In a few days, once Brek is settled, we'll talk again."

Noren had indeed thought it over, and had been more curious than worried. He wasn't bothered by the fact that Stefred evidently didn't plan to explain whatever it was he'd be getting into, for he had learned that many of the things a Scholar met could not be explained. They had to be experienced. All the experiences he'd undergone so far had proved worthwhile: unpleasant at times, but on the whole exciting or at least enlightening. Training did involve pressure, but it wasn't a sort of pressure he disliked. Just one comment of Stefred's had made him wonder.

"The issues I'm referring to have nothing to do with your training," Stefred had said. "They are real."

Now, entering the familiar study which, like the conference room where he'd met Brek, was one of the few places in the City that had windows, Noren began to piece things together. He had been too absorbed in his own problems, in Brek's, to do so before; he'd dismissed Grenald's remark about the Prophecy's coming true as the kind of wistful speculation sometimes heard from older Scholars who had few years left in which to see the research progress. *Maybe it will begin sooner than you think*, Grenald had said. . . . There could be a connection with the issues Stefred had mentioned, and with the unusual meeting to be held that night. Scholars did not meet formally except on matters of gravest importance, and even then the uncommitted—those who had not assumed the blue robe and the obligations of priesthood it symbolized, and who therefore had no vote—were rarely included. Sudden hope lifted Noren's spirits. Perhaps a breakthrough was imminent! Perhaps there was no need to worry that he might have sanctioned an empty promise.

One look at Stefred confirmed the hints that something crucial had arisen. He was obviously troubled, more troubled than Noren had ever seen him, and he did not seem at all eager to proceed. "I must do some things I'd like to put off," he declared without preamble. "First, there are questions I've got to ask you. If it were possible, I would wait till you're further along in your training; failing that, I'd at least delay until your responsibility to Brek is finished. That's no longer feasible. You must cope with them now. Bear with me, Noren, if this hurts; I won't probe deeper than I have to."

"I don't mind questions," said Noren, settling himself in the chair next to Stefred's. "We've always been honest with each other."

"Yes. You will be more honest with me than you've been with yourself lately; that's why I would prefer not to do this yet. In time, you would confront the difficult parts spontaneously, but you're not quite ready." Stefred sighed. "Your tutors confirm what I already knew from the computer's measurement of your aptitude. Grenald in particular tells me that, potentially, you have one of the most brilliant scientific minds of your generation, and that if I upset it, I'll be accountable for any effect on your future contribution to the research. He is probably right. Yet I promised you that you'd have a choice, and even if I hadn't, it's guaranteed to you by fundamental policy—which Grenald knows as well as I. Given such a choice, do you want me to continue?"

Confused, Noren groped for an answer. Stefred, he knew,

34

expected more of him than simple assent; he must attempt to analyze the problem. It would not be spelled out for him. At length he ventured, "You couldn't upset my mind except by telling me something I'm not aware of. And if you're asking whether I'd rather not be told, well, you know the truth's more important to me than anything else."

"More important than the scientific work on which fulfillment of the Prophecy depends?"

"Is there a conflict?"

"For the sake of argument, assume there is."

"Then the truth—the whole truth—is more important. A part couldn't be more important than the whole."

Stefred, with evident reluctance, fixed his gaze directly on Noren and in one skillful thrust stripped away the armor built up through many weeks past. "Is that consistent with the fact that you've devoted practically every waking moment to technical studies since the day after your recantation?" he inquired softly.

Noren gasped, overcome by the extent of his own self-deceit. How had Stefred known? He had never hinted to Stefred that doubt about the work's ultimate outcome had entered his thoughts; not until he was watching Brek recant, in fact, had he admitted to himself that there might be truths from which he had hidden. Yet underneath he'd been aware that they existed. They'd emerged gradually from his increasing knowledge of science, and only concentration on its technical aspects had kept them back. The worries they'd raised could hardly be unfounded. . . .

"Forgive me," Stefred said. "That was brutally abrupt, but it told me something I had to be sure of: you don't wish to use science as a shield. If you did, I couldn't have opened your eyes so quickly. Some Scholars take years to recognize what you just grasped." There was no reassurance in his tone, though the usual warmth came through; Stefred's honesty was what inspired people's confidence in him.

35

Straightforwardly he continued, "We have no time to go into this problem right now; you must grapple with it alone. And it's only the beginning, Noren. I'm leading up to more upsetting things."

"I—I hope you're not going to ask how I feel about wearing the robe," Noren faltered, sensing the direction events seemed to be taking. He was to be offered some challenging new task, one for which full commitment was undoubtedly a prerequisite . . . and much as he might want to accept, he could not yet become a High Priest—not when deeper reservations were mingling with his original ones.

"I must, Noren. You need give me no decision—you will never be pressed for that—but if you have strong leanings one way or the other, I've got to know."

"I honestly don't know myself, Stefred. If that's what you meant when you said I'd choose involvement—"

"It is not what I meant. I wouldn't presume to influence you in regard to commitment; it isn't a step to be taken lightly." As relief spread through Noren, Stefred went on, "Don't answer this next question if you don't want to; I have valid reasons for asking it, but not ones that entitle me to invade your privacy. Do you attend Orison, Noren?"

Turning away, Noren felt his face redden. "Not often."

"You've no need to look so guilty. Attendance isn't required of you, and surely you know that none of us thinks less of you for not going, as villagers and Technicians would. There are committed Scholars who serve as High Priests before the people but take no part in our private religious rituals."

"I don't feel guilty," said Noren. "I never felt any guilt for not having faith in religion, and I don't now." He paused, deciding what had caused the flush of shame; with Stefred there was no alternative to complete candor. "I'm embarrassed, I guess," he continued slowly, "because the private rituals like Orison are the one thing I've encountered here that makes no sense to me. I just don't see what they accomplish. The symbolism of religion was designed by the Founders to give hope to those who couldn't be told our secrets, to express truths that couldn't be stated in plain language. Yet as Scholars, we've learned the truth; our hope is in science. To the people we must speak of the Mother Star in symbolic words, but we who know the facts about it—what use have we for such symbols?"

"That's a perfectly legitimate question, and not one to be ashamed of."

"But look—I'm supposed to be so intelligent; I should be able to figure it out! There's got to be something I'm missing. *You* go to Orison. Every time I've been, I've seen you there, and I—I've seen you enter while I stayed outside."

"Have you lost any respect for me because I do go?"

"Of course not. Why should I?"

Stefred smiled. "You might, if you were staying away merely to assert your independence."

Startled, Noren confessed, "It was that way in the beginning . . . though I don't think I knew it. But not any more." He had found that among Scholars, one's right to independence was so plainly acknowledged that one had no need to assert it, and his boyhood antagonism toward religion had given way to genuine puzzlement. Though he'd been too busy to devote much thought to the problem, it was apparent not only that the villagers and Technicians expected more of the Mother Star than fulfillment of the Prophecy's promises, but that the High Priests endorsed this view. Were it not so incredible, he might even have concluded that they shared it.

"You've come further than you realize," Stefred commented. "Last year you wouldn't have believed that there were any mysteries you couldn't comprehend." Then, with a penetrating look that warned of disquieting words to come, he once more broached a painful topic. "Do you think it possible, Noren, that if you don't wholly understand my attitude toward the Mother Star, you also missed something in Talyra's?"

At the sound of the name Noren winced. First Brek and now Stefred, when for so long he'd repressed all thought of her! "There's no comparison," he asserted.

"If you see none, I won't pursue it. But there are other things you don't understand about Talyra, and in fairness to you I can't let them pass."

"What use is there in discussing them?" Noren burst out, a bit too sharply.

Quietly Stefred declared, "I called you here this morning to find out if you still love her. Your face tells me that you do."

Astonished, Noren abandoned all defenses. "I'll always love her," he agreed miserably.

"Enough to take on the burden of a relationship that would never be truly open—that would require you to conceal much of your inner life, respecting her beliefs without explaining yours?"

"It doesn't matter, really. You know I'll never see Talyra again; she'd have to take the initiative—"

"Which you've been sure she would not do. But she has."

"Talyra . . . requested audience?" Noren whispered, suddenly cold. "When?"

"Shortly after you recanted. I did not grant it then; I had to be sure that your feelings for each other would not be changed by separation. She was told merely that I would see her before she left the training center to return home as a village nurse. However, something's developed that makes it necessary for me to act at once."

"And you—you want me to decide whether she's to stay here as a Technician? It's too soon, Stefred! I can't say whether we'd ever be able to marry." Such a marriage would not be permitted unless he revealed his true status by assuming the robe, for no Scholar could take a wife who was unaware of his obligation to keep major secrets from her. Yet not all the secrets could be kept. Once admitted to the Inner City, Talyra would know too much to leave; Technicians who entered were, like the Scholars themselves, subject to lifelong confinement. And they too had to give up their children for adoption by village families, since a child who grew up knowing that Scholar rank wasn't hereditary would have been doomed to a confinement not of his own choosing. These sacrifices were made gladly by those who considered Inner City work a high honor; but to let Talyra make them for the sake of a love that might remain hopeless. . . .

"The final decision will be mine, based on her wishes as well as yours," Stefred told him, "but I cannot admit her without your consent. The problems are difficult and complicated. With Talyra there's a special complication, since she was present at your recantation and therefore knows that you were not only a heretic, but impenitent. That knowledge will make her ineligible for Scholar status once she learns you have attained it, even if she becomes a heretic herself."

"Talyra would never do that!" Noren exclaimed.

"No, probably not. Though she is braver than you realize, I don't think she has that particular sort of mind. Nevertheless, the opportunity is every citizen's birthright, and it would be unjust to bar her prematurely from it; yet no person who realizes that heretics needn't repent to become Scholars can qualify. Your marriage must therefore be postponed; you must promise to delay any revelation of your rank until we're sure that adjustment to City life won't cause her to develop heretical views."

"I see that," Noren concurred, "though in her case it's just a formality." Inner City Technicians did not witness recantations and naturally assumed that any heretic who was made a Scholar had been penitent. The few who'd accidentally learned otherwise before entering the Inner City were necessarily excluded from candidacy because they alone, of all non-Scholars, were aware that unrepented defiance of the system could result in personal gain; the tests of incorruptibility were for them not valid. It was right that care should be taken to ensure that no potential heretic gained such awareness. But as far as Talyra was concerned, he was more worried about another injustice. "There'll be no difficulty about postponement," he continued, "because if I do decide to assume the robe, it won't be soon. That's the trouble: it's so unfair to her—"

"She has no expectation of marrying you, Noren, and if she loves you and has continued to grieve for you, she'll be happier here than outside, believing you a prisoner. She can serve as a nurse as well here as in the village, after all. She might even study to become a doctor."

"I—I'm not sure she could adapt. She's so unwilling to change the way she looks at things."

"Is she? That doesn't follow from the fact that she wouldn't give up her faith on your say-so. I suspect that Talyra can adapt quite well; the question is whether you can. The stress on you will be very great—too great, Grenald thinks." In an impassive voice Stefred added, "In his opinion I'd be a fool to let you involve yourself with a girl."

Indignantly Noren protested, "Look, I have every respect for Grenald, but—well, he's old enough to be my great-grandfather."

"Yes. He is an old man who has devoted most of his life to research that he won't live to see completed, and who gave up his children as infants. He may have grandchildren and great-grandchildren, but he knows neither their names nor the villages where they live. Now you've come—and

40

you are his heir, Noren. Of all the young people he has taught, you are the one most likely to advance the work that his generation cannot finish. Can you blame him if he doesn't want you distracted from it?"

Again Noren flushed. Stefred was the most compassionate man he had ever known, but he could be harsh at times when he had to be, and he'd implied from the outset that this was one of those times. Didn't the priority of the research override all other considerations? "You're telling me I have no alternative," Noren said, striving to keep the emotion out of his own voice. "If I'm really dedicated—if I'm sincere in what I've always claimed about my willingness to sacrifice anything necessary to make the Prophecy come true—I should forget Talyra and commit myself to the job, whether or not I go so far as to accept the role of High Priest."

Surprisingly, Stefred frowned. "That would be the easiest way," he said after a short silence.

"Easy?" Noren echoed in bewilderment. Stefred was usually so perceptive. . . .

"It would be easiest," Stefred repeated, "but if you elect that course, I'll thank you not to do so under the illusion that I advised it. I thought you knew me better by now; but if you don't, at least bear in mind what we established a few minutes ago. The work, vital though it is, remains part of a larger whole."

"But if I've used study as a shield against . . . problems," protested Noren, "they're problems related to our work! They're connected with—with fulfillment of the Prophecy; if I face them, I'll be more absorbed by that than ever. I don't see the comparison you're drawing."

"I don't suppose you do," Stefred conceded. "You are very young, and martyrdom still has its appeal." He leaned forward, saying gently, "Under other circumstances I would not go into this when you're unready to work it out on your own. In one brief talk I'm having to cover ground that should be explored over a period of weeks, perhaps years—and it's unfair to demand a decision that you are not mature enough to make with full understanding. Yet in the real world I'm bound not by what should be, but by what is, and the events of the moment force us to decide Talyra's future today."

Noren, thoroughly baffled, gave up the attempt to resolve the issue and asked humbly, "Will you help me, Stefred?"

"If you mean will I choose the shape of your life for you, no. But I'll tell you my own view of it." He turned toward the window, looking out beyond the City to the open land that he himself had not walked upon since youth, and said slowly, "I've been quite frank about our hope for you as a scientist, a hope that was born during your childhood when Technicians under our direction watched you and subtly encouraged you in the path of heresy. Grenald is not the only man who believes you'll someday be instrumental in achieving the breakthrough that's been sought since the First Scholar's time. But you were not brought here to be an extension of the computer complex. You are a human being with the right and the responsibility to become enmeshed in human problems, personal problems. You must make sacrifices, yes—we all must, for we are stewards of our people's heritage, and the ultimate survival of the human race rests upon us. But we do not sacrifice our humanity. We do not give up the thoughts and feelings and relationships of our individual lives. If we did, our dedication would in the end be self-defeating; we would have no more chance of fulfilling the Prophecy than computers alone would have."

Staring at him, Noren saw the Chief Inquisitor in a way he never had before, despite their weeks of friendship. Stefred himself had once been married. His wife had been a

Scholar, one of the few village girls to seek knowledge beyond the station in which custom had placed her. She had been killed accidentally during a nuclear research experiment. There had no doubt been children who'd become craftsmen or farmers somewhere, proud of their status as adopted sons and little dreaming that their true father still lived. Or perhaps they had become heretics; perhaps they were now Scholars themselves! Stefred would not know. Even if he had presided at their inquisitions, he would not know, for though babies were placed only with good and loving families, no records of parentage were kept. Chagrined, Noren began, "What you said about Grenald—"

"Was meant merely to remind you that he too is human."

"I—I've oversimplified things, I guess."

"Sometimes one must in order to keep one's balance."

"I don't really want to, though. And I do want Talyra here if she wants to come."

"So I thought." Stefred rose. "I'm sure you've guessed that I'm concerned about more today than you and Talyra, that this issue is related to a larger one. At tonight's meeting you will learn the facts. Noren, there are two things you must go through before you learn. I would not subject you to them in quick succession if it were not an emergency."

"That's all right," Noren assured him, though inwardly he was already more deeply shaken than he cared to admit. The day was apparently to be as demanding for him as for Brek.

*

Several hours later, after introducing Brek to the computer room where one was free to call forth any information one cared to about the Six Worlds, Noren met Stefred in the courtyard beside the inner gates that led to the City's exit dome. "It's best for you to be present when I interview Talyra," Stefred had told him. "It will not be an easy thing to witness, and you won't be allowed to speak; but she will need you, Noren. Merely seeing you will give her confidence."

Noren shuddered. It would be necessary, he knew, to determine not only Talyra's willingness to enter the Inner City, but her ability to adapt to customs totally unlike those under which she'd been reared; and neither issue could be approached directly. "If I'm not convinced that she'll be happy here, I shall send her away," Stefred warned. "You will have to watch her go, knowing that you won't see each other again, and she'll be unaware that it might have been otherwise. Do you love her enough to endure that?"

"Yes," Noren said steadily. "But Stefred, she can't be given enough information for her to decide whether she'll be happy until it's too late for her to go back."

"She won't need information; she will judge and be judged by her feelings and her sense of values, just like a Scholar candidate, during my talk with her."

Noren frowned; Stefred's talks with people were apt to be grueling. "Will you—test her, then?" he asked worriedly.

"Yes, briefly, but there's no danger in it; I promise you she won't be hurt in any lasting way."

As they walked down the wide corridor that stretched toward the main Gates and outer platform where public ceremonies were held, Noren's pulse accelerated. He had not been in this dome, nor indeed in any other, since the day of his recantation; the huge domes that ringed the area of closely spaced towers were Outer City, off limits to Scholars and Inner City Technicians. Exceptions were made when it was necessary for a Scholar to appear publicly, to interview someone, or to investigate trouble with equipment such as the nuclear power plant, which was normally maintained by ordinary Technicians who lived in the domes and were free to go outside. But Noren had as yet done none of these things. The research laboratories, where he'd sometimes assisted, were located in the towers themselves. Those towers were also immense, for although of smaller diameter than the domes, they soared so high they could be seen for miles by awed villagers.

Walking beside Stefred, Noren thought back to the last time he'd passed through the corridor, recalling how clear-cut the Founders' decision had seemed to him then. Prone though he'd always been to question, he had not questioned their conviction that the sealing of the City would result in discovery of a way to change the world. He had known too little of science to guess that the essential research might fail. He'd acknowledged the Prophecy's truth only because he'd believed that it *was* true, literally, despite its symbolic form; nothing could have induced him to recant on any other basis. Nothing else could have justified his acceptance of a rigid caste system under which most people were deprived both of technology and of all but the most rudimentary education.

When, in recanting, Noren had endorsed the system, he had done so in the belief that synthesization of metal was only a matter of time. He had assumed that if the Scholars went on doing their job, there could be no doubt about cities and machines someday becoming available to everyone. Once he'd begun to study, however, he had found that research didn't work that way. If scientists didn't know how to do something, then they had no real proof that it could ever be done. And so far the Scholars hadn't learned how to achieve nuclear fusion of heavy elements. Their progress over the years had consisted mainly of eliminating once-promising possibilities. To be sure, the current experimentation offered hope of another possibility; but hope was not the same as assurance. Would he have proclaimed the Prophecy to be "true in its entirety" if he had realized that? Noren wondered. Would he have freely renounced his opposition to the Scholars' authority as "false, misconceived

45

and wholly pernicious?"

Those statements echoed in Noren's mind as he and Stefred continued along the corridor leading toward the platform where he had made them. The memory was all the more vivid because Stefred was robed; as a known Scholar, he could not show himself to Talyra—or in fact to any villager or Outer City Technician—without covering his ordinary clothes. And even so, such face-to-face discussions were few; routine business was carried on by radiophone, for only thus could the air of mystery surrounding the Scholars be preserved.

The small windowless room they entered contained a desk and several chairs, all made of the white plastic material with which the starships had been outfitted. Most City furnishings were similar and had been in continuous use throughout the generations since the Founding. That would have been thought strange on the Six Worlds, Noren had been told; there, people had recycled things long before they wore out simply for the sake of variety. Variety was one of the luxuries the City could not afford. Even the homes of the villagers, who made their own furniture from softstone, wicker and the hides of work-beasts, were less monotonous. For that reason Outer City Technicians sometimes bought village-made furniture although it was relatively uncomfortable; their quarters were more spacious than those of Inner City people, and unlike the Scholars —who, as stewards, were not permitted to own anything— they had money.

Waiting, Noren turned his mind to Talyra, trying to quell the hope that had risen within him. Even if she wanted to join him, she might not measure up. She was so very devout, so unwilling to question the superiority of the Technician caste, that she could easily give a wrong impression; Stefred would not accept anyone who believed that being a Technician meant having the right to look down on the villagers.

46

She is braver than you realize, Stefred had said. She must be, Noren reflected, if she had requested the audience. Any village girl would feel terror at personal contact with the awesome High Priests who, under ordinary circumstances, were seen only at a distance; Talyra had additional cause to be afraid. Supposing them omniscient, she would fear that they were aware that she'd once helped him elude their custody.

"You won't let on that you know about her part in my escape from the village, will you?" he asked anxiously.

"I shall have to," Stefred told him. "She'll expect it; since those who request audience are informed that their past lives will be investigated, her coming here is tantamount to an open confession. And though a villager normally can't be accused by Technicians or Scholars unless first convicted by his peers, a student at the training center is under our jurisdiction."

"She took the risk deliberately," mused Noren. "Why?"

"Why did you take the ones you took? You wanted something, wanted it so much that you ignored everything reason told you and followed your heart instead."

"But she has no hope of even seeing me."

"She hopes to help you through intercession on your behalf. Also, though you may find it hard to fathom, it's likely that she's torn by guilt over what she did—which is not the same as regretting it—and is seeking to declare herself and take the consequences. That is a form of honesty, Noren."

Maybe it was, Noren thought, recalling the suggestion that he might have misinterpreted Talyra's attitude. In the village they'd argued from opposite premises: she, that Scholars could do no wrong; he, that they could do no right —and neither view had been based on any real knowledge of the situation. Yet of the two, his had been the more dogmatic. There had been no doubt in his mind that it explained everything. Talyra, on the other hand, had believed both in the goodness of the Scholars and in the injustice of his imprisonment. Honesty was simple when one's convictions didn't conflict; now that he was facing doubts and conflicts of his own, he was beginning to see why she had seemed so bound by unexamined assumptions.

"She'll accept your reassurance," he said, "but as for the rest, it may be hard to get across. The very idea of becoming a Technician may—well, shock her. Talyra's awed by Technicians; she won't admit to herself that she's as smart as they are."

"She will admit it to me," Stefred said. "I've dealt with many candidates, Noren, and I know how to find out what they really want." He paused. "I'll have to frighten her a little in order to be sure of her true feelings; and to make her aware of them herself, I'll need to be a bit cruel. You must be silent and let me handle it; you must not offer any encouragement, for if you do, her choice will not be wholly free."

Nodding, Noren strove to master his turbulent thoughts. Not since their parting had he dared to envision Talyra deliberately: her face; her long dark curls; her slim figure clad in a tunic and underskirt of the light green worn for holidays and other religious affairs, adorned by blue glass beads of spiritual devotion and today, perhaps, by the red love-beads he'd once given her. . . .

The door opened; she stood there between two uniformed Technicians, pale but with her head held high. At the sight of him her face was illumined with a brief, astonished joy that turned quickly to anguish. She thought him a prisoner, Noren realized miserably; she would feel terror for him as well as for herself. He longed to go to her, comfort her, but he knew he must not. Talyra must have a fair chance to withdraw.

Stefred dismissed the Technicians, motioning Talyra forward, and she knelt at his feet. "That is not necessary," he said brusquely. "It is done only on formal occasions. Sit

48

beside me, Talyra."

"Yes, Reverend Sir," she replied, using the form of address employed in public ritual. She rose and took the chair offered her.

"'Sir' alone is sufficient." Glancing at Noren, Stefred added reflectively, "It would be well, Talyra, for you to become somewhat less worshipful in regard to Scholars."

Noren gulped. If Talyra were ever to address *him* as 'Reverend Sir,' he would be too embarrassed to speak.

"You have requested audience with us," Stefred went on, "ostensibly to plead clemency for someone you love. Yet we think perhaps you may also seek our pardon on your own behalf. Surely you know what has come to our attention in our review of your past."

"I—I think so, sir." Though her voice wavered, she appeared less dismayed than Noren himself by the directness of Stefred's approach and his use of the cold, ceremonious "we."

"We must accuse you of having once helped this man, a self-proclaimed heretic, to escape. You cannot be required to confess to us; it is your right to demand a civil trial. If you waive that right, however, you must swear to answer my questions truthfully and to accept my judgment."

"I do waive it, sir. I have no wish to deny the charge."

"Swear, then."

"I swear by the Mother Star that I will tell you the truth." Talyra drew a breath and added hastily, "But I wouldn't, sir, if it were not that Noren is already condemned! I'd never tell anything that would hurt him; I only hope I can make you see that he doesn't deserve such a terrible punishment as—as was announced."

"You must pledge also to accept my judgment, Talyra."

"I so swear, as far as my own case is concerned—but not for Noren's!"

Stefred leaned forward across the desk, fixing his gaze

49

on her. "You must care deeply for him to feel yourself a better judge of his heresy than I. Or are you too an unbeliever? Do you perhaps consider denial of the Prophecy no crime at all?"

Talyra looked horrified. "Sir, I believe the Prophecy! I have never questioned it! Upon my oath—"

"Your oath by the Mother Star is worthless as a defense," the Scholar said dryly, "since if you were indeed an unbeliever, it would have no meaning for you." He frowned. "Talyra, heresy is a very grave charge. You say you do not think Noren deserves life imprisonment, yet have you ever heard of any heretic who was seen again after his recantation? And not all heretics recant. Some are not even charged publicly, for if they waive civil trial, as you have just done, their cases are not made known in the villages."

Talyra met his eyes. "I did not waive a heresy trial," she declared firmly. "I am not a heretic, and no court would convict me. You told me merely that I am accused of helping Noren, and that is the only crime I've admitted."

"That's quite true," Stefred agreed. "I wasn't trying to trap you, Talyra, but I had to assure myself that you have the wit not to incriminate yourself falsely. If you didn't have, it would be improper for me to continue this interview without appointing someone to defend you, for though you are not yet formally charged with heresy, it's possible that I will find grounds for such a charge in your responses."

"What reason could you have for even suspecting me?" cried Talyra indignantly. "I helped Noren because I love him, but I never agreed with what he said—he'll tell you so himself!"

The Scholar eyed her intently. "What would you say if I were to tell you that he has said the exact opposite: that he has not only reported your part in his escape, but has claimed that you shared and encouraged the false beliefs that he has now abjured?"

50

By great effort, Noren avoided her incredulous stare. One look from him, and she would know what to say; he must not give her any clue. Stefred, he realized, was testing them both by these tactics, for if he feared her answer enough to influence it, it would be proof that he was unwilling to accept a decision based on Talyra's feelings alone.

In a cold dull voice Talyra declared, "I would say that you were lying. I didn't think Scholars could lie, but if you tell me *that*, I'll have to believe they can. You are setting a trap for me after all, sir. To accuse a Scholar of lying would indeed be heresy."

"You have nothing to fear from me as long as you are honest," Stefred assured her. "The point at issue here is your motive for helping Noren. To have helped him simply because you love him is one thing, but to have done it because you held heretical beliefs yourself would be something else. So you see I must determine whether you really do love him. If you do, it would be impossible for you ever to believe that he'd done what I suggested. He hasn't, of course. I did not say he had; I merely said *if*."

Talyra's tense face relaxed into a faint smile. "You're very wise, sir. I just can't think you'll really lock Noren up for the rest of his life! He—he was always honest, too; doesn't that count for something? He was wrong, and he's admitted it—but he believed what he said. Would you have wanted him to lie? Would you have wanted him to repent not having lied?"

"Certain things have inescapable consequences," Stefred said quietly. "Noren is to be confined within the City permanently and nothing can change that; it is the consequence of heresy. But you don't really know much about the City, after all. Has it occurred to you that life inside may not be so terrible? The Technicians live here; I live here myself."

"But not as a prisoner, sir!"

51

"No? Have you ever seen a Scholar outside the City?"

She shook her head, confused. "Yet you could go outside if you wanted to. You could do anything you wanted to."

"Why is it," said Stefred, sighing, "that people so often think that those above them can do anything they want? It works the other way, Talyra. I have a good deal less choice than you do. If Scholars did whatever they liked, Noren's suspicion would have been all too accurate; they would be unworthy guardians."

To Noren's relief, Talyra's expression showed that she was thinking, and the new thoughts didn't seem unduly disturbing. His concern had been groundless, maybe; he'd feared that the process would be more painful.

There was a short silence; then Stefred began an innocuous line of questioning quite evidently designed to lead directly to the decision. "Is there anyone outside the City for whom you care more than for Noren?"

"No."

"Not even anyone in your family?"

"I love my family, but I was planning to marry Noren. Now I'll never marry anyone."

"What are you going to do, then? Do you really want to be a nurse?"

"Yes, I like the work at the training center."

"Yet you turned down the appointment when it was first offered."

"That was because it meant delaying our marriage."

"Why was getting married right away so important? Were you eager to have children?"

Noren held his breath. He and Talyra had never discussed that, for it had been assumed as a matter of course; in the villages a woman who bore few babies was scorned. The rearing of large families was considered a religious virtue. He did not know whether a family was important to her for

52

its own sake, but if it was, she should not enter the Inner City, and Stefred would undoubtedly send her away.

"You don't understand," Talyra said. "Noren and I were in *love*."

Slowly Stefred continued, "I do understand. Suppose, Talyra, that you had to choose again whether or not to help him; would you do the same thing?"

"Yes."

"What if it meant that you would suffer the consequences of heresy even though you yourself had not incurred them? What if it meant that your family and friends might never learn what had become of you?"

Talyra met his eyes bravely. "I'd do it."

"Then you're as unrepentant as he is? You still love him, and you won't ever be sorry?"

"That's right, sir."

It was going to work out, thought Noren joyously. In a moment Stefred would tell her, and the ordeal would be over. . . .

And then he saw that the true ordeal had not yet even begun.

*

With Stefred's next words, Noren knew what the Chief Inquisitor was going to do; and he was appalled. Talyra's wits were sharp, but she would be defenseless against an expert assault on her misconception of herself. He wished heartily that he had never agreed to let her be questioned.

"When a girl loves a man that much," Stefred was saying, "it's only natural for her to be influenced by his opinions. Surely you did not disagree with all of Noren's ideas."

"Of course not, only with the heretical ones," Talyra said confidently, too naive to sense her peril.

"He must often have told you that the things here in the City should be available to everyone, and not just to Technicians and Scholars. Did you agree with that?"

"It is not in accordance with the High Law."

"I know the High Law, Talyra. I am asking whether you agreed with that particular idea of Noren's, and you are bound to answer truthfully."

She dropped her eyes. "I—I agreed that it would be good for everyone to have things," she admitted in a low voice. "But they will have them after the Mother Star appears."

Oh, Talyra, thought Noren hopelessly, *the orthodox answer won't do for Stefred! For the village council that would be a clever reply, but Stefred will hang you with it.*

"Yet what if when it appears," the Scholar went on, "the Technicians decide to keep everything for themselves?"

Shocked, Talyra protested, "That couldn't happen."

"How do you know it couldn't? Have you never met a person who might want to?"

"Yes, but such people aren't Technicians."

"Noren believed otherwise. He believed that Technicians were ordinary men and women like the villagers. Suppose, for instance, that you yourself were a Technician—"

"Don't mock me, sir," she pleaded.

"I am not mocking you. Suppose you woke up one day to find yourself a Technician: would you feel glad to have things that other people don't, or would you wish that the Mother Star would appear sooner so that you could share them?"

Talyra was almost in tears. "How can I answer? I'd want to share, of course, yet if I picture myself in that position, I'm committing blasphemy by thinking of myself as Noren used to."

Ruthlessly Stefred drove the point home. "Come now, Talyra: do you really, deep inside, believe that you'd be unable to do the work of a Technician, or that you would not enjoy it?"

She buried her face in her hands. Noren's grip tightened on the arms of his chair and he half-rose, but Stefred shook his head, going himself to Talyra and laying a firm hand on her shoulder. "You have sworn by the Mother Star that you'll tell me the truth," he said impassively. "To break such an oath is a worse offense than the other."

"I am guilty, then," she sobbed. "I didn't even know it before, but you were right about me!"

"You acknowledge these ideas? Think, Talyra! Your answer may determine the whole course of your future."

"I can't deny them. My guilt's greater than Noren's, for he at least was not a hypocrite."

Her despair was more than Noren could bear. He would never forgive himself, he thought; he should have known that Stefred's relentless approach to truth, so exhilarating to himself, would destroy Talyra. She'd been happy with her illusions; why had he let himself be convinced that she could remain happy after those illusions were gone?

"No!" he burst out. "I'll not let you do this to her!"

"Be silent! If she's to face what's ahead, she must see herself for what she really is."

"Let her go free," Noren begged, his lips dry. "Don't make her face it for my sake."

"Having gone this far, Noren, I must proceed for her own sake; to stop now would be misplaced mercy."

Raising her head, Talyra faltered, "I—I never asked for mercy, sir. Even for Noren I asked only justice."

"And you seemed convinced that in the end I would be just. I promise you that I shall be."

"I believe that. You have exposed my impiety, which I most heartily repent; I don't expect to escape—consequences."

Noren cringed. To him, the kindness in Stefred's tone was evident, but to Talyra, who had been forced to confess what she thought was an unforgivable crime, it would not be; and he knew that Stefred would probe her further. Underneath she could not actually feel she'd done any wrong; she must

55

be compelled to admit that, too. Otherwise she'd remain forever unconvinced of her worthiness to be a Technician.

"So be it, Talyra," the Scholar said decisively. He returned to the desk and faced her. "Because you have helped and defended Noren and have even accepted some of his ideas, you must share his fate. You shall be confined within the City, as he is; you will never see the village of your birth again."

She swayed, staring at him, obviously overwhelmed by the seeming severity of the sentence. She had expected punishment, but not the punishment she'd considered too great even for Noren. In panic, Noren clenched his hands. Stefred had promised that there would be no danger! Yet he had gambled and made a pronouncement from which there could be no turning back; what would happen if she failed to rise to the challenge? As long as she was contrite, she could not qualify.

"Do you want to retract anything you've said?" Stefred asked.

"N—no, sir," Talyra whispered.

"Do you think the verdict too harsh?"

"I—I deserve it, I guess."

The Scholar shook his head. "Talyra, you're being dishonest either with me or with yourself. You know in your heart that you've never harmed anyone and that your inner thoughts are not evil; you can't possibly feel that you deserve life imprisonment any more than Noren does. Tell me what you do feel, not what you think I want to hear."

"I feel such a penalty's heavy in proportion to the offense," she admitted, "but if it must be Noren's, I'm willing to share it. You've shown me that I'm no less presumptuous than he."

"And is presumption to be punished equally with crimes of violence? For that matter, is any form of heresy? Here in the City even a murderer would receive no worse! Really, Talyra—is that fair?"

56

Talyra stood up, flushed, at last jolted into questioning the shaky premises of the villagers' brand of orthodoxy. "No," she said, "it's not fair. My thoughts may be blasphemous, but they are my own, as Noren's were his; and as you've said, they never hurt anybody. I came here believing myself innocent of all heresy, but your effort to find it in me has fanned its flame. There's no need to goad me into any more incriminating statements. I will give you one freely: I hereby abjure my penitence, for you have made me see that Noren's doubts about the High Law were justified."

Good for you, Talyra! Noren cried inwardly. A mere indication that she was no longer sorry would have been enough, but by stating it formally, she had shown her true courage. In her view, if there was anything worse than a heretic it was a relapsed heretic—one who returned to heretical beliefs after having retracted them—and she had laid herself open to that charge.

She trembled a little, awaiting retribution, and then bewilderment crossed her face as Stefred answered, "I did so deliberately, Talyra. Later you will understand why." To Noren he said, "All right. It's finished; go to her now. The rest will come better from you than from me."

Noren, with pounding heart, came forward to take Talyra in his arms. She clung to him, her eyes glistening. "I'm glad it turned out this way," she said softly, giving him no chance to speak. "I could never have been happy in the village thinking of you here in prison; now at least I'll be close by. And I—I see things clearer, Noren. Some of what you used to say makes more sense. Underneath I must have known it did; the Scholar judged me rightly."

"He wasn't mistaken, then, in deciding you'd rather be here with me than return to the village where we'd never see each other again?"

"Be with you? You mean I'll be allowed to see you— often?"

"As often as you like," Noren told her, smiling. "We're

57

not going to be punished, Talyra. I didn't understand either when I was sentenced—we weren't meant to—but the Scholar Stefred never said we'd be put in prison; he simply forbade us to leave the City."

"But—but only Scholars and Technicians live in the City! And besides, we've broken the High Law—"

"I broke it, but I've recanted and been pardoned. You never broke it at all. In the Scholars' eyes you're completely innocent."

"How could I be, Noren? Helping you to escape may have been just a civil offense, but I'm still guilty of blasphemy."

"No," said Noren gently. "I was right about some things; it's not blasphemous to think you'd like to be a Technician. Talyra, you are a Technician now! Stefred had to make sure you wanted it before he passed judgment, because no one who's aware that not all Technicians are born to their status can be released."

She stared, wide-eyed. "Are *you* a Technician, too?"

Noren had learned long before that one could conceal without lying. "As you said, only Scholars and Technicians live in the City," he told her. "A heretic who recants is confined here because of the secrets he knows, but he lives and works like the others."

Talyra, for the moment speechless, turned to Stefred in a mute appeal for confirmation. His smile was warm, yet solemn. "There is nothing in the High Law that prevents a villager who is qualified from becoming a Technician or even a Scholar," he said. "There can never be anything wrong in a person's wanting to know more than he knows, or be more than he has been; the Law specifies only that those who do choose that course can never go back."

He rose and walked to the door. Freeing herself from Noren's embrace, Talyra followed, holding out her hands in the ritual plea for blessing. As Stefred extended his, she knelt, and this time he did not forbid her; she would have felt crushed, rejected, if he had, for she sought not to pay homage but to receive. But before the words could be pronounced, she looked anxiously over her shoulder. "Noren?"

In dismay, Noren watched her new glow of confidence fade to troubled confusion at his failure to kneel beside her. He moved to do so, but with a barely perceptible shake of the head Stefred stopped him. No pretense would be permitted. Not yet High Priest, he was nevertheless a Scholar, and one Scholar could neither kneel to another nor receive from his hands what faith alone could bestow; Talyra's distress could not alter that. And this would not be the last time he would have to hurt her.

The flowing sleeves of Stefred's blue robe hid her face as he intoned the formal benediction: *"May the spirit of the Mother Star abide with you, and with your children, and your children's children; may you gain strength from its presence, trusting in the surety of its power."* Surety? thought Noren bitterly. But there was no surety! One could not trust that man's heritage of knowledge would lead to a transformation of the world, for it was quite possible that it would not. That was the truth he'd hidden from, the thing he was learning from science, and there was indeed no going back. He wondered how Stefred could sound so sincere.

III

ALONE TOGETHER, NOREN AND TALYRA FORGOT ALL DOUBTS and fears in the joy of their reunion. Then, later, he took her through the corridor into the Inner City that was to be her whole world; and though it was strange and awesome to her, she did not seem to mind. To Noren the high spires of the towers that had once been starships were beautiful because of all that was preserved there; he'd thought that Talyra, who must remain ignorant of their origin and who had never craved more knowledge than was useful in the village, would find them disturbingly alien. She did not. She found them holy. In her own way, she too considered them the abode of truth.

They stood hand in hand, with the sun streaming down between the lustrous towers to the incongruously rough pavement of the courtyard, while he told her all he could about the life in store for her, amazed by the serenity with which she confronted it. Talyra had always thought it proper for the Scholars to have secrets, so the fact that anyone who learned some of those secrets must be kept permanently within the walls was in her view very logical. That among Technicians Inner City work was an honor seemed natural to her; that she herself should be so honored filled her with gladness. Slowly, Noren began to see that he'd underestimated Talyra. She had never been unwilling to accept new ideas. Her convictions were entirely sincere, and the discovery that the exaggerated teachings of the prevalent religion weren't officially endorsed merely strengthened those convictions. "I've said all along that our sacred duty is to the spirit of the Mother Star," she declared. "If some of what people think about it is mistaken, so what? Do you suppose I'd take my *family's* word over a *Scholar's?*"

She was surprised, of course, to learn that Scholars were not born, but appointed; yet this did not shock her either. "How are people chosen?" she asked curiously.

"That is a deep secret," Noren replied gravely. "Only the Scholars themselves are allowed to know that." It was an answer that satisfied her completely.

All the things he had expected to have trouble in presenting—that Scholars wore robes only for ceremonies and audiences; that one did not kneel to them on other occasions; that Inner City people, whether Scholars or Technicians, commonly ate together, shared leisure time, and even intermarried—proved easy for Talyra to accept. There was just one point that was awkward. "Noren," she asked hesitantly, "can former heretics marry, too?"

He was prepared; he'd known well enough that the matter must be discussed. "A heretic must have the permission of the Scholars," he told her, "but in time, it is often granted." He drew her toward him, fingering the red necklace she wore, the betrothal gift he had bought in the village with coins hoarded throughout his boyhood. "You know, don't you, that we'd get married right away if I were free to?"

"Of course."

"There are reasons why I am not free, and I—I don't know when I will be. There may be a long wait. It may never be possible at all." Painfully he added, "You are not bound by such restrictions. If someone else were to ask you, you could marry him whenever you wished."

"Oh, Noren! As if I would!"

"It's likely that you'll have suitors," he said frankly. It was all too likely, since far more men than women became heretics; although unmarried Technician girls who requested Inner City work were frequently brought in, they did not stay unmarried long. He could hardly ask Talyra to wait for him. Yet neither could he pretend that he had left her free, he thought miserably, for obviously she *would* wait, whether he asked it or not. He'd known that when he'd consented to her admission, and he had also known that she might wait in vain. Perhaps he'd been selfish . . . but much as he loved her, he could not assume the robe on that basis.

She regarded him with concern, sensing his anguish. "You couldn't receive the Scholar Stefred's blessing, nor can you yet marry—is the penance so harsh, Noren? I thought at first, when you said you'd been pardoned—"

"There is no penance. The Scholar Stefred has conferred more upon me than you can imagine; underneath he's as kind as he is wise."

"But he told me that even he is not free to do as he likes."

"Not if it would interfere with his duties as a guardian of the Mother Star's mysteries," Noren agreed. "He wouldn't want to be; no Scholar would. Sometimes he has to do things he hates doing, things that seem cruel."

He was referring to the interview just past, but Talyra grasped more than he'd meant to reveal. "You've been hurt," she observed sadly.

"No," Noren insisted, but she was not convinced; he had never been a good liar. "I haven't been hurt in the way I feared once," he assured her. "Not the way you must have

62

thought when I recanted."

"Physically? I never thought that! I knew they'd done something that showed you how wrong you'd been. Why, I told you long ago that the Scholars wouldn't want anyone to recant unless he really meant it."

She had, and he'd considered her naive; yet her guesses had come closer to the truth than his own. *Perhaps it's like the innoculations Technicians give,* she'd said. *The needle hurts, but without it we'd all get sick and die. . . .*

"When the Scholar Stefred questioned me," Talyra reflected, "I felt awful; he made me say things I'd been afraid even to think. It seemed as if all the firm ground would crumble away and leave me falling. But afterward—well, I was surer of myself than before. Even though I saw I'd had some false ideas, I liked myself better—" She broke off, watching Noren, realizing how much older he looked than when they'd parted. "What happens to heretics is like that, isn't it? Only it's harder, and goes on longer?"

He nodded. "Something like that. We're not permitted to tell the details."

There were so many details he could not tell, so many areas in which there could be no communication between them: she must not ask about his work; she must not question his absence if for hours or days she did not see him; though she might speculate about the hidden mysteries, she must not do so aloud. That was the Inner City's way, he explained; Technicians did not discuss such things. They didn't seek information about the duties of friends who were assigned jobs inside the Hall of Scholars, or about why some were given such jobs far oftener than others. Neither did they discuss each other's past lives.

"For instance," he cautioned, "you must never describe my recantation to anyone; you mustn't even mention that you saw it. What a heretic has been through is best forgotten."

"I'm glad," she said simply. "I want to forget. I know

63

what you had to do was necessary, and—and you were awfully brave . . . yet you suffered for something you couldn't help! I couldn't believe you deserved to suffer just for having been mistaken; that's haunted me so long."

"It's over. It needn't haunt you any more, darling."

"Nothing will, now that I'm here with you. The spirit of the Mother Star has blessed us both."

They kissed again, and for a few minutes he felt carefree, lighthearted, as if he too need no longer be haunted by anything. But after he'd left her with the Head Nurse, who was to find her lodging space and introduce her to the other Technician girls, Noren found that his perplexity had grown. If Talyra's belief in the Prophecy and the Mother Star was genuine—if she was not, as he'd always assumed, merely sticking by what she'd been taught—then on what grounds was she basing that belief? He himself had been shown the facts, and knew that she wasn't deceived; at least she wasn't unless the Scholars were also deceived about the Prophecy's eventual fulfillment. It was easy to forget that she had never been given any proof. Without proof, could one really be deeply convinced?

*

Two things you must go through, Stefred had warned: two trying experiences before the mysterious, suddenly called meeting that evening, and as to the nature of the second, Noren had been given no clue. An hour remained before the time appointed for him to report back to Stefred's office.

He found Brek still in the computer room. "It's—tremendous," Brek said, his eyes shining. "I never conceived of a setup like this, not even after the dreams. You can ask *anything*—"

"The trick is in learning what to ask," said Noren. He entered Brek's console booth and sat down next to him, preparing to key in a question; there was a principle of chemistry he wanted to verify.

"I know; I've been experimenting," Brek agreed. "Most of the time I couldn't understand half of what showed up on the screen. And once I had to press DISCONTINUE just to get a chance to rephrase."

"What had you requested?"

Grinning sheepishly, Brek admitted, "I'd asked for a full description of the mother world's history."

Noren smiled, knowing that the response to such an inquiry would have gone on for days if uninterrupted. He was past the stage of unrestrained eagerness himself. Yet communication with the computers never lost its fascination for him; study tapes were marvels, but the thought of direct access to an infallible repository of all truth thrilled him in a way that nothing else could match.

In theory, he knew, it would be possible for every Scholar to have a computer console in his own room; on the Six Worlds such arrangements had often existed. The limitation was less one of technical feasibility than of materials—not only the materials for manufacturing the consoles themselves, but the metal wire that would be needed to link them and to provide power. Computer equipment could not run on solar-charged power cells as lights and study viewers did. As it was, relatively few of the consoles that had been installed aboard the starships were hooked up.

The computer complex consisted of the separate computers that had served the ships of the fleet, now interlinked under a single control program. No one memory unit could hold all the knowledge brought from the Six Worlds; the Founders had planned carefully, distributing information among the various ships in such a way that the most vital portions had duplicate backup, and had reprogrammed the system upon assembly to operate as a unified whole. It was self-monitoring and, in regard to its programs, self-maintaining —fully protected against inadvertent erasure of data—and no accident short of power failure could damage it. Such a failure would, of course, destroy all the information through loss of electronic memory impulses; for that reason maintenance of the nuclear power plant was in the Scholars' eyes a task of the highest and most sacred priority.

To be sure, under the High Law all machines were sacred, as was metal itself. Villagers viewed them with reverence and awe, believing them to be of supernatural origin, for they had been told—quite truthfully—that they came from the Mother Star. Noren had doubted this; in the days of his heresy he had held the very unorthodox opinion that machines were made by Technicians and Scholars. To his great surprise, he had found that he was mistaken. Machines were irreplaceable, except insofar as worn parts could be recycled, a process carried out under the computers' control. It was not just that there was no more metal for making parts; some, in fact, could be made out of plastics derived from the planet's native vegetation. The problem was more complicated than that. There was also a lack of the machines needed to fabricate the parts. The Founders had brought what equipment they could, but they'd been unable to transport enough to reproduce the industrial facilities of the Six Worlds.

Though villagers stood in awe of machines, they assumed that the Technicians—in their eyes superior beings—must have no such feeling, but this was not so. Villagers did not handle machines at all; Technicians, who bore responsibility for them, were reared to view the mishandling of a machine as a sacrilege. To damage a machine beyond repair was a mortal sin, punishable by deprivation of Technician status. This provision of the High Law was entirely just; the loss of a machine could cause serious harm to generations yet unborn; enough instances of damage would bring about the extinction of mankind. Yet Noren had been startled by the diffidence with which Brek had first approached the computer console. "Are you sure it's fitting for me to touch it without more instruction?" Brek had asked incredulously.

"Fitting? You're a *Scholar*, Brek." Noren had frowned; he too considered the computers sacred, in the sense that all knowledge was sacred to him; but he had never doubted his own worthiness to use them.

"But the Law is more binding than ever now that I know its justifications," Brek had protested.

"The Law . . . oh, you mean the part about mishandling. Yes, of course, it is; but you don't need a High Law any more—none of us do. We'd be careful anyway, wouldn't we? Besides, you can't hurt a console by pushing buttons, and the computers themselves are sealed behind that partition."

With that assurance, Brek had lost his anxiety; but Noren saw that in some ways new training might be harder for a Technician than for a villager. He himself had never hesitated to touch whatever he found in the laboratories.

Now, turning to him, Brek said, "I still can scarcely believe I can come here whenever I want without supervision."

"We're not supervised at all," Noren told him. "We were put through a lot to prove ourselves trustworthy, but now that we have proven it, we're trusted."

"In everything? What happens if we break the rules?"

"There aren't any rules. Well, there are, I suppose, but they're called policies, and they're not arbitrarily imposed; they're simply principles no Scholar would violate." He paused, trying to think of a concrete example. "About ten weeks ago, before your arrest, you were living in the Outer City, I suppose. Was there any water shortage?"

"Water shortage? Of course not; there's always plenty of water."

"There is when the purification plant works. When it doesn't, like the week I'm talking about, most of the pipes to the Inner City are shut off. People too old to have children drink unpurified water, and the rest of us ration ourselves so that there'll be no interruption of the Outer City or village supply. No one checks up, but would you have drunk enough to keep yourself from being thirsty?"

"I see what you mean," Brek mused. "But Noren, weren't you scared? Knowing what could happen if the breakdown lasted?"

"We were all terrified," Noren admitted, without going into detail about what his feelings had been before he'd heard that breakdowns were periodic occurrences to which the older Scholars, who had seen many repaired, were well inured. "It's the same way with everyday things," he continued. "All goods on this planet are in short supply—at least processed ones are, since there are so few machines for manufacturing them—so we in the Inner City restrict ourselves to the barest minimum. Only what's absolutely essential is bought from the Outer City merchants. As heretics we arrive with nothing, not the smallest token of our former lives, and we never acquire anything, Brek. We have no personal belongings but the clothes we wear."

It was an unnatural way to live, and not, according to what he'd been told of the Six Worlds, one that fostered the progress of a society. But the Inner City wasn't a society; it was an association of people who, for one reason or another, had voluntarily given up normal life to pursue a special goal. Most were dedicated in a religious sense. Moreover, having grown up with the idea that Scholars belonged to a supreme and privileged caste, most could not have felt comfortable had no austerities been practiced. Noren had found that Inner City privations were not merely tolerable, but welcome.

Outside, there was no privation except what the planet itself imposed. The villagers and Outer City Technicians traded freely in what goods the existing machines could turn out, as well as in the few that could be handmade from the world's limited resources. There were not many such, since no trees grew and wood was unknown; there wasn't even any fuel, other than tallow and dried moss, so glass had to come from the Outer City's domes, as did cloth, paper produced from rags, and other essential commodities. Villagers had plenty of money to purchase these things; the Technicians paid them well in plastic coinage for food. Food was abundant, although, Noren had been told, it was by his forebears' standards even more monotonous than furnishings: the hybrid grain once developed to meet the nutritional needs of the overpopulated mother world was the sole crop, aside from an herb tea, and it was supplemented only by the flesh and eggs of caged fowl. Workbeasts were inedible, having been adapted through controlled mutations to a diet of native fodder.

"The First Scholar often went hungry," reflected Brek, recalling the dreams. "Do we?"

"We would if the harvests were small, as they were in the Founders' time. There's no need nowadays. On Founding Day, though, it's traditional to fast in remembrance." Noren thought of how strange that had seemed to him; in the village where he'd grown up, Founding Day had been a time of feasting.

"All this . . . our policy of assuming hardships to avoid imposing them on the villagers and Technicians . . . is it what was meant by 'discipline' in the sentencing?" Brek asked.

"In a way. But for those of us who choose to study, the real challenge is mental discipline: learning to use our minds efficiently."

"I don't see," Brek admitted, "how I'm ever to absorb all I'll need to know to become a nuclear physicist, or a scientist of any kind, for that matter. The computer told me that on the Six Worlds people my age had been studying for

69

years and still weren't ready to specialize."

"That was the custom, one started long before anything was known about faster methods. But now it's possible to catch up in a hurry."

Noren went on to explain how it worked. One learned mental discipline through a "game" played with the computer, a game that demanded logic and fast thinking. "It almost threw me at first," he confessed, "because in the village school I'd never had to think; all we did beyond learning our letters from the Book of the Prophecy was to memorize parts of the High Law, figure a little, and listen to the teacher talk. The computer measures your capacity the first day and holds you to it. You have to score at your level or admit defeat—you aren't given any other type of training, except in non-scientific work, until you've passed that hurdle."

It had been a harsh lesson, but not one Noren had minded; having based his whole defense during his trial and inquisition on the idea that he was not the Scholars' inferior, his pride hadn't let him quit. Nobody had forced him. He had simply been told that before he could work with tutors or receive study tapes he must earn an acceptable score in the "game." When first informed that the game was merely a matter of pushing the proper buttons, he had thought it would be ridiculously simple, and indeed, the initial session had been great fun. What was so hard about watching colored lights and following the instructions on a screen?

That had been before the lights multiplied, the instructions grew complex, and the pace increased to the point where he was given only a few seconds to react.

Intense concentration had never been required of him before and he'd been prone to daydream as a defense against the dullness of village activities. In the game one could not afford to let one's mind wander. Noren had been appalled

70

by the lowness of his scores and yet, during the first week or so, he'd been unable to improve them; he would freeze, find himself worrying over the unexpected failures, and the seconds allotted for response would be gone. The computer was infinitely patient; it never got tired of presenting comparable, although somewhat altered, instructions, and in fact would not proceed to the next degree of complexity until the current one had been mastered. Noren himself got exhausted; several times he kept at it all night. Eventually, after passing from despair through anger and grim determination, he'd learned to focus on the task and had begun to make progress. Thereafter, the game was exhilarating.

He still spent considerable time at it, he told Brek, for its scope had been expanded to include rigorous testing of his academic progress. The computer was programmed to keep close track of this and to guide each Scholar's course. Study tapes, generated in sequence to meet one's individual needs and aptitudes, were the foundation of instruction. These were requested at a console, produced by the tape output machine, and taken to one's room; a person went through them at his own speed. Upon return the tape was reused for something else, since the supply of it was very limited, whereas the information remained perpetually in the computers. Direct questioning of the computers—either on matters unclear in the tapes or on any other subject of interest—was permitted whenever there was a console free. The best way of learning about the Six Worlds' civilization, however, was through dreams. The Founders had recorded a great many memories as a means of passing their heritage on to posterity, and all novice Scholars, scientists and non-scientists alike, experienced controlled dreaming frequently.

"Don't you have books?" Brek asked, puzzled.

"No." Noren laughed. "I was horrified when I discovered

71

that; I'd always longed to own books, and I thought Scholars must have lots of them. But they would have been too heavy to import, of course, and the printing press here can barely supply the Technicians and the villagers. We don't need them, not when we can request literature tapes as well as factual ones."

"Stefred has books in his office."

"Those were written here—on this planet, I mean, by people with literary talent. They're copies of what's sold in the Outer City and by village traders. Stefred keeps them in sight to show new candidates that he's human, but any of us can borrow them, and even some of the ones by village authors are as good as literature from the Six Worlds. Not all the gifted people become heretics, after all."

"But surely many do. Aren't there writers and artists among the Scholars?"

"Yes, of course, and musicians, too; but they don't devote full time to it as they probably would outside. They could if they chose, but they feel that the vital jobs have priority. Plenty of Scholars pursue the arts on the side, though, and work that doesn't involve our secrets is sent to the markets under assumed names. You may well have seen some without guessing it came from the Inner City."

"I've always wondered about the music at public ceremonies," Brek declared. "It's completely different from flute music, and it can't be supernatural the way we used to think—what produces it, Noren?"

"Most of it was recorded on the Six Worlds," Noren explained, "and stored in the computers' memory. The sounds are reproduced electronically. A few Scholars have composed new music by programming the computers to rearrange such sounds, which originally came from instruments made of metal or wood, instruments we can't have here."

They talked on for a while, Noren describing the rest

72

of the important training techniques: hypnosis for memorizing technical data that would otherwise require years to absorb; discussions, both formal and informal, with one's tutors; active assistance in the laboratories. Brek listened with avid interest, yet he seemed preoccupied. "Noren," he asked finally, returning to a topic that evidently still troubled him, "about the water plant breakdown . . . I didn't know things like that could happen. Is our survival on this world so precarious in spite of all the safeguards?"

"The more you learn, the more you'll realize how precarious it is," Noren said, hoping he would not have to elaborate. The conversation was coming all too close to matters he still did not want to ponder.

"I don't see how Scholars cope without—without anything to hold to," confessed Brek. "People on the outside are afraid at times, but they've got faith in the Mother Star; they think there's some mysterious power controlling things. It doesn't seem quite right to give that up."

Noren stared at him. "It's funny you should say that. You're a heretic—"

"Not in the same way you are. I—I never doubted the Mother Star, Noren. I challenged only the Scholars' authority. And now, since I've learned what the Star really is . . . I'm torn. I feel empty! Something's lost that I can't ever get back again, though I respect the Prophecy for what it is and what it means for the future. I lay awake last night thinking that that might be the hardest part of being a Scholar." Shamefaced, he mumbled, "I guess you think I'm crazy; certainly all the others would."

Slowly Noren replied, "Perhaps not. To most Scholars the Mother Star means more than the Six Worlds' sun. It's become a sort of symbol."

Brek looked up, surprised. "A symbol of what?"

"That's the strange thing . . . I can't tell you. I don't understand it at all. The private rituals leave me cold."

"What private rituals?"

"Orison, mainly. It's like the Benison held each morning outside the Gates, only there's much more to it than reading from the Book of the Prophecy—references to the Six Worlds' traditions, for instance, and a liturgy that seems to convey something I can't grasp. I've tried to analyze it, but I don't get anywhere."

"Can't Stefred explain?"

"You know Stefred; he likes people to find their own answers, especially about anything serious. And he takes Orison seriously. He goes himself."

"Doesn't everybody?"

"No, and most of the time I don't."

Soberly Brek asked, "Will you go with me, Noren?"

Fighting an odd reluctance, Noren nodded. If Brek felt that he'd lost something, something akin to what ordinary people got from believing the Mother Star was magic, Stefred must know, he realized; the pyschiatric examination a candidate underwent was very thorough. Perhaps that was one reason the subject of Orison had been raised that morning. Perhaps Stefred had been hinting that since he'd been given the responsibility of initiating Brek into the Inner City, he should be prepared to enlighten him about its religious observances.

Was it possible, he wondered suddenly, that in this Brek didn't need enlightenment? Inside, was he afraid that Brek would make sense of the symbols and consider him blind? For the first time it occurred to Noren that they might be intended to learn from each other.

*

The computer room was built into the foundation of the Hall of Scholars; Stefred's study was on an upper level of that tower, which, having been designed as a starship rather than a building, was a baffling maze of compartments, juryrigged lifts, and passageways leading off at odd angles. Its interior partitioning had been altered by the Founders, of course, since in space the outer walls had been "down" in terms of the artificial gravity.

Noren knew all the shortcuts. Hurrying to keep his appointment, he passed through the narrow corridor off which the Dream Machine was located, and to his surprise, overtook Stefred. "We've no need to go back to the office," Stefred told him. "I'd have asked you to come here in the first place, Noren, but I didn't want you anticipating a dream."

"A dream—now?" Under ordinary circumstances, for controlled dreaming one reported at bedtime and slept through the night. Moreover, Stefred's presence indicated that he had just dismissed another dreamer, and it was rare for him to operate the Dream Machine personally. Routine sessions didn't require the attendance of a skilled psychiatrist.

As he entered the cubicle, Noren smiled, remembering how terrifying it had seemed the first time, when he'd been allowed to give his imagination free reign as to the sinister purpose of the equipment. He would never be afraid in that way again, not of anything!

He settled himself in the reclining chair and leaned back against the padded headrest, awaiting the hypnotic preparation that would send him into receptive sleep. During his dream sessions before recantation, drugs had been used, but these were scarce and precious; a Scholar—who trusted the therapist as an unenlightened heretic could not—had no need of them. Hypnosis was employed for various purposes in training, and one learned early to be a good subject.

But this time Stefred did not proceed in the usual way. "I have reasons for not describing this dream to you in advance," he said evenly, "and also for plunging you directly into it without any type of sedation. It will be rather frightening, in some respects a nightmare, but I think you'll find the experience interesting."

Normally one was unconscious when the Dream Machine's electrodes were applied to one's head; despite himself, Noren tensed during the process, wondering what new challenge lay in store for him. It was apparent that what was ahead could not be merely educative. Only once before had he been awake at the time the machine was switched on, and that had been a deliberate test of his susceptibility to panic; no doubt he was again to undergo an evaluation of some sort. Yet the surrounding array of wires, control knobs and dials was no longer dismaying to him, nor was he likely to be thrown by the abrupt shift of location and identity that would occur when the sensory inputs to his mind were replaced by electronic ones. The point at issue must be his ability to adapt to the conditions of the dream world itself: to adapt quickly, unassisted by the relaxing effects of a preliminary sleep phase. Then why not get it over with? he thought irritably. Stefred could have started the machine long ago, and the delay was nerve-wearing. . . .

It was meant to be, Noren realized. Reason told him that he had nothing to be apprehensive about, yet an attempt was being made to arouse apprehension through subtle forms of stress. That wouldn't be done without a constructive aim. He willed himself to remain calm, to enter into the game with confidence; and in the next instant he heard the switch close. There was an explosion of colors before his eyes, followed unexpectedly by total blackness.

Everything around him was black; he was adrift in blackness, falling endlessly into a pit that had neither sides nor bottom. In desperation Noren groped for something to catch hold of. Failing to find it, he reached out with his mind, attempting to draw on the knowledge of the person from whose memories the dream had been recorded. To

76

his dismay, he could grasp no such knowledge. He did not share the man's thoughts as he had the First Scholar's, and, to a lesser extent, the thoughts of the recorders of dream visits to the Six Worlds. His personal identity, however, remained stronger than usual, strong enough to reason that the limitations imposed on him must be the result of drastic editing. The recording was composed less of ideas and emotions than of pure physical sensation; his mental reaction to it would be almost entirely his own.

Resolutely he mastered his initial fright. It was impossible that he could be falling; it had gone on too long. There was no such thing as a pit with no bottom. Besides, there wasn't any sense of motion. Yet his body felt very peculiar, as if it had no weight, and his most basic subconscious instincts interpreted that as a fall. Perhaps he was failing to detect motion merely because he had nothing to relate to, not even the rush of air. . . .

No air? But that *was* impossible! He was breathing, after all . . . or was he? The second onslaught of terror was worse than the first; he wondered whether this was death. Could one dream of death—not of dying, but of death itself? Obviously a dead person could not record any thoughts. But this was unlike former dreams, for he had no real alternate identity; maybe it had not been recorded and then edited, but had instead been simulated from the beginning. It was technically possible to do that: once, some weeks after his recantation, when his growing comprehension of science had led him to conclude that he had no objective grounds for belief in the authenticity of the original dreams, Stefred had let him sample one induced by a faked recording. The difference had been indisputable, but a major part of that difference had been the lack of genuine emotions separate from his own—just what was most noticeable now.

There had been another distinction, however. In the faked dream, the sights and sensations too had seemed unreal. He had been confined to a narrow segment of normal perception, sure that what was apparently taking place could not be happening, could never have happened—yet unable to escape. This was not like that. Unnatural though it was, it *had* happened, somewhere, to someone! It was true . . . so true that it occurred to him that he might actually have died. Perhaps he was no longer dreaming at all.

The truth isn't to be feared, Noren told himself, clinging to the one principle that to him was beyond question or compromise. Slowly the wave of panic passed. There was no doubt that he was breathing; he inhaled and exhaled naturally enough, although no wind touched any part of his body. And his inability to see was probably caused by blindness. He had supposed that the blind knew a softer dark, more like the closing of one's eyes at night than the jet-black expanse before him, but that evidently had not been the case with whoever had made this recording.

Noren resigned himself, surrendering to the realities of the dream. Suddenly he became aware that he had begun to move—though his fall continued, he was also moving by his own effort. There was purpose in the movement; though he still had no external reference points, his muscles worked and he was going somewhere. . . . A dazzling flash of light hit him. He was not blind; the darkness really existed! In its midst was radiance so bright he could scarcely bear to look upon it. He turned aside and for the first time observed his own body, encased in a thick white garment that covered even his hands. Incredibly, he found himself close to one of the City's massive towers—but the tower lay on its side. It had no ground beneath it, or any sky overhead.

Something had gone wrong, Noren decided. This dream must be natural, not controlled; only in natural dreams could one's disorientation be so extreme. Controlled dreams had logic. One met the unknown, the incomprehensible, but never the incongruities that arose spontaneously while one slept. He had been neither drugged nor hypnotized; he could will himself awake if the dream was indeed natural . . . yet he wasn't sure he wanted to. The weightless feeling, now that he had gotten used to it, was really quite pleasant.

He put out his hand to touch the silvery surface of the horizontal tower, feeling a kind of wonder. Disoriented he might be, but his mind was clear; the impressions he was gathering were sharp, detailed, not hazy as they'd been in dreams where he had struggled with abstractions that were beyond him. He was near the tower's top, at least what would have been the top had it been standing. Seizing a handhold that projected from the wall, he reached for another above and began to pull himself around—"up" in terms of his present position, though there was little of the effort involved in climbing—curious as to what might be visible from greater height. To his astonishment, he got no higher. He passed handhold after handhold, only to see the convex wall stretch on and on above him as if its span had become infinite.

Once again fear stirred in Noren. A black shadow cut sharply across the wall, coming ever closer; if he kept going he would soon re-enter darkness. And he had no choice. He had no volition as far as the actions of his body were concerned; when he tried to control them, he discovered that the Dream Machine was doing so after all. His only freedom was in his personal inner response. To be sure, that had been the case in the previous dreams, but always before there had been the compensation of shared thought. He had not been compelled to proceed into the unknown with no idea of what his alter ego's goal had been. Then too, he had not been so alone. There had been people around, talking to him, listening to words that came from his lips and by their reaction guiding his adjustment. Here he was isolated; it was all taking place in utter silence.

79

He approached the shadow, thinking how very odd it was that the tower, when first seen from a short distance, had been fully illuminated. Something behind him must be casting that shadow, some monstrous thing that was advancing. . . . If only he could turn his head! His heart thudded painfully and he felt chills permeate his flesh, yet his hands were firm as he moved them from grip to grip. The physical symptoms of fear must be his own, he realized; they were occurring in his sleeping body, while the recording contained only the confident motions of a man who had not trembled. He held to that thought as his right arm disappeared into the dark.

Then, without any foreknowledge of the intent, he did turn for an instant, looking back over his shoulder toward the source of light he was leaving behind; and it so startled Noren that he felt he was not only falling, but spinning. Though the tower was still there, he was sure that he'd lost contact with it, that he would fall forever toward a fire that was worse than darkness. There was no shape to cast a shadow. There was only a vast black sky dominated by a sun, immense and horribly brilliant, that looked much as it had on film and in his first controlled dream and in all too many of his natural ones; but he had no shelter from it now. He was in the presence of the nova. . . .

One glance was enough. It was a relief to creep on into the dark where that intolerable flame could not reach him. Why couldn't it? Noren wondered, momentarily baffled. A sun, when it shone, shone everywhere. Why wasn't it shining on the whole tower? His head and shoulders were by this time enveloped in blackness; he raised his free hand to turn a knob on the helmet he hadn't realized he was wearing. Instantly there was light again: not sunlight, but innumerable swarms of blazing points that could be nothing but stars.

Awestruck, Noren clung to the wall of the tower, facing

outward, while comprehension flooded into his mind. It came not from the recorder's thoughts, to which he still had no access, but from his own power of reason; the pieces at last began to fit. He'd been climbing not up, but around —around the circular tower to the side opposite from the sun. And it wasn't really a tower yet; it was still a starship. He was in space!

Noren had seen space from the viewport of the First Scholar's starship during the first controlled dreams he had experienced, but that was not at all the same as being outside such a ship. Aboard the starship there had been artificial gravity; he had encountered neither weightlessness nor the absence of "up" and "down," although he'd since been told of these conditions. He had also been told that stars would appear abnormally bright outside the atmosphere of the planet on which he'd been born, which was even thicker than the Six Worlds' atmospheres, and that the sun, too, would be brighter—but mere words had not prepared him for the actuality.

It was not the nova he'd just glimpsed, he perceived. The nova had been observed only from the escaping fleet, which had gone into stardrive minutes after the explosion; no one could have been outside a ship then. He must have seen the Mother Star at some time before it novaed. Yet he had never heard of thought recordings having been brought from the Six Worlds, and this dream seemed so real, so immediate, that he felt sure it had been recorded in real time rather than from memory.

The stars . . . he could not grasp what it meant to be seeing the stars this way! Obscured by the polarization that had protected his eyes from the naked sun, they'd burst into visibility when he, the astronaut, had changed the filter setting of his helmet. The astronaut had no doubt seen them often, but Noren did not share his thoughts and was still overpowered as he clambered further around the ship—

and came face to face with the most awesome sight of all.

It was a planet, a huge planet half-filling his field of vision, that except for some yellow splotches was shrouded in grayish-white. Noren turned cold. Not one of the Six Worlds had looked like that! He had seen films showing all of them; most had been predominantly green or blue, with their white areas forming clear, though shifting, patterns. Was this then an alien solar system, one judged unsuitable for use and quickly abandoned? There had been many such. The planet looked inhospitable enough: some deep, racial instinct told him that it was not right for colonizing, that it could not support life of his kind. As a human refuge it would indeed be useless. . . .

No, he thought suddenly. Inhospitable, yes, but not quite useless. It was not an abandoned planet. It was his own.

*

The waking was as it had frequently been in recent weeks: slowly, naturally, Noren slipped back into the real world, feeling not the relief of escape from nightmare, but a sense of loss, of exile from a place he had not wished to leave. Before he reached full consciousness, there were flashes of memory from other dreams: a surging ocean, a broad green meadow dotted with shade trees, a city without walls where men and women partook freely of wonders past description; but he clung longest to the glory of the unveiled stars.

"You adapted." Stefred's approval seemed tinged, somewhat, by a trace of feeling Noren couldn't identify. Turning from the panel of dials that enabled him to monitor a dreamer's well-being, he continued, "If I asked you to go through that again, with some variations—perhaps to do so repeatedly—would it bother you?"

"No," Noren replied confidently. "It's only a dream, after all. Besides, I understand it now, and there were parts that were—exciting."

Stefred smiled ruefully. "Some people find them so, others don't. I was practically certain that you would."

"Who recorded it?" asked Noren. "The other dreams, except the First Scholar's, were of the Six Worlds, but this was here. I looked down on *this* world."

"We don't know his name. He was one of the shuttlecraft pilots who dismantled the starships and brought them down to be reassembled as towers." With odd hesitancy, as if it was painful to go on, Stefred added, "For him, of course, it was more than a dream."

"It was his job, and he—he must have liked it," Noren commented, making a guess as to Stefred's own immediate job and resolving to face what must be faced squarely.

"Would you like it if it were yours?"

To consider that was frustrating, but Noren made no attempt to evade the question. Part of the discipline of a Scholar's education, he knew, lay in coming to terms with the fact that the vast universe beyond this one deficient planet—the universe accessible to his forefathers—could not be reached outside of dreams. This was necessary. Scholars were not supposed to be content with what they had; they were supposed to long for the unattainable, since only in that way could the goal of restoring the Six Worlds' lost riches be kept constantly in view. People who want what they don't have progress faster than those who are satisfied. The Prophecy itself had been created to ensure that the villagers would never stop wanting the changes it promised.

"You're tantalizing me," he said, determined to take it in stride.

"Not this time," Stefred replied. "This time I'm doing something quite different." He drew breath, then persisted, "How would you feel about going into space not in a dream, but in reality?"

"That's impossible."

"No. A space shuttle still exists. Some of the starships are still in orbit, though in the First Scholar's time they were stripped of all useful equipment."

Yes, awaiting the Time of the Prophecy, when each hull would become the nucleus of a new city; Noren knew that. He tried to make light of the matter by stating the obvious: "I don't know how to bring down a starship."

"You know as much as anyone on this planet, or at least you will after you've been through that dream in its complete and unedited form often enough."

Looking into Stefred's face, Noren exclaimed, "You're . . . *serious!*"

Stefred nodded soberly. He detached the Dream Machine apparatus, saying, "Save your questions, Noren. I realize that's difficult, but there is no time for them now, and at the meeting tonight they will be answered."

Dazed by the overwhelming implications of what he was hearing, Noren sat up. "One thing more," Stefred cautioned. "I must ask you to say nothing of this dream, particularly not to Brek."

"Can't you let him be involved, too?" protested Noren, thinking that when Brek did find out, he would be justifiably envious.

"I intend to, and the test isn't valid unless a person comes to it unsuspecting, as you did." With a sigh Stefred admitted, "Quite possibly it's not valid even then, but there's a limit to what I can devise on three days' notice."

Noren knew better than to prolong the discussion. He took leave of Stefred and headed downstairs to meet Brek, in such turmoil over the momentous happenings of the day that he found it hard to keep his composure. Only a little while remained before the meeting. There wasn't time to go to the main refectory open to all Inner City residents, where he had hoped to see Talyra; he and Brek must again eat at the one in the Hall of Scholars. It was crowded, for the coming assembly was on everyone's mind and few had wished to interrupt their speculations about what might take place, as would have been necessary in the presence of Technicians. Steering clear of that topic, Noren talked instead of Talyra. If she had arrived on any other day, he would be sharing supper with her, not with Brek, he thought ruefully. He would never have spent her first evening in the City at the Hall of Scholars, the one tower she was barred from entering unless summoned for specific duties. He was torn; he longed to be with her, yet excitement about what lay ahead outweighed everything else. If the starships were to be retrieved from orbit, that could only mean that a breakthrough in the research was much closer than anyone had guessed!

They went to Orison. For that also, more Scholars were present than usual; even regular attendees did not come every night, since they often worked late, but this evening all work had been stopped. Besides, the room in which Orison was held was the only one large enough for a general assembly, and people had already begun to gather.

Noren did not know the liturgy well, except for the parts that were direct quotations from the Book of the Prophecy. He was aware, of course, that in ritual created by the Scholars for their own use the Mother Star was meant to be viewed neither in the villagers' way, as a magical power in the sky, nor in the scientific way, as a sun that had become a nova. It was representative of something else. The difficulty lay in grasping what the "something else" was. "You told me that some things Scholars do can't be explained in advance, but have to be experienced," Brek reminded him as they went in. "Maybe this is one of them."

"But when I come," Noren objected, "I don't experience anything."

This time he did.

Perhaps it was the larger group, the air of tense expectancy; perhaps too it was the fact that he was already thoroughly shaken by the events of the past two days. There was nothing different in the dimly lighted room itself, with its prismatic glass sunburst, larger than the one in the refectory, affixed to the ceiling's center; nor was there anything unique in the Six Worlds' stirring orchestral music that no longer overwhelmed him as it had when he'd first heard it outside the Gates. There was no apparent difference in the ritual. The presiding Scholars were robed, as was customary, but all the others wore everyday clothes like his own. The words, presumably, were the same ones always used, allowing for a normal amount of daily variation.

He was standing, staring upward at the light glinting from myriad facets of the sunburst, and had allowed his mind to drift. Talyra . . . some of the words were those Stefred had used to bless Talyra, except for being expressed in first person plural: *"May the spirit of the Mother Star abide with us . . . may we gain strength from its presence, trusting in the surety of its power."* But there was no surety! That was the truth he'd hidden from. . . .

All day it had lain at the surface of his thoughts; still he had not dared to consider its full significance. *You must grapple with it alone,* Stefred had said, yet he hadn't done so. What was the matter with him? Noren wondered in dismay. He did not want to shrink from the truth! Truth had always been what he cared most about, and though he'd known it could sometimes be painful, he had not ever meant to let that deter him. He had not faltered when confrontation of the facts had required him to give up his most cherished theories and to undergo the ordeal of recanting. He would not falter now. Grimly, Noren forced himself to face the thing his recent doubts implied: it was possible that he would someday find that recanting had been a terrible mistake.

86

It was not just that he'd unwittingly affirmed a promise that might not be kept. As matters stood, the Scholars intended to keep it; they were struggling toward that end; they were not deceiving the people for any reason but to attain the end. If it was attained, there would have been no deceit. But what if at some time in the future they were to learn that the Prophecy could never be fulfilled? What if the research were to end in utter failure? There would then be no justification for secrecy, no justification for withholding either machines or knowledge from anyone. The First Scholar himself would not have justified such policies on lesser grounds than the saving of mankind from extinction; he wouldn't have concealed truth from people to uphold a vain hope any more than the Six Worlds' leaders had concealed news of the impending nova. He had assured his companions that he was not asking them to establish a false religion. But the religion he'd created had been the center of people's lives for generations now, and somehow Noren couldn't picture its High Priests abolishing it if it proved invalid, although the restrictions it placed on the villagers would then be unwarranted.

The ritual words went on: *"For there is no surety save in the light that sustained our forefathers; no hope but in that which lies beyond our sphere; and our future is vain except as we have faith. . . ."* He had heard them before, but he hadn't grasped them. He had thought them a reference to the necessity for preserving the knowledge of the Six Worlds. Yet they weren't that at all! The Scholars knew such knowledge was insufficient, that research based on it might fail, and that hard work wasn't enough to ensure that the Prophecy would come true. The words were an admission of these things. No wonder even the scientists clung to religious symbolism; it kept them from having to say in plain words that their own hope might be a delusion.

Noren wrenched his mind away from the thought. It

didn't matter now, not now, when there had evidently been some unexpected new development, when there were plans to retrieve the starships. . . . And yet, he realized suddenly, Stefred had not acted as if he knew that a breakthrough was close. He'd been clearly aware of what was to be discussed at the meeting, but he had not been happy; he'd been troubled. Even about the starships he'd been troubled. In no way had he behaved like a man who was privy to good news.

As the solemn ritual proceeded, Noren stood transfixed, his eyes uplifted less from custom than from inability to look away. The Mother Star . . . symbol of a delusion? All at once he swayed giddily, gripped by an intangible terror unlike any he had ever encountered. If there was delusion, it concerned not merely the Prophecy, but survival itself. In theory he had known that survival could not continue unless metal became available. Yet he hadn't followed his fears to their logical conclusion. He had never imagined the death of the human race occurring not through anyone's lack of effort, but because synthesization of metallic elements turned out to be inherently impossible.

There were more words, but he did not hear them. The sunburst blurred, and in its place the desolate planet, alien and inhospitable as he'd seen it in the dream, swam before his eyes. Trembling, he lowered them and slowly, deliberately, surveyed the people around him. Brek's face was grave, reverent; that was understandable because Brek did not yet know that the nuclear physicists had no proof that their work would ever succeed. But the older Scholars surely knew, whether they were scientists themselves or mere observers. And they did not seem afraid. Some showed no emotion at all; the rest appeared at peace with the world, as if there were indeed something in which they could trust.

"Noren?" At the touch of Brek's hand on his arm, Noren

88

was jolted back from the precipice. He noticed that the lights had brightened and that most of the people were now sitting down, awaiting the start of the meeting. The rite of Orison was over.

A hush fell as the chairman of the executive council rose to speak. "I'll come right to the point," he said quietly. "As some of you already know, we face a crucial decision. The purpose of this meeting is to discuss whether or not we should make an immediate attempt to found a new city on the other side of the Tomorrow Mountains."

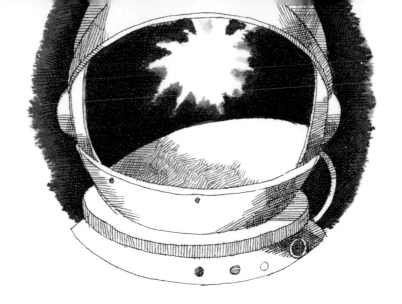

IV

AFTERWARD, WHENEVER HE RECALLED THAT MEETING, Noren found it hard to believe that he could have sat through it so impassively; yet impassive he was. Already in shock from the impact of the fear that had overpowered him during Orison, he was incapable of feeling the shock that the prospect of another city would otherwise have aroused in him—and did arouse in those of his fellow Scholars who weren't on the committee that had engaged in advance discussion. A new city had not been thought possible prior to the success of the research. They had barely enough equipment to keep the existing one going; how could any be diverted? There was nothing most Scholars would like better than to be in on such a project, but how could it be justified?

"As heretics, you were warned before the secrets were revealed to you that you would be confined here for life," the chairman told them. "It was repeated at your sentencing and again later, when the conditions of your confinement were explained. No release was anticipated. Never since the First Scholar's expedition arrived has a Scholar been farther than the platform outside the Gates: at first because the risk of disclosing the Six Worlds' destruction was too great, and then because for us to mingle with the villagers—even when we wouldn't be recognized as former heretics—would rob us of the remoteness that's essential both for maintaining general respect and for recruiting people with inquiring minds. There have been several other reasons."

The traditional sacrifice of one's physical freedom could not be abandoned lightly, they knew; for one thing, it caused the desperate urgency of man's dependence on time-worn machines and his vital need to solve his basic technological problems to remain uppermost in one's outlook. And there had been no constructive purpose in abandoning it. Technicians had been exploring beyond the Tomorrow Mountains since soon after the Founding, using as many of the precious aircars as could be spared from the top-priority task of transporting land treatment machines to the villages. Scholars might have gone along, since no contact with villagers was involved, but they had not done so, not only because of tradition but because they couldn't take time from their own vital work in the City. It was more efficient for Technicians to survey the land, verifying the detailed orbital surveys that had been made prior to the Founding, and bringing back minerals for analysis. There had never been talk of a permanent outpost; yet apparently, the situation had changed.

The explanation and ensuing debate continued most of the night. The executive committee, composed of department heads and elected council members, had already held debates and had decided, by a slim margin, to recommend the project; but anything involving a major policy change must be put to a vote among all the fully committed. Even relatively small matters, like whether a particular tool should be melted down and its elements allocated to research, were so decided, for such things were of far-reaching significance. The disposition of one kilo of metal might conceivably determine whether future generations lived or died. The disposition of enough materials to set up an outpost could very easily determine it. Yet no one could be sure, Noren thought in horror. How could they dare to vote on an issue when they were not sure? It was fortunate that he, as an uncommitted novice, had neither the right nor the responsibility to do so.

"Normally, a decision of this magnitude would demand many weeks of deliberation," the chairman said. "For reasons I'll explain presently, we must hold the vote tonight—"

An astonished gasp from the assembled Scholars made him pause; then, calmly, he continued, "But before I go into that, I think we should consider the less urgent factors, those related to the status of our work."

Noren had not yet acquired the technical background to follow the discussion fully; his study, aside from mathematics, had thus far been limited to underlying principles. The emphasis had been on understanding the fundamental basis of the research, for details, when needed, could be quickly memorized under hypnosis. He'd been told that to be creative, one must have a thorough comprehension of a task's nature. That had to be gained slowly, in the case of the Scholars as a group no less than in the case of each individual trainee. At first he had been impatient with the slowness of the way the work had progressed over the years. He hadn't been able to see why the current experimentation was designed not to produce metal, but simply to verify certain aspects of the theory that seemed most promising. Wasn't there some shortcut? he'd demanded. Wouldn't it be quicker to try out the theory by actually attempting fusion of heavy elements?

It would not, Grenald had explained. If they proceeded that way and failed, no one would be able to tell what had gone wrong; the various ideas involved must be tested separately. Moreover, having no materials to waste, they could not build the equipment for a full-scale experiment until they were sure that the theory was sound. Everything done so far showed that it was, for it had been developed gradually as, one by one, the conflicting theories had been eliminated. All the same, no matter how many things pointed to a theory's accuracy, a single demonstrated fact that didn't fit would be enough to disprove it.

Although Noren did not have a full grasp of the theory itself, he was familiar with the mathematics involved in it; he always absorbed rapidly any math he encountered. And he was well aware of what was at stake in the experimentation in progress. If it verified everything it had been planned to verify, an attempt to achieve fusion might conceivably be made soon. Experiments rarely worked out that well, however, and it was more probable that a need for further tests would become apparent. To progress directly to the synthesization of usable metal would require a true breakthrough: an outcome even better than could be foreseen, one that revealed facts nobody had guessed. And if by any chance some facet of the theory proved to be not merely unverified, but definitely erroneous, then the theory would have to be modified. That could take years of work. No one talked about that.

At least they hadn't talked about it until the meeting.

As he listened to the discussion, Noren soon saw that the Scholars were divided into three factions: one that favored sticking to the Founders' original plan; one that felt a breakthrough might be imminent enough to justify getting a head start on another city; and one that feared a setback would occur, a setback too serious to be dealt with except by drastic measures. It was this last group that had first proposed that preparation for the establishment of a distant outpost should begin. "We must be ready," its spokesmen declared, "because if our current theory proves inadequate, there is only one way we can turn—toward techniques that will eventually entail experimentation too risky to be tried in an inhabited area."

That nuclear fusion was potentially dangerous was something that had astonished Noren when, soon after beginning his studies, he had been shown a film of something called a "thermonuclear bomb." It had been quite horrifying, especially when the purpose of the bomb—for which nothing in his own world had prepared him—had become clear; he'd been thankful that he had not been introduced to it through a dream. There were no such dreams, since thermonuclear bombs had not existed in the time of the Founders and had in fact been abolished long before thought recording had been invented. But the film had been preserved, for there were lessons in it, and among them one of particular importance to potential experimenters: extreme care must be taken in the effort to achieve controlled nuclear reactions lest they produce an uncontrolled one.

The danger had not been great so far. Long ago the scientists of the Six Worlds had learned to control nuclear fusion and had harnessed it for the generation of power; the City's main power plant was a fusion reactor, as those of the mother world had been after its supply of organic fuel was exhausted. Fusion power was clean and safe; it did not even create radioactive wastes. But nuclear fusion of heavy elements was far more difficult and complex than the type of fusion employed in a power plant. If it could be achieved at all, it would be achieved only through methods unlike the proven ones, and the approaches as yet untried were not without peril.

To men of the Six Worlds, it would have seemed obvious that all nuclear experimentation ought to be done far away from the City. It wasn't that simple, however. The facilities necessary for such experimentation did not exist anywhere but in the City, and they couldn't be moved without dangerous depletion of its reserves. The villagers were dependent upon the City for weather control, purified water to supplement rain catchment, and the periodic soil treatment and seed irradiation; without those things, they would perish. The hazards of splitting the City's resources had until now been greater than the chances of a serious accident. Yet if new failures were to affect those odds. . . .

The Founders had expected failures. They had realized that they and their successors were facing a task considered impossible by the science of their own era; and this, after all, was why they'd set up a social system that was in most respects morally repugnant to them. It had been the only way to buy time, enough time for the impossible to be accomplished. Transmutation of the elements . . . it was an old dream; before the dawn of science, men had tried to transform base metals into gold. Later men had laughed. No one had imagined a situation in which man's survival would hinge upon a variation of the alchemists' laughable, impossible goal: the changing of other elements into metals.

The very existence of a planet without usable metals had been a surprise to the Six Worlds' scientists when, after the initial fruitless explorations that had followed the perfection of the stardrive, they had come upon it. They'd been looking for worlds to colonize, and had previously found none with suitable gravity, climate and atmosphere; at first this one had elated them. Its soil contained poisons, but technology could deal with poisons. There had been no expectation of discovering planets where advanced technology would be unnecessary, for it had been assumed that if such planets existed, intelligent life forms would have evolved upon them, making them unavailable for claim. It had been recognized that a people that had fully populated its own solar system could continue to survive only by means of technology: the technology to build starships, and the technology to utilize otherwise-uninhabitable worlds. That was the natural way of things. When survival was threatened, technology developed to meet the threat. Even the nova could not have endangered the survival of a star-faring race, had it not been for the unfortunate chance that the sole refuge located before tragedy struck lacked the metal on which all technology depended.

Astronomers had long known that some stars were metal-poor; whether their planets were also metal-poor—or even whether they had planets—could be determined only by exploration. Some had been found to have planets without solid ground. This world, however, had been a puzzle at the beginning. It was solid, composed primarily of silicon, yet its proportion of metallic elements was even lower than that of its sun. There was no metal ore at all; the orbital surveys, made with sensitive and trustworthy instruments, showed that clearly. Only traces were present, traces too small to be extracted without prohibitively complex equipment. Baffled, the first landing parties had investigated further, and had come to an awesome conclusion: what little usable metal the planet had once had was already exhausted. It had been mined in past ages by visitors from some other solar system who had depleted the ore and gone on.

Nothing was known of these mysterious visitors of the past, for though the signs of their excavations were unmistakable, they had left no artifacts. No one could tell where they'd come from or where they had gone. Since this was their first proof of intelligence elsewhere in the universe, the scientists of the Six Worlds had been excited; such a find had seemed ample compensation for the fact that the planet could never become a self-supporting colony. But that, of course, had been before the nova wiped out all sources of off-world support.

The Founders had known in advance that the Six Worlds' sun would nova—but only a few weeks in advance. The starfleet had been small, and there were frustrating limits to what it could carry. Life support equipment had first priority; the computers with their irreplaceable store of knowledge second; facilities for conducting research, although also vital, had of necessity been confined to an absolute minimum. No expansion of those facilities was possible without metal.

It was a vicious circle. By scouring the planet, the remaining traces of suitable metal might have been located; but such traces could not be utilized without equipment that wasn't obtainable. Once the breakthrough occurred—once even a small amount of metal had been synthesized—it would become possible to manufacture the equipment. Then the world's limited resources could be tapped. Perhaps metal could then be reached by drilling into the planet's core. But would there ever be any breakthrough when the laboratories weren't adequately outfitted?

Never before had Noren heard pessimism from the scientists, but at the meeting there were some who expressed it openly. "We're fools if we don't recognize that our present line of thought may have to be modified," one of them asserted. "Within weeks—half a year at the most—this series of experiments will be finished; without better facilities we may find ourselves facing a dead end—"

"No!" Grenald interrupted, rising to his feet in anger. "It's not a dead end. This time we will succeed."

There was silence. Everyone respected Grenald, and he had been head of the nuclear physics department for many years. Yet he looked old, tired; it was obvious to all that with the culmination of his work close at hand, he himself had become uncertain and afraid. Stefred's words came back to Noren: *He is an old man who has devoted most of his*

97

life to research that he won't live to see completed. Stefred knew, he thought sadly. Stefred knew that Grenald's hope of an imminent breakthrough was based on wishful thinking.

"We will succeed," Grenald repeated, "and because we will, we should take the preliminary steps toward founding a second city. We betray our trust if we delay by a single week the Transition Period's beginning."

The Transition Period was the time during which the groundwork would be laid for the keeping of the Prophecy's promises. They couldn't be fulfilled all at once, of course. The people had been told that when the Mother Star appeared there would be machines and cities for everyone, and most pictured those cities rising out of the ground overnight; but it would not happen that way. Building would be a slow process even after metal was available and factories had been established. Furthermore, villagers who stood in awe of machines would not be ready to move into cities, much less to share the job of construction. During the Transition Period, villagers who so wished would be given the opportunity to become Technicians; they would be free to enter training centers, work on the new cities, and then move there. People who preferred to remain farmers, but were willing to sell their land and start farms near the new cities, would rank as Technicians, too. By the time the Star became visible, the promised things would indeed be available to all.

At Grenald's words, there was a murmur of agreement; all Scholars were anxious for the Transition Period to begin. Moreover, the Inner City was crowded. Though no children were reared there, the population outside had grown rapidly over the years, and that meant the number of people who became heretics steadily increased; before long no more doubling up in quarters would be feasible. Then one of the Outer City's domes would have to be taken—an unthink-

98

able step, for it would mean imposing hardship on the Technicians who would be ousted. Some Scholars felt a new city could be justified on those grounds alone.

Others, however, were cautious. "You speak to bolster your own confidence," they told Grenald. "Do you think acting as if the research has already succeeded will somehow bring it to pass? It won't! If we weaken this City by a premature attempt to establish another, we'll certainly betray our trust. The equipment we've safeguarded so long will be lost."

The proponents of this view outnumbered Grenald's supporters, but the proposal for the new city was also backed by the third faction—the group that believed failure of the current experiments would demand an outpost for more dangerous ones. "We know there's risk in weakening the City's reserves," they maintained, "but it's less than that of nuclear accident if we must turn to the avenues saved for a last resort. So in either case the project makes sense. If we succeed soon, we'll have a head start on the Transition Period, and if we don't, we'll be prepared for what may have to be tried next."

Back and forth went the argument, until at last someone contended, "Wouldn't it be simpler just to wait and see? As we've said, it will be no more than half a year until we know the outcome of Grenald's work. Surely we could make a much wiser decision then; I fail to understand why the committee has brought up the matter at this point."

It was then that the chairman rose once more. "I did not wish to reveal this until all sides had been considered," he said, "since if there had been a strong majority either for or against the proposal, it would have outweighed the immediate considerations. But the fact is that if we're going to set up an outpost beyond the Tomorrow Mountains, we should do it now. A new base will require retrieval of a starship from orbit, and the starships can be reached only if

99

the space shuttle homes in on their electronic beacons, beacons that have been monitored by the computers since the time of the Founders. Three days ago there was a signal failure alarm. The solar-powered beacon in one of the starships is no longer functioning at full strength; and the computers have warned us that if we do not retrieve that ship at once, it will be lost to us forever."

*

In the end, when the meeting was over and Noren and Brek walked back to their lodgings to spend the few hours until morning, there could be little doubt that the outpost would be established. The vote had been cast by secret ballot and was not yet counted; but the prevailing opinion had been clear. The beacon failure alarm had become the deciding factor.

The two looked up at the stars, faint dots speckling the gaps between towers that almost touched overhead. Noren thought of them as they had been in the dream: blazing points of pure, unfiltered light. He would perhaps see them so in reality! But Brek knew nothing of that, and so they could not talk of it.

Elated, Brek began, "To go beyond the Tomorrow Mountains—"

"You don't know that you'll be one to go. They said that except for certain specialists, the choice would be made by lot."

"They also said that the place would be staffed on a rotation basis, that no one would stay there permanently. We're young, Noren! Sooner or later we'll get there even if we're not among the first! It's life imprisonment against . . . hope."

"Does it bother you that much—the confinement, I mean?"

"I—I don't know. I haven't had as long as you have to get used to the idea. I'm willing, certainly. But I can't pretend that it doesn't matter to me."

Noren was detached, numb. "I don't think I ever felt that way, even at first," he reflected. "The Inner City has everything I was seeking—"

"It's different for you. You're gifted; someday you'll be a top scientist."

"Where did you hear that?" Noren demanded.

"In the computer room today, when you were off with Stefred. Everyone knows it. If Grenald's work should fail conclusively, it would take years to prepare for a new series of experiments, and you're the best prospect for coming up with some brand-new approach."

But that was awful, Noren thought. They were counting on him for something that might not even exist! He did not doubt his ability to learn; he would surely seek out whatever truth was accessible to him; but suppose the truth was that there were no new approaches? He would not become like Grenald, defending an unproven theory with the idea that sheer stubbornness would *make* it true.

The next morning Brek was summoned to see Stefred, and after supper Noren too was called. He was relieved, for though he'd planned to spend the evening with Talyra, sharing the day's meals with her had been a strain. She had not understood his preoccupation; she'd been confused, thinking him tormented by some lingering result of heresy, and had plied him with questions he could not answer. For more reasons than one, he found himself eager to be involved in the retrieval of the starship.

A small group had gathered in Stefred's office, all young men who had experienced the dream. Brek had been through it and was as excited as the rest; an opportunity for space flight was beyond the wildest hopes any of them had ever cherished. Who could worry about the future when the present offered so much?

It was not as fantastic as it seemed, Stefred explained.

101

The space shuttle had an automatic pilot, which, as they'd heard at the meeting, was programmed to dock with the starship's electronic beacon; no piloting skill was needed. The crewmen's task would be to dismantle the ship so that it could be brought down piece by piece. They would, to be sure, have to work in spacesuits under zero gravity conditions. No one living had ever done anything like that —but neither had the first men to walk in space, back in ancient times when five of the Six Worlds had yet to be colonized. And those men hadn't had the advantage of a detailed and accurate introduction to it through dreams.

The Founders had planned well. As Noren had guessed, the shuttlecraft pilot had recorded his thoughts not from memory, but in real time during an actual flight, knowing that those who would make such flights again would have no prior experience even with high-speed aircraft, let alone spaceships. "On the Six Worlds boys of your age would not have been given this job," Stefred said, "since years of training would have been required. We have no trained astronauts. The older Scholars are engaged in other work for which they're vitally needed, and besides, they're not in condition physically. Your youth is an advantage in both those respects; the only other qualification is that you be willing to risk your lives." He eyed them intently. "You must understand from the beginning that it's dangerous. The space shuttle has been unused for generations. It has been maintained according to the instructions left us by the Founders, but we have no guarantee that it will perform. And that's not the only hazard—"

"Do you really think any of us would turn down a chance to fly into space?" someone interrupted indignantly.

"I don't," Stefred admitted. "That's why I'm not happy about offering it." Sighing, he continued, "I will tell you frankly that I voted against the proposed new city both in the executive committee and at last night's meeting. The majority was with me until the matter of the beacon failure arose; I suspect that those who changed their minds on that basis were following emotion, not reason."

"But surely, if an outpost is likely to be needed soon anyway, we shouldn't waste the last chance to get this starship!" Noren exclaimed. There were no materials left for constructing domes like those of the Outer City, and certain vital equipment could not be installed in village-type buildings of rough stone or brick, which couldn't be air-conditioned; so a prefabricated "tower" would be needed in every city until the planet's industry was well established. Moreover, to villagers, a city without any of the unique and spectacular towers would not be a City at all. They would not consider the Prophecy fulfilled unless their own area had one. "There'll be barely enough towers for the Transition Period as it is," he argued. "Losing one could affect the outcome of the Founders' plan."

"Some of us," Stefred said soberly, "feel that it may affect it more if we risk six promising young Scholars in attempts to home in on a signal that's known to be unreliable."

Noren drew breath. "You mean it may fail completely . . . while we're in space."

"It may. In that case the automatic pilot may abort the mission successfully—or it may not. Have you wondered why I made the test dream so rough, Noren? Why I plunged you alone into a blackness you could not com-prehend, leading you to think you might be confronting death? If that shuttlecraft fails to dock, it may go into an extrasolar orbit, an endless orbit! Have you any conception of what that means?"

The thought, though sobering, did not alter anyone's enthusiasm; and Stefred, convinced that they were genuine volunteers, went on to discuss the details of their prepara-tion, setting up schedules for intensive use of the Dream

Machine. But it was plain that he was not really comfortable about the project. Noren was uncomfortable also, but for a different cause; when Brek and the others left, he stayed behind a few minutes.

"Stefred," he asked, "why, when you knew I'd be away erecting the tower at the new outpost, did you bring Talyra in yesterday? Why did you say that the decision could not wait?"

Stefred hesitated for a long time. "Someday I'll tell you, Noren," he said finally. "It's complicated." He made a gesture of dismissal; then, abruptly, burst out, "If you have any reservations about what you said yesterday during our talk, any doubts about preferring to know more than can be learned through exclusive concentration on science, then you should not join the space crew."

Numerous though Noren's doubts had become, there were none on that score. He said nothing, realizing that no reply was expected.

"Grenald begged me to disqualify you arbitrarily, but it wouldn't have been fair to do that. The choice had to be yours. Nevertheless, he does have logic on his side; the risk, in your case, is perhaps excessive—"

Slowly, Noren shook his head. "It won't do, Stefred," he said. "You've been trying to scare me but you know I won't back out no matter how scared I am. We both know that the Scholars who voted in favor of this project are just as concerned about the risking of life as you are, and that it's basic policy to respect the decisions of volunteers. You've admitted you can't bar me from volunteering. You can't even tell me to consider my potential as a scientist; yesterday you advised the exact opposite! There's some other issue that's worrying you, and you still aren't giving me all the facts."

"Maybe I'm not," Stefred conceded. "But did it ever occur to you that perhaps I don't have them all?" He stared

104

out into the night, where the glowing windows of the adjacent tower obscured the stars. "I don't know why I blame myself," he muttered, more to himself than to Noren. "If I followed Grenald's urgings and my own best judgment, you would hate me for it. You've got too independent a mind to want protection from the perils to which skepticism can lead; you also have youth. That's a dangerous combination; yet if the salvation of the world lay solely in old men's caution, why would young people be born?"

Noren left the room quietly, pressing the point no further. Though the reply he'd received was cryptic, it was obviously not meant to be otherwise. Always before he had felt secure under Stefred's guidance; now he sensed that something was wrong, terribly wrong—something Stefred himself was disturbed by. This time the challenge was not a planned lesson. It was real and unavoidable, and Stefred trusted him to find a way to meet it.

*

From then on the days were too busy for brooding over anything. The training dreams, unlike the edited one Stefred had devised as a test, had no element of nightmare; both Noren and Brek found them fascinating. Dreaming, they experienced not only zero gravity and the techniques of maneuvering in a spacesuit, but the specific process of dismantling starships—which, having been originally assembled in orbit, were designed to come apart. The starships were made not of metal, but of a semi-metal alloy that could not be reshaped by any means available on the planet. Had it been possible to melt them down, the material would have been used long before to make tools and machines. As it was, special tools were needed to separate the sections of airtight shell, and only a few had been kept: enough for two men to use at a time. That meant the job would be a slow one. Many trips would be required to get an entire starship down using a single small shuttle; since only two

105

men could work, only two would go on each flight. The fact that this also appeared to minimize the risk seemed of little comfort to Stefred.

Noren did not see Stefred often; the Dream Machine was turned over to the young women who normally operated it, and the six prospective astronauts used it in rotation, day and night. In between, they scrutinized the Inner City's towers closely, tried on the carefully preserved spacesuits, and—following the detailed instructions of the computers —checked out the shuttlecraft itself. It was stored in its original bay in a tower that had not been fully converted. The first ascent was to be made under cover of darkness so that the villagers would not observe it; after that, of course, all traffic would be on the other side of the Tomorrow Mountains.

Ten days were allotted to preparation, the maximum number that could elapse, according to the computers' projections, if the starship beacon was to function until all the work was finished. Lots were drawn whereby Scholars not held back by essential duties were designated for the first staff of the outpost; they too began to get ready. Until the tower was assembled, only a few would go; but more would follow, and with them, Inner City Technicians. That was necessary because some of the chosen Scholars were married to Technicians, and also because others, like Noren and Brek, were uncommitted. The secret of the outpost's existence could not be kept from the Inner City Technicians, and once they saw people not known to be Scholars going there, they would want an equal chance for themselves. Everybody wanted to go beyond the mountains. Yet life in the settlement would be anything but easy. There would be backbreaking work with an absolute minimum of equipment, not only in construction, but in the raising of food. Aircars couldn't be spared to transport food indefinitely; the Scholars would have to spend part of their time farming by the primitive Stone Age methods they'd been taught in the villages as children. Noren was not looking forward to that, though he considered the founding of a new city well worth it.

Meanwhile, whatever free time he had he spent with Talyra. He had thought she would be lonely and frightened in the City, that she would seek not only his love, but his comfort; it didn't work out that way. To his astonishment, Talyra did not seem to have any difficulty adjusting to her new situation. She liked it. When she was unhappy it was not for her own sake, but because he could not convince her that he himself was all right.

Talyra had been given a job in the nursery, which horrified Noren when he first heard of it; it seemed unnecessarily cruel. Talyra didn't agree. She informed him that this was the first assignment for all Technician girls. They were supposed to be under no illusions as to what they would face if they married: the bearing of children they could not rear. Because Talyra had been trained to deliver babies, which was one of the chief functions of a village nurse, she was classified as a midwife; but she also took care of the babies as the other girls did, and she didn't mind at all. "But Noren," she declared, "I *like* babies! Why shouldn't I enjoy the work?"

"Doesn't it bother you to see the mothers come in to nurse their children, loving them, yet knowing they'll have to give them up when they're old enough to be weaned?"

"That is the High Law," she answered soberly. "How else could it be? There is no room for families in the Inner City, and we who are privileged to serve here must accept it. It's hard, but everyone knows that Wards of the City go only to homes where their new parents will love them, too."

Noren could understand that view in the Scholar women —who knew why the sacrifice was necessary—although in one way it was worse for them because they also knew that on the Six Worlds, where it had been possible to get milk from animals, babies whose mothers couldn't keep them had been adopted at birth. It was more difficult for him to see why Talyra took it so calmly. Was she covering up on his account? he wondered. Or did she still trust the High Law blindly? She had remained as devout as ever, certainly; she attended the Inner City's open-air vesper service daily. When he could, Noren went with her, telling himself that he did it to make her happy, yet knowing inside that it was to avoid accompanying Brek to Orison, which was held at the same hour.

As a nurse, Talyra occasionally assisted in the medical research laboratory, a fact that apalled Noren still more until he realized that she was completely unaware of the true nature of what went on there. She did not know that the people she tended had volunteered to be made sick. Technicians, of course, were not permitted to do that. The volunteers were all Scholars. He himself had already been through it once, and it wouldn't be the last time. Medical research was, after all, the only type that could be of benefit to the present generation of villagers, and it would be unthinkable to try things out on *them*. There were no animals with a biological resemblance to human beings, as there had been on the Six Worlds. Some diseases that had been conquered there were no longer curable, because of a lack of drugs and facilities; then too, there were still local ills for which no help existed. Noren had tried to exact a promise that if they ever found an antidote for the poison that had killed his mother, they would test it on him; but since the same one had also killed the First Scholar, his name was far down on the volunteer list.

Inner City customs were so unlike village ones that Noren marveled at Talyra's quick adaptation to them. It was strange to see her dressed in City women's trousers instead of the skirts she had always worn; but she found them comfortable, she told him, and she was awed by the quality of garments cut with scissors and stitched with metal needles, since villagers had only bone. Because there weren't enough scissors and needles to go around, all City clothes were made by seamstresses, and Talyra declared that she hated sewing anyway. That surprised him, for she had never complained as he had about farm chores. He was also surprised to learn that she disliked cooking and thought the arrangement whereby even married couples lived in tiny rooms, taking all their meals in the refectory, was a fine system. Talyra was not one to rage against the world; she simply went ahead with what had to be done. Yet though she'd seemed satisfied in the village, she found the Inner City more truly satisfying—or would have, Noren saw, had it not been for his own evident turmoil.

He hadn't quite realized how hard it would be to conceal his problems if he and Talyra saw each other every day, and the problems had intensified. His feeble attempts to hide them did little good. Repeatedly he asserted that he had not been punished for his heresy, yet Talyra remained doubtful. Finally, after nearly a week of her desperate probing for reassurance, he said sharply, "Have you ever known me to lie? You broke our betrothal because I wouldn't lie about being a heretic; you defended me before the Scholar Stefred on the grounds that I'd always been honest. Why should you think I'm lying now?"

She raised her eyes to meet his, saying in a low voice, "Will you swear to me by the Mother Star that they have given you no punishment?"

"Yes," he maintained. "By the Mother Star, Talyra." As he said it, he recalled the day long before when they had quarreled over his refusal to hold such an oath sacred, thinking that on that point at least, they no longer differed.

To his amazement, she burst into tears. "Then it's as I feared," she whispered. "You—you still don't believe,

109

Noren. I see it in your face. You're still a heretic; that's why you aren't able to accept all they offer you."

Later, lying sleepless on his bunk, it occurred to Noren that Talyra's keen intuition had again brought her very close to the truth; but at the time he was outraged. "Are you suggesting I lied at my recantation?" he demanded angrily.

"No. You wouldn't do that. You'd been forced to concede that the Scholars are wise; yet in your heart you have no faith."

"You're not being reasonable," he insisted. "Faith? What is that but to be content with ignorance? I *know*, Talyra! I know that the Mother Star exists, that it will someday appear as the Prophecy says—"

"And that we need fear nothing as long as its spirit remains with us?"

He turned away, knowing that although he could scarcely acknowledge such a belief, he was not free to deny it; and suddenly it came to him that perhaps the book of the Prophecy would not be "true in its entirety" even if the research succeeded. *"So long as we believe in it, no force shall destroy us, though the heavens themselves be consumed. . . ."* He had not lied. He had believed it; he had supposed that man's survival was certain. The First Scholar had been certain! If he hadn't been, he could never had done what he did, nor could he possibly have borne what he had to bear. Moreover, the feeling of certainty had been strong in the dreams. Yet not only was the creation of metal in doubt, but the human race was vulnerable to other disasters. Had the First Scholar, a scientist who must surely have known that, been deluded himself?

"You still can't be happy," Talyra said sorrowfully, "because you aren't whole. Before, you were sure what you believed, so sure . . . and I used to think that once you saw how mistaken you were, that would fix everything. I— I've been stupid, Noren. Heresy isn't a sin, it's something you're born with, and recanting can't give you faith you just don't have. The Scholars don't punish; that's not their way—you simply have to live with the consequences of what you are."

Noren did not try to talk about it again; although more than once after that night Talyra sought statements from him to allay her fears, he found that his own fears led him invariably to anger. That was not her fault and he had only a few days left to be with her, so he stifled it, kissing her instead of speaking. And when they kissed he could not regret her entrance to the City, unlikely though it seemed that the barrier to their marriage would ever fall. He now felt that the revelation of his Scholar status must be postponed indefinitely; nothing short of concrete proof that the Prophecy's promises were fulfillable would make him willing to assume the robe. How could he have imagined that his misgivings would lessen with time?

Rooming with Brek did not help, for although Noren welcomed his friendship, shared problems couldn't be pushed into the back of one's mind as easily as those not constantly discussed. "This is good, what we're doing now," Brek declared. "To build a new city, one that will eventually be open to everybody—that's fine, and rank won't make much difference there. But as far as commitment to priesthood's concerned, we're just evading the issue. When our shift at the outpost is finished, we'll have to come back . . . and probably the Transition Period can't begin that soon."

That it might never begin was something Noren had not mentioned to Brek; he could not bring himself to mention it to anyone, for once he did, he'd feel compelled to take some stand. He did not know what stand to take. As a result, he shared little more openness with Brek than with Talyra, and to be less than frank had always been painful for him. Day by day the pressure built up until he found himself counting the hours until the shuttlecraft's ascent. In space, at least, he would be free!

The space crew had been divided into teams by Stefred. Noren and Brek were paired, and when the lots were cast to decide who would make the first trip, they won. The computers monitored the starship's orbit and set the time of departure at three hours past midnight. No announcement was to be made to the Technicians before the tower was assembled, since its source couldn't be explained; they would later assume that it had been "called down from the sky," as the Book of the Prophecy described. So when Noren bid Talyra goodbye he told her only that he'd been chosen for special service that would prevent him from seeing her for some time. The possibility that he might not return he refused even to consider; the perils of the undertaking seemed unreal beside his desire to escape to a place where there'd be no abstract problems.

Talyra had no reason to suspect that he was leaving the Inner City, of course. "You look more cheerful than usual," she observed. "I know I musn't ask about the things people do when they serve inside the Hall of Scholars, but if what you've been called to do makes you look this way, it must be good." Her voice faltered briefly. "It—it must be worth another separation, even though we've just found each other—"

"It's good, darling," he agreed quickly. "It can't bring anything but good." Then, because he knew it would please her, he sought words that fit the formal religion she cherished. "The Scholar Stefred does me honor in judging me qualified," he added. "You must think of it as—as a journey, though the service to which I go is not like any journey in the world. I shall glimpse mysteries that few ever see, Talyra."

"Then I'll say farewell as for a journey," she told him, her face lighting with joy. "May the spirit of the Mother

Star go with you!"

"And may its blessings be spread through my service," he replied gravely. He took her in his arms then, and they said less solemn things; not till he'd left her did he realize that for a few minutes he had spoken sincerely and naturally in the language a priest would use.

He'd been advised to get a few hours' sleep, but he could not imagine doing so. Instead he went on up to his lodging tower's top level, where, in a small compartment that had been the observation deck of the starship, windows looked out on all sides. Each tower had such an area, used as a lounge and normally crowded; but at midnight he had it to himself. He sat gazing out at the stars, tingling with the thought that he would soon be seeing them from an identical compartment that floated free in space.

A quiet voice broke in on his growing exhilaration. "Since you weren't in your room, I thought I'd find you here," Stefred said.

Noren turned, startled. If Stefred had any last-minute instructions, why hadn't he sent for him earlier? Often enough they'd talked informally at meals and in the recreation areas, but never before had the Chief Inquisitor sought him out in his own quarters.

Stefred's face was worn, almost harrowed, though in the dim light of the observation lounge it couldn't be seen clearly. "You go to hazards of which you know nothing," he said with evident distress. "I can't explain them; yet you trust me, and I owe you honest warning."

"Look, you don't need to say anything else," protested Noren. "I've already been told how hazardous it is, and even if I hadn't, the hazards are pretty obvious."

"Not all of them."

"I've risked my life before, Stefred!" Noren exclaimed impatiently. "At least I thought I was risking it, as we all did when we became heretics. Haven't I proved that I'm

113

not going to panic?"

Stefred sat on the molded white seat that encircled the room, leaning against the window next to Noren; for a while neither of them spoke. This tower was not central like the Hall of Scholars, and nothing stood between it and the stars. None of the moons were up, not even Little Moon, so the silhouette of the Tomorrow Mountains wasn't discernible. The world was empty, Noren thought suddenly . . . empty except for the City, and the cluster of villages surrounding it. He had never pictured it that way, but from space he would see how empty it really was.

"You've proved your courage," Stefred said slowly. "You've shown more than one kind: the courage to risk death, to face unknown horrors, to stand up for what you believe against various sorts of opposition—I could list quite a few others. You know them. But there are kinds of courage you don't know, Noren." He paused, groping for words that he apparently could not find. "The demands of this job may be greater than they seem at first."

They could hardly, Noren felt, be greater than those of coping with the problems that had descended on him in the past two weeks, from which any diversion—even danger—would be a relief. "Must we keep on talking about it?" he burst out.

"No," said Stefred, sounding oddly apologetic. "You've made your decision, and I've made mine; I shouldn't have come. As long as I'm here, though, I'll say one thing more." He faced Noren, declaring decisively, "In the past I've tested you sometimes, taught you a good deal, and I've never led you into anything beyond your ability to handle; you've learned to rely on that. You must not rely on it now. I believe you'll come through this all right, yet it's possible that you'll meet experiences you're unready for. If the going gets rough, you will need more than courage."

Puzzled, Noren asked, "What? Further knowledge?"

"In a sense."

Hot anger flashed through Noren, overriding the apprehension that had begun to grow in him. "You're deliberately withholding information that would help me? Stefred, you've no right—"

"I'm withholding information," Stefred admitted. "It would not help you; at this stage it would do the reverse. The kind of knowledge that will help is one you must gain for yourself. It exists, and you will have access to it—whatever else happens, Noren, don't let yourself forget that."

*

They had been through it so often in dreams that it seemed they were dreaming still: donning their spacesuits, settling into the padded seats of the shuttlecraft, strapping themselves down, and then the waiting. . . .

It would be soundless, they knew, and they would hardly feel the motion. The shuttlecraft was not a rocket; Noren and Brek had read of the rockets used in ancient times, but the nuclear-powered shuttles that had been carried aboard starships were far more advanced. The craft would simply move out of the tower's bay and rise vertically into the dark. The lift-off would be totally out of their control. They would be in the hands of the automatic pilot and of the City's computers, which for countless years had held the program for this maneuver in unchanging memory. To the computers the passage of generations had no meaning; the last docking with an orbiting starship might have been yesterday.

Noren trusted the computers implicitly, for they were, after all, the repository of all knowledge, and if they were fallible in anything, the whole cause of human survival might as well be given up. Brek too was confident, although the role of passive crewman seemed less natural to him than to Noren because as a Technician he'd occasionally flown aircars. Neither of them had any real doubt as

115

to their safety; the computers had checked the failing beacon signal and had pronounced it strong enough to home in on. In preprogrammed sequence, they had tested every circuit in the shuttlecraft and had certified its functioning. There was nothing tangible to worry about.

Nevertheless, as he waited through the automatic countdown, Noren was more terrified than ever before in his life.

He had not been seriously alarmed by Stefred's warning. When they'd taken leave of each other, he'd been angry, and he still was; if Stefred had purposely tried to infuriate him, he could scarcely have done a better job of it, Noren thought bitterly. To be challenged was one thing, a thing he'd always enjoyed, but to be told that this was not mere challenge and then to be denied full knowledge of the facts —it wasn't fair! He'd arrived at the shuttlecraft hot with the desire to get on with the job.

There had been a sizable group gathered to see them off —the other space teams, their tutors and closest acquaintances, Scholars with whom they'd be working at the outpost—and at first Noren had felt a sense of belonging that he'd never had occasion to experience. Having been a loner throughout boyhood, he hadn't formed many relationships in the City, despite people's friendliness. He found the warmth of their send-off surprisingly moving. But then had come a bad moment: a small incident, unimportant, yet somehow of sufficient impact to change his enthusiasm to dread.

The council chairman had been present, clad, strangely, in his blue robe, which seemed inappropriate since it was the middle of the night and not a ceremonial occasion. At least Noren hadn't anticipated any ceremony. But just before he and Brek entered the space shuttle, the group had fallen silent; people had stood, eyes lifted, and the chairman—a down-to-earth man who a short while before had been talking casually to Noren about the expedition that

116

had previously been dispatched to pinpoint the landing site —had suddenly become all priest. "We embark this night on a mission of utmost gravity," he'd said. "May the Star's spirit abide with us, and in committing ourselves to its guidance, may we be mindful that only in trusting have we any hope of success. We have made all preparations that are within our power to make. We have calculated the risks and herewith incur them, though there has been honest division among us as to whether they are justified; it is possible that only our descendants can judge. We can do no more than act in the light of such knowledge as is accessible to us. . . ."

They were frightening words, yet Noren sensed that in some way they were meant to comfort. If so, it was cold comfort, certainly. The robed priest continued into ritual: " '. . . There is no surety save in the light that sustained our forefathers . . . our future is vain except as we have faith. . . .' " followed by some of the Prophecy. The memory of that last Orison engulfed Noren, and he recalled with vivid clarity the dream-image that had shaken him so. In the training dreams he'd concentrated on the ship, not the view of the desolate planet, and he had shared enough of the original astronaut's thoughts to be unaffected by the sight of it. Confronting that sight in reality would be less easy.

". . . May the spirit of the Mother Star safeguard you," the High Priest had concluded, clasping Noren's hands and then Brek's. Now, strapped down inside the sealed cabin, Noren was kept from panic only by determined pride. This was the most thrilling opportunity he would ever have, he told himself. Space . . . zero gravity . . . the stars . . . all the things he'd been looking forward to with such eagerness— was he losing his sanity? How could he be chilled, shaking, unmanned not by fear of death but by some nameless foreboding he could not even define?

Unable to endure the silence, he said the first thing that

came to mind, hoping that his voice revealed no tremor. "Did Stefred talk to you tonight, Brek? Alone, I mean?"

"Yes," Brek said. "He came by our room; he wanted to see us both. I'm sure he was sorry to miss you, though the ceremony just now was much the same as what he said."

That was an odd comparison, Noren reflected, for the ceremony had been mostly ritual, and he'd never known Stefred to use ritual terms in private conversation. "How do you mean?" he questioned.

"Why, he wished me the Mother Star's protection—that sort of thing."

"Stefred spoke to you privately . . . as a priest?" Noren asked incredulously.

"Not exactly; it was more like any two people saying a formal goodbye."

"But he used the symbolic phrasing."

"Of course. Didn't you and Talyra use it?"

"Talyra doesn't know any other kind," Noren pointed out.

"Noren, there isn't any other kind, not for this. Would you have expected him to say just 'good luck, and I hope the shuttle works'? To invoke nothing greater than his personal friendship for me?"

He'd have expected Stefred to be honest, Noren thought in bafflement; one couldn't conceive of his being anything else. The protection of the Mother Star . . . well, that could be translated as the protection of the Founders' knowledge in building the shuttlecraft and programming the computers, or perhaps as the protection of one's own knowledge passed down from the Six Worlds. But Brek hadn't interpreted it that way; like Talyra, Brek had read in some sort of magic. And Stefred knew Brek's mind too well not to have foreseen that he would do so.

A vibration, noiseless but powerful enough to penetrate

118

one's bones, spread through the craft, passing into their firmly restrained bodies. "We're moving," Brek whispered. They looked at each other, and Noren's terror receded, replaced by excitement.

Yet as the vibration intensified a new thought struck him: he was leaving the City—the City, the citadel of knowledge he'd sought so long and finally reached. He would be in the wilderness for many weeks to come, and though he wanted to go, he found himself once again torn. The City had never seemed a prison to him. He would miss it.

To rendezvous with the starship did not take long. As in the dreams, Noren and Brek felt the abrupt shift to weightlessness when the engines cut off; they saw the series of colored lights that told them they were docking; they felt the bump that meant the shuttlecraft had come to rest in a bay like the one it had recently left. They put on their helmets, marveling at the feel of moving under their own volition in a realm without gravity, a realm where up and down did not exist. They threw the switch to start cabin depressurization, waited for the large green light, unfastened the hatch . . . and emerged into a "tower" vestibule whose outer doors stood open to a vast black sky.

No stars were visible, for the faceplates of their helmets had been darkened lest on exiting, they confront the sun. It was like the test dream, where one fell blindly and in utter silence. To Noren it was silent, anyway, for there was only one radiophone for communication with the City, and Brek —whose job as a Technician had been the servicing of radiophone equipment—was carrying it; there had been no real justification for allocating two, although Stefred had seemed to feel that two were needed. He'd been overruled, since radiophones were vital for intervillage communication and like everything else had to last until the Time of the Prophecy. Noren did not mind. He could talk to Brek

119

when necessary by touching helmets with him, and anything he might wish to say to the ground team could be relayed.

He was no longer afraid; he felt free, euphoric, just as he'd expected he would. To float in limitless vacuum, restricted only by the thin tether that anchored him to the ship; to move almost without effort by means of a skill that had become familiar to him in dreams; to take up the tools and use them upon a Machine more awesome than any from which village taboos had once barred him—that these things were possible filled him with elation. He and Brek, grasping the handholds, made their way out to the tail of the starship where dismantling was to begin. The sun at their backs, they worked without speaking. There was no need for speech. Absorbed by the task and by the wonders of their situation, secure in their trust of each other and of the technology that enabled them to do what no man had done since the Founding, they encountered no difficulty in performing the job assigned to them.

They had been told to work steadily but unhurriedly; Brek was to report their progress at intervals over the radio-phone. Noren could hear neither the reports nor the replies, but he knew that if any exchange of significance took place, Brek would tell him. Each section of hull, once unjoined, was to be fastened to a line and pulled into the shuttlecraft bay; the plan was to stow them all aboard later, when there were enough to fill the hold. Brek motioned that he would take the first one in. The thing wasn't heavy, of course, since it too lacked weight, and a slight push from Noren was enough to give it momentum.

While Brek was gone Noren paused to rest; he was not really tired, but he'd never been one to stick unceasingly to a task when there was something interesting to think about—and in space there certainly was. He pulled himself around the ship to the side away from the sun, not wanting to miss this chance to adjust his helmet's filters for one

120

quick look at the stars.

They were overwhelming. He had seen them in the dream, but not like this: not immediate, tangible, many of them brighter and more splendid than Little Moon. He was no longer dreaming. The stars were *real*.

And all at once everything else became unreal. The villages . . . the City . . . the Six Worlds that were now mere space dust . . . those were no part of reality! He was detached from them. It was they that were dreams; he, Noren, was alone in space, unshielded from the boundless void and the stars that burned with a beauty he could not bear. Suns . . . all of them suns . . . how many of them had worlds where peoples beyond contact lived and worked and sought knowledge? How many still had worlds? They were light-years away; some, like the Mother Star itself, might have novaed long ago . . . he might be seeing only their ghosts . . . but if so, was anything in the universe less illusory?

He turned cold, for it was an appalling thought. Always he had trusted in the existence of truth that was firm and absolute; he had searched for it unceasingly, and had supposed he was on his way to finding it. Yet if all was illusion, if the uncertainty he'd found so dismaying involved not only human survival but the very nature of things, then he had no more of an anchor to true reality than to the planet from which he was adrift. He could not even depend on the workings of his own mind.

Once again Noren was engulfed by terror he could not understand. He wanted to cry out, to call and be answered by Brek or by someone; but there was no means of doing so. He wanted to run, to feel air touch his face, to feel life surge through his weightless body; but that was impossible too. He was paralyzed. He was cut off from life. In desperation, knowing himself powerless to combat what was happening to him, he reached out for the next handhold. At first he could not make his arm move. But in time—he was not sure whether it was a long time or a short one—he was floating in a place where he saw not only stars, but the immense rim of the gray, mist-shrouded world.

It was, as he had known it would be, empty. He had always known that no one lived anywhere but in the one small settlement maintained through the Founders' wisdom, but he had not sensed it as he did now, isolated from all contact with that settlement—that island in a huge expanse of emptiness. And there might well come a time when there would be no island! The human race would have no refuge once the City's equipment gave out. Somewhere in the immeasurably great region of dark, Noren thought, were the rays of light from the nova—the Mother Star—traveling at inconceivable speed but not yet close to him. He would die before they came close; soon after their arrival, his people might all be dead. If there was no scientific breakthrough. . . .

Had other human races perished also? Abruptly, as he looked out into the depths, new horror assailed him; he questioned in a different way from before. Those blazing suns . . . uncounted billions, he had been told, in the whole universe . . . why did some become novas? He had heard the facts in terms of astrophysics; he knew what triggered the change physically—but that was not the answer he sought now. Why did such facts exist? Why should a star consume its worlds, its people, exiling the escapees to an alien land where the attempt to survive might be futile? For that matter, why did either stars or people come into being at all?

For the first time since learning the truth about the Mother Star, it occurred to Noren to ask not *how* things happened, but *why*.

His mind could not cope with such questions. Yet it had never failed him in the past! He'd relied on it to reason things out, to find meanings. . . . Maybe there were no meanings. Or maybe no effort of his mind was valid. He had broken away from the world; he was drifting, falling, into a black starlit cosmos he could not comprehend. There was nothing solid or concrete to hold to. In the grip of panic, Noren lost touch with the starship itself. A remote part of him knew that if he could clutch the safety tether, he could pull himself back; at least he should shut out the view that was so unnerving.

But this time his hand would not obey his will. This time he was truly paralyzed and could not turn the knob to remove the stars from his sight. He could not even close his eyes. He remained staring, no longer in command of either his body or his thoughts, while his panic overmastered him.

V

IT WAS BREK WHO GOT HIM BACK INTO THE SHUTTLECRAFT,
Brek who activated the automatic control sequence that took
them down to solid, but hitherto unexplored, ground. Noren
had no memory of it afterward. He was told that Brek had
contacted the City by radiophone and had been advised to
return at once without cargo.

The ship landed according to plan at the site of the new
outpost, to which a guide-beacon had been transported by
aircar, since descent to the City by daylight was undesir-
able and Brek was not judged competent to reset the automatic pilot in any case. A vague impression of gray rolling
mossland under an even grayer sky was all Noren recalled
of his first steps beyond the Tomorrow Mountains. Yet the
sky seemed studded with flaming suns. Later, in the night,
he was not sure whether this had been dream or hallucina-
tion; but he found his mind clear enough to know the circumstances and feel the shame.

Waking in the dark to the dry oppressive heat of the

planet's natural climate, he at first thought himself back in the village, but there were no buildings; he lay on a blanket spread upon moss, and overhead was open sky. Open sky! Noren turned onto his stomach and buried his head in his arms, for he knew that if the clouds should disperse he could not bear even a glimpse of starlight. He remained still, paralyzed once more, conscious that men slept nearby and that he did not want to be seen by them. After a while he became aware that his face was wet with tears.

He had not experienced failure before, at least not of a kind caused by any personal inadequacy, and certainly not in a venture that affected the welfare of others. Tears stung and sobs wracked him, though he made no sound. The trip useless . . . precious hours of the beacon's functioning wasted . . . some later crew might well be endangered by his loss of nerve, and completion of the tower might prove impossible. He could not live with that knowledge! He could not face those who had trusted him. He could not face anyone, least of all Brek, who had witnessed his weakness. But it was worse than that. He could not face the world itself. Fear swept through him again as he saw that to him, the world was not the same place as it had been; it still seemed unreal, without meaning, like some of the ancient films he'd been shown that bore no relationship to anything he could interpret. This had nothing to do with space flight, Noren realized. Space had merely opened his eyes to a less substantial view of reality.

He had thought he could not rise and move and speak, but when morning came he found otherwise. It proved possible to go through the motions. An image came into his mind: a creature he'd heard of, a tiny mother-world creature that had over a hundred legs . . . he'd wondered how it knew which to move next. Had it stopped to ponder the matter it couldn't have known, yet it walked. He too

125

would proceed without pondering. To do so was better than to reveal that what had happened to him was more than a temporary spell of panic; in any case, he could scarcely lie there and let people assume he was sick. He got up, washed his face in the basin that stood on a stone table at the edge of camp, and joined the group clustered around the breakfast fire, marveling that his muscles seemed to function just as they always had. People greeted him cordially, with studied matter-of-factness; and when he opened his mouth to reply, words came out, despite his conviction that he would find himself mute.

The camp's leaders wanted him to go back to the City at once by aircar; Noren flatly refused. "I'm all right," he maintained, feeling inside that he was not all right, that very probably he would never be, but determined to let no one suspect it.

They frowned and shook their heads, but Noren was so insistent—and outwardly so composed—that they agreed to let Stefred decide. He shrank from talking to Stefred even by radiophone, but since he was gently informed that if he didn't, he would be sent back without his consent, there was little choice. They went away and allowed him to make the call in private.

"Don't you want to come for a day or two, at least?" Stefred asked. "You can go out again with the next supply car—"

"No," Noren declared. It was not merely that he wasn't willing to admit any need to consult a psychiatrist, for he was sure that once he met Stefred face to face and confessed the whole truth, as he would feel compelled to do, he would not be allowed to go out again. He would not be trusted to do anything. And furthermore, he could not endure the thought of confronting Talyra.

"I won't force you, Noren," Stefred said slowly. "If you need help, I'm here—we're all here, and we'll stand by you.

126

But quite possibly this is something you have to resolve alone. Perhaps work at the outpost is the best thing for you right now." There was a long pause, so long that Noren wondered whether the radiophone was malfunctioning. Finally Stefred's voice continued, "There's a good deal I could say, but I don't think you're ready to understand it. Just remember what I told you the other night."

Noren was too numb to be angry, and though his impulse was toward rage when he recalled their talk in the observation lounge, he was too honest not to know that it was mostly rage against himself. There had been plain suspicion of his vulnerability to panic. Stefred had been troubled from the beginning, and had offered warnings that he, Noren, had chosen to ignore. Still, it was unlike Stefred to take an "I told you so" attitude.

Avoiding Brek, Noren went to the camp leaders and asked for work. There was plenty to be done. The camp was in wilderness, and not all the allocated equipment had yet arrived. Little would be provided in any case; the occupants would live under conditions of extreme difficulty, much as the first-generation villagers had, but with the added hardships of the Founders. They would receive nothing but what was necessary to sustain life.

The first priority was construction of a foundation for the tower. It was being built of stone and mortar without the aid of either machines or metal tools. Scholars had arrived some days earlier to start it, but the job was not finished, and Noren's strong back was welcomed. He in turn welcomed hard physical labor that left him no time to think.

He worked ceaselessly, finding that hands that had learned masonry in boyhood did not forget their skill. In the villages stonesetting was not a trade, but a measure of manliness, for whenever a new house was raised all the neighbors came to help. Most Scholars had been reared as

127

villagers; they'd known well the ancestral methods of building that had been passed down from father to son. Like all of the other unchanging village ways, the methods were effective. They were not subject to improvement, for the engineers of the first generation had been ingenious people quite competent to devise the most effective uses of stone.

It was more laborious in camp than in the villages, since there were as yet no work-beasts. Getting a work-beast into an aircar would have been an utterly impractical undertaking. Aircars were not very large, and work-beasts were not very cooperative; their adaptation to unpurified water and native fodder had, of course, been detrimental to their intelligence. Moreover, there were more vital things than beasts of burden to be carried aboard the few aircars available. Nor was it feasible to herd any beasts by land, for aside from the length and difficulty of the journey—which would necessitate climbing to high altitudes and packing enough food and water to last many weeks—there were savages in the mountains: the now subhuman mutants whose ancestors had fled there after heedlessly incurring genetic damage. They too had lost their intelligence, but they were fierce and dangerous. So work-beasts could be brought only in embryonic form after the laboratories were ready, and until they arrived and matured, the wicker sledges on which stones were moved must be pulled by hand.

Wheels would have been a tremendous advantage; villagers, having never heard of them, did not miss them, but the Scholars never ceased regretting that the one invention most basic to the civilization of the old worlds had proved impossible in the new. Each and every person who learned anything of the Six Worlds found it hard to believe that there wasn't some way a wheel could be made. It was simple to cut one from softstone, as sledge runners, furniture, and the like were cut; but softstone wore away quickly from friction, and besides, stone wheels would not turn properly on stone axles. They just weren't efficient enough to be worth the trouble. It was equally impractical to manufacture plastic wheels, for though plastics of the required hardness had been developed from native vegetation, there was no metal to build the high-pressure equipment needed to mold them. Small plastic parts for the maintenance of existing machines were the most that could be managed. Villagers had potters' wheels and millstones, but for transport the primitive sledges were indispensable.

Sledges were meant to be drawn over sanded roads, but in the camp there were no roads at all. The road-grading machine—and there was only one in existence—was being used by Technicians in the establishment of a new village. Under the High Law whenever forty families petitioned for a village of their own, they had a right to hire the Technicians' services: road-building, clearing of farmland, initial fertilization and treatment of the soil, purification of the clay for a pipeline to connect another common cistern to the City water supply—all the necessary jobs that could be done only through the use of the sacred Machines, climaxed by the installation of a Radiophone Machine in the new village center as a symbol of religious sanction. That took precedence over the Scholars' needs. Until the obligation to the villagers had been met, the camp would do without machinery.

The site of the settlement was anything but attractive. Noren, once he became clear-headed enough to survey it, observed that it was very much like the land he had known all his life: undulating gray country, in this case unrelieved by the fresh green of quickened fields. There were fewer knolls, perhaps, and fewer of the purple shrubs that grew mainly on high ground. Then too, the mountains were closer, and their crags of white and yellow rock rose further above the horizon. But somehow he had expected

129

"beyond the Tomorrow Mountains" to be a more novel region.

Maybe it was, he thought ruefully. He was really in no condition to judge. He was still detached from the world; it was flat, unreachable, as if an invisible screen stood between him and what he saw. It was more dreamlike than any of the controlled dreams had been, and far more frightening. . . .

Grimly he turned to the work, swinging his stone pick with a strength he'd not known he possessed. He was thankful the sun was not out, and not merely because of the heat; the sun was too vivid a reminder of those other suns that had overwhelmed him. Could it be possible that he was insane? he wondered in terror. Should he have told Stefred the whole story? He was repelled by the idea; his mind, the sharpness of his mind, had always been what he most valued. Unable to keep his thoughts blank, he allowed them to drift, feeling a strange astonishment that despite the seeming unrealness of his surroundings, he'd lost none of the knowledge he had acquired.

He thought of the mother world. Impressions from controlled dreams returned, arousing sudden longing. One dream in particular had taught him much about the lacks of his planet; a dream in which he'd immersed himself in cool water . . . immersed himself fully, so that he was floating in it! Both the City and the new outpost had been purposely located far from deep bodies of water. Maps made from orbital surveys showed many big lakes, yet no lake could be approached safely until such time as synthesization of metal made large-scale purification feasible; although the High Law was an adequate deterrent to drinking impure water, a taboo against all swimming would be impossible to enforce. As he labored in the dry outdoor heat for the first time since his enlightenment, Noren understood that, and he raged anew at the cruelty of his race's exile. Before, he

130

had simply accepted it. Now every turn of his mind led to the unanswerable *why . . . why. . . .*

At midday everyone paused to eat. Noren had no appetite; he scarcely noticed the meagerness of the meal, though he knew that the plan was for the expedition to subsist on as short rations as possible. While there was plenty of food to spare in the settled area of the planet, room for transporting it aboard the aircars was very limited, and until a local harvest could be produced, hunger would be the rule. Hunger—and also thirst. So far all pure water, too, had to be transported, and the likelihood of rain was small. The general overcast that had made the planet look predominantly white from space rarely produced rain, and the equipment for weather control could not be duplicated. The purification plant, when installed, would have to serve for irrigation of crops as well as for drinking and bathing; strict water rationing was destined to continue.

These discomforts were not discussed. No one complained; no one reminded anyone else to be abstemious. The rations for the day were set out on a crude softstone table and each man helped himself. People sat around in informal groups to eat, talking and laughing, with inward resolve to accept the demanding conditions of camp life as a personal challenge; their morale was high. After all, everybody had wanted to come. The thrill of the venture was ample compensation for the drawbacks.

Noren stood apart, reflecting with bitter dismay that the thrill could no longer reach him. He ate because one must eat to work, but the bread seemed tasteless and his mouth was so dry that it was hard to swallow, although he took his fair share of water. The fear in him grew steadily: fear not of any external threat, but of a self he had not met before and did not wholly trust. His normal confidence in himself was gone. If only, he thought numbly, there were some way to reverse time . . . to get back what he'd had before confronting the naked stars!

Yet if there were a way to reverse time, it would also be possible to get back all that had existed before the nova. Why must time be as it was? Why, for that matter, must any laws of the universe be as they were? The science he'd studied explained them, but it did not explain their reason for being. It did not explain why six worlds should be destroyed by a nova, nor, in fact, did it tell why even one world should exist in the first place. . . .

Seeing Brek approaching, Noren gulped the last of his bread and went back to work. He spoke to no one, and, once he'd rebuffed them, the others let him be, respecting his desire for privacy. Toward evening the clouds broke, and he avoided glancing at the sun that burned down on him, confining his thought to the effort of handling stone.

He stopped for supper with reluctance. Everyone else was exhausted, since even the former villagers were not yet reconditioned to heavy labor, and those born as Technicians, like Brek, had never performed it before. Noren welcomed the pain of his muscles as a sign that he was still in bodily touch with the world. Ordinary things—the smoke of cook-fires, the spongy feel of the moss on which he sat, the sound of people's voices—seemed like random bits of a cup smashed beyond restoration.

Brek came toward him again, and this time Noren could not escape. "Look," Brek began, "we don't have to talk about it if you'd rather not. But I want you to know that I —I understand, and—well, that I don't blame you—"

Understand? thought Noren wretchedly. Brek couldn't possibly understand what had happened; nobody could. It would be impossible to describe even if he wanted to confide in someone. "I'm all right now," he said sharply. "I just want to be left alone."

"Aren't you coming to Orison?"

"Orison—here?"

"Well, not the formal kind, but everybody's getting to-

132

gether around the fire. You can't just sit here in the dark by yourself."

Noren got up and strode away, his back to the flickering glow of the bonfire on which, now that the cooking was done, more moss was being heaped. He could not, he felt, maintain his composure at such a gathering. The idea filled him with panic.

But as darkness deepened across a clear sweep of sky, the panic became worse; and resignedly Noren turned toward the light that outshone the distant, disquieting stars.

*

One day was much like another. The stone foundation was finished and erection of the tower began; its sections were brought down from orbit in the proper order for reassembly. Noren had little aptitude for work requiring manual dexterity, but he had been taught the use of the special tools and was thoroughly familiar with the starship hull's design; moreover, he was determined to perform flawlessly. It was the only way to stave off the solicitousness of well-meaning fellow Scholars. He did not want their pity. He knew that they sincerely wished to help, but there was no help for what had befallen him.

At first he didn't think he could possibly find the courage to walk in space again, but when the other two teams had made trips, so that it was rightfully his turn—and Brek's— Noren knew there was only one course. Steeling himself for the most blatant lie he had ever attempted, he approached the camp leaders and begged for another chance, insisting that he was not afraid. "I panicked before," he confessed grimly, "but by the Mother Star, I won't let it happen again." He had met panic repeatedly since the flight, panic just as severe although even more groundless in terms of tangible cause, and he'd managed to keep it under control. He hoped no one guessed how much weakness he was hiding.

It was no use. His request for further space flights was

133

denied. That was scarcely surprising in view of all that hinged on the success of each one, but it was a blow to his faltering self-esteem. He went away hating himself because inside he felt more relief than resentment.

Though he was sure Brek must despise him, there were no outward signs of it; Brek tried to go on as if nothing had changed. Noren, to whom the whole world had changed, was irritated by this and sometimes hot-tempered, for he could not endure any friendly gestures of sympathy. Before long a new space partner for Brek was sent out from the City, and the flights proceded on schedule. Brek never spoke of anything that occurred during those flights within Noren's hearing, but he talked incessantly of other subjects. He went out of his way to ask advice, and although Noren was brusque, his pretense of normalcy demanded that he offer what he could. It proved to be a strain even when the queries concerned science.

For the prospective scientists in the group, training was soon resumed. Gradually the camp started to take on some semblance of a civilized community. Though no effort could yet be expended to build shelters, which were not required by the climate, people chose personal living areas and began to spend some of their evenings away from the community bonfire. A few of the City's study viewers were sent out and new tapes for them, along with recharged power cells, came aboard every aircar. At first Noren was pleased, since his practice in disciplined concentration enabled him to shut out the world through study whenever he was not working. But the experiences he'd undergone had left their mark. Science was not the joyous pursuit it once had been; its lack of certainty had robbed it of weight, and the basic questions that were tormenting him had raised doubts as to how much of it could be considered valid. Brek did not know that. To Brek it was all new and exciting and authoritative. As his tutor, Noren found himself

134

more and more a hypocrite.

He had never expected to be one of Brek's permanent tutors, and in fact the appointment was not official; but everything was informal in camp, and since no one else assumed the role, it fell to him by default. The Scholars who would normally have held the responsibility, specialists fully trained in nuclear physics, were not at the outpost; they were all in the City devoting themselves to the culminating experiments. Brek did not need their guidance, for he was still at an elementary level and his immediate job left little leisure for study. There was no possibility of his progressing beyond Noren's ability to instruct.

Insofar as he could, Noren kept their sessions strictly technical, and there were plenty of safe topics to occupy Brek's attention. First, there was the matter of why the natural resources of the planet could not be utilized for the building of machines. That they could not was something a new Scholar accepted uncritically, for no villager or even Technician had the background to realize that certain metallic and semi-metallic elements did exist in the native rock; but once a trainee's study of chemistry began, simple explanations became inadequate. It quite naturally appeared that since the Six Worlds' scientists had been so knowledgeable, they ought to have been able to find substitutes for the metals they'd used at home. But in this, at least, Noren was on firm ground. He could assure Brek categorically that it was impossible to obtain usable metal by mechanical or chemical processes. Not all metallic elements had the same characteristics; metals with the properties needed for machines—strength, durability, and so forth—had never been present in large quantities, and what deposits there once were had been taken by the mysterious alien visitors of the past, whose technology had apparently surpassed that of the Six Worlds.

Thus the Founders had pinned all man's hope on trans-

135

mutation of specific elements through nuclear fusion, in full knowledge of their audacity in setting such a goal; only recently had Noren come to see how audacious they had been. Foolishly so, perhaps. Still, they'd had no alternative. The orbital surveys had shown the entire solar system to be metal-poor; if there had been a chance of getting metal from any of the moons or other planets, the Founders would have tried it, but there'd been no such change. The Visitors who'd preceded them had done a thorough job.

Speculation about the Visitors had never ceased among the Scholars, although without more data no conclusions could be reached. In the City the topic was mentioned occasionally, but in camp, around the evening fires, it was attacked with renewed interest. In the back of everyone's mind was the wild hope, "What if we should *find* something? What if we should uncover evidence not only of their presence, but of their origin, or of how long ago they came?"

Noren sat frozen during these discussions, unnaturally silent, cold with an apprehension he could neither analyze nor push aside. His people were not the only sentient beings . . . they had absolute proof that they were not . . . yet they could make no contact with their predecessors or even determine whether any of them still lived. What sort of a universe was it where such barriers prevailed? Were all human races isolated, condemned to perpetual ignorance of the rest? Did others, too, rise to greatness and then, through senseless, futile tragedy, die out—like grain shoots crushed beneath the hoofs of work-beasts loosed into a field? Perhaps the Visitors' sun had also ceased to exist except in the form of light rays out somewhere between the stars, invisible because no one was there to see. Were stars, like men, inescapably doomed to death?

He had never thought much about death except in an abstract way. He'd believed himself beyond reprieve during his trial and inquisition and had been afraid; he had felt vague surprise while sharing the dying thoughts of the First Scholar, who as an old man had given up life without fear; he had, earlier, grieved over the deaths of his mother and of a boyhood friend. He had been horrified by the concept of racial extinction and had pledged himself unhesitatingly to its prevention. But he had barely begun to face the implications of prevention being impossible, and somehow, doing so raised the awareness that he himself would someday really die. Alone in the darkness of the outdoor nights, Noren let himself consider death not merely as an abstraction but as a future certainty, feeling terror such as he had never imagined. He, to whom knowledge was all-important, confronted the depths of the unknown, and was overpowered. Had this been buried in him all along? he wondered in dismay. Had his panic in space been based on physical fear after all? The idea added both to his inner shame and to his determination to show no further weakness, but the memory of that paralyzing moment continued to haunt him; though he drove himself to exhaustion in an attempt to suppress it, it followed him into his dreams.

Exhaustion was the common lot of the entire team, of course; strenuous work on short rations had its effect on everyone. Yet all the men had their pride. Moreover, as village youths many had taken pleasure in competition, and camp life brought back remembrance if not full prowess. Stewards and High Priests they might be, but there was nothing somber about them; before long somebody suggested a stonesetting contest, a proposal adopted with great enthusiasm. Though the accompanying festivities could not take place without women and children to watch, to reward the victor, and to prepare the traditional feast, it seemed a good way to initiate work on the water purification plant, which in the absence of domes would have to be installed in an ordinary stone structure.

137

The stonework of such structures was crude, since without metal tools it was necessary to rely mainly on rocks small enough not to require cutting. Fortunately these were abundant in the area; the men not engaged in erecting the tower had been able to gather them without too much difficulty. Everybody wanted to take part in the contest, so on the day chosen, tower construction was temporarily suspended, and only the current space crew had to miss out. As was usual in the villages on such occasions, people rose and ate before daybreak, and by the time the sun appeared the workers were in place around the square marked off in the gray earth where the building's walls were to be. Sunrise came late beyond the Tomorrow Mountains. The nearby ridges to the east blocked all rays long past the normal hour of dawn. Noren stood facing them, wondering as he waited how they could look so tall when from space, they'd been merely a yellowish blotch. He felt no excitement; the high spirits of his companions lowered his own by contrast; but he was resolved that as far as stonesetting was concerned, he was not going to make a poor showing.

At sunup the men began a song, taking stones into their hands in readiness. It was the folk hymn prescribed by custom, passed on from one generation to the next as the building skills themselves had been passed on:

> *May our strength be everlasting,*
> *May our skill be sure.*
> *Till the Star's light shines upon it*
> *May the stone endure.*

Noren did not join in, not even when the work started and the songs became livelier and, before long, bawdier. He was kept from it by more than the new depression; his boyhood had not been happy enough to be brought back willingly. Some of the others, apparently, had had fun in the villages, heretics though they were; they were enjoying this chance to relive bygone years. Or was it simply that they were hoping to forget what they knew of the future?

Not once in camp had Noren heard anyone express doubt about the successful outcome of Grenald's experiments. The issue had been argued at the meeting in the City, but after the vote, even the skeptics seemed to have convinced themselves that they, here beyond the mountains, were the pioneers of the Transition Period. Had not another city in fact begun to rise? Was not real evidence of the Prophecy's fulfillment at last before them? Surely the breakthrough would come soon, people declared; surely the vision they saw when they surveyed the drab and desolate camp would be transformed into reality! Noren had always felt that villagers were prone to believe in things because they wanted to, but it was disillusioning to find that Scholars were no different.

He attacked the work that day as never before, conscious only of the stones he handled, not bothering to count them or to notice the rate at which his own section of wall grew in comparison to others; not even noticing when fresh mortar was brought by one of the men too old for heavy labor. As the sun rose higher and the day's heat increased, he stripped to the waist, throwing aside his tunic without a glance; sweat poured from his body and ran into his eyes so that he could scarcely see. He could not see anyway; he was giddy; but it did not seem to matter. Vaguely he perceived that the pain in his arms and back was more severe than any he could remember, yet that did not matter either. He did not pause except during the rest periods called at intervals, when he waited apathetically for the signal to resume work. His body moved of its own accord. It was as though it were no part of him.

Eventually the light began to fade, and Noren decided that he was on the verge of passing out. He did not mind; it might, he thought, be a good thing. Not until men surrounded him, thrusting a mug of ale into his hands, did he become aware that the sun had dropped below the horizon and that the contest was over. And even then he could not take in the fact that he had won.

Dazed, he looked around at the stone walls that had not been there that morning. Stone was real, stone was tangible; it would indeed last till the Mother Star's light shone upon it . . . but what did that mean? The stone might well outlast the men, and perhaps, in some dim future age, other Visitors would come and wonder who the builders had been. Such things ought to fit together in a pattern, Noren felt, but he could see no pattern at all. He let his fellows carry him to the bonfire, and he drank the ale that, in lieu of a feast, was to supplement the usual food ration; but he knew no joy of victory. The best he could manage was grim satisfaction in not having disgraced himself.

Sparks from the blazing moss flew upward, mingling with the stars. Noren's eyes did not follow them; he had avoided looking up of late; but a recollection of other campfires came to him: fires in the village square, where he and Talyra had sat together in the first season of their betrothal. "If she were here—" Brek began, congratulating him, and Noren turned away. If she were here, she would place the victor's string of polished pebbles around his neck, and she would kiss him while the people watched and cheered; but later, when they were alone, it would be no good at all. She would sense his emptiness, and Talyra's pity was one thing he could not bear.

He drooped with a weariness that was as much of spirit as of body. The singing, which had not continued past early morning, was taken up again: not only the bawdy songs, but slow, sad ones, love songs and laments for nameless things lost in the haze of legend. One after another men recalled ballads they had not heard since boyhood, marveling that those from different villages knew them. It was not really surprising, considering their common ancestry and the fact that the traders who traveled from place to place spent their nights in taverns; yet somehow the provincial attitude of one's youth was hard to shake.

"You know, we have one great advantage in this world," someone remarked during a lull. "Despite the reversion, despite all that was taken from us, we still have the part of our heritage our forebears struggled longest and hardest for. We have unity."

"What do you mean?" asked Brek, who had not yet studied much of the Six Worlds' history.

"We have a single culture that's expanding instead of many that must eventually merge. That wouldn't be good, of course, if it hadn't been based on a combination of the mother world's cultures. Diversity is valuable. But it means we won't have to go through the painful business of resolving cultural conflicts all over again."

"The Founders spared us that," another man agreed. "Think what we'd have faced if mankind had reverted to more primitive customs without keeping any sense of common identity! All the villagers' frustration over their inability to progress would have been turned into disputes between separate villages."

"I'm still confused," Brek admitted. "We're united by the Prophecy and the High Law; we couldn't survive without them. But those of us who know the secrets don't like the system. We're working to get rid of it. So how can you call such unification an advantage?"

"We're working toward the time when we can reveal the secrets, relinquish our control of the City, and abolish stratified castes. We're not trying to get rid of the High Law, though. That will always be necessary here."

"Well, yes. People won't ever be able to drink unpurified water, or cook in pots made from unpurified clay. And religion's certainly not going to become obsolete."

141

Wasn't it? Noren thought. What good would it do, once its promises had been kept? And if keeping them should prove impossible, it would become a hoax, an inexcusable deception; the Founders themselves had been horrified by the idea of upholding a *false* religion. "Brek," he protested, "surely you don't think heresy should be a crime after the Prophecy's fulfillment is . . . settled."

"I didn't say that."

"Heresy is not a crime under the High Law," someone else reminded them. "Only village laws forbid it, and those laws aren't going to be changed overnight; it will take time for intolerance to be outgrown."

"But can't we issue some kind of proclamation?"

"Certainly not. We mustn't interfere with democratic government then any more than we do now."

"The point I was making about unity," explained the first man, "is that in the culture that's grown up on this planet, religious tradition will never be a cause of strife. Individual heretics may be persecuted—although we as priests will always offer them sanctuary—but groups of people with different symbols for the same idea will never go to war over it, as happened on the mother world when intolerance prevailed."

"They went to war over the *symbols?*" Noren burst out incredulously. He had learned enough about the mother world to know what war was, and he could understand why it had occurred when dictatorships had tried to rule by force. But over religion. . . .

"Think of how the people among whom you grew up felt about heresy," the man suggested, "and then imagine them deciding that all the citizens of the next village were heretics. Or picture a case where quite a few of them agreed with some new interpretation of the Prophecy, and were condemned as a group, including their families—"

A sharp cry interrupted him. On the opposite side of

142

the bonfire, one of the older men had collapsed.

*

It was Derin, the camp's Chief Mason. A heart attack, the doctors called it; an attack brought on by the exertion of the contest, in which he had won third place. No one could have predicted it, for he'd been pronounced fit upon examination in the City; still, because of his age, his friends had tried to persuade him to be content with designing the structure. Derin had laughed at them. Stonework was his pride, and he had won setting contests before. Unlike most Scholars, he had lived in his village until middle life, and had been a highly respected craftsman. City confinement had been a real sacrifice for him, though his natural engineering talent had been put to good use in the drawing of plans for the building to be done during the Transition Period.

People clustered around. "It is good construction," Derin whispered. "The stone will endure—"

"The stone will endure," his friends agreed. Two or three of them knelt beside him, clasping his hands. There was nothing the doctors could do. On the Six Worlds, physicians had been able to replace failing hearts, but on this one the equipment for such surgery was unavailable. Even therapeutic drugs were lacking. As in so many other ways, things had moved backward.

Noren watched in horror as Derin, half-conscious, went on, lapsing into the viewpoint of his youth. "My great-grandfather built the arch of the meeting hall; his name's over it still. This will stand as long; it will stand until the Star appears, and the Cities rise to replace it."

"It will stand far longer," people assured him. "It is part of a City; the Prophecy's fulfillment has begun."

"Yes . . . yes. I forget. . . ." He sighed, and Noren saw from his face that he was still in pain, though he was trying to conceal it. "In the village we thought Scholars were

143

immortal. We thought they knew all the answers. I . . . I think I wish it were true."

"The answers exist, Derin."

Although the City was contacted by radiophone, all knew that return could not save Derin even if he lived until an aircar came. The outpost's chief brought a blue robe, which he laid over Derin's helpless form. "May the spirit of the Star abide with you," he said gently, as one of the doctors began induction of hypnotic anesthesia.

Abide with him? thought Noren, aghast. Abide with him *where?* The man knew he was dying, and there were no non-Scholars present; surely this was not a time for pretense.

But the words seemed a solace, somehow, for when Derin closed his eyes he was smiling.

In the morning, when the aircar arrived and everyone gathered for the formal ritual of sending the body to the City, it took all Noren's self-control to attend. He had been to such ceremonies before, not only his mother's but those held for other people of his village—but that had been before he knew what was done with bodies. The idea of one's mortal remains being sent to the mysterious City, where they were given into the custody of revered High Priests, was accepted by villagers as entirely fitting. Even Technicians viewed it so; they were unaware of the necessity for recycling all chemical elements and had no information about the converters that had once been standard equipment aboard the starfleet. Yet to Noren the use of corpses for the same purpose as other human wastes, however well disguised, did not seem dignified. And the recitation of words designed to mask deception ought not, certainly, to be practiced among Scholars who knew the facts.

". . . *Now to the future we commit him, our beloved friend, knowing that in death he will continue to serve the hidden end he served in life, as shall we all, being eternally*

144

heirs to that which has been promised us through the spirit of the Mother Star. . . ." Staring dizzily at Derin's body, wrapped in its blue robe as a villager's would be wrapped in white, Noren feared that he was going to be sick before the ceremony concluded. How could these men listen to such words? Many of them had been close to Derin, had loved him!

Yet the words went on. *"For as this spirit abides with us, so shall it with him; it will be made manifest in ways beyond our vision.* . . ." That, Noren perceived, did not appear to fit the case. That kind of statement was applicable less to one's body than to one's mind. He frowned, puzzled; all the symbolism of public ritual was supposed to be translatable by the enlightened. He must be overlooking something.

As a child, when he had asked what happened to people's minds when they died, he had received the usual reply. "That is a mystery," his mother had said serenely. "People cannot understand such things as that; only the Scholars know them." It was a matter in the same category as how Machines worked, why soil must be quickened before crops would grow, and by what means the Prophecy had been transmitted from an invisible star to the hand of whoever had first written it down. About these other things he'd gone on wondering, and his curiosity had in due course been satisfied; to the first he had not given much attention —not, that is, until recently.

The Scholars around him did not seem perplexed. What if he were to ask someone what those words were meant to signify? His pride, of course, was too great for that, since it would mean confessing that the issue troubled him; yet a Scholar would reply honestly. . . . *"He is forever of Mankind, holding a share in Man's destiny; his place is assured among those who lived before him and those who will come after, those by whom the Star is seen and their children's children's children, even unto infinite and unending*

145

time. . . ." That was all right for villagers . . . or was it? Would that particular bit of poetry contribute to mankind's permanent survival, or had the High Priests, in this at least, exceeded their bounds?

The rites ended, the aircar rose and hovered silently over the circle of people whose faces were still turned devoutly upward toward the sky, the original source of man's knowledge and the domain of all secrets. He had seen that sky more clearly than most, Noren thought; he could still see fierce blazing stars beyond the soft blanket of life-sustaining air, which from above was not blue, but gray and foullooking. So had the Founders, however. How had they endured such a view? Had they closed their eyes to the question of meaning, of whether there was any logic at all to life, to death, to the evolution and destruction of worlds?

All his life Noren had questioned, but never so deeply as this; he had never encountered problems that seemed to make less and less sense as he continued to ponder them. He had assumed that the City held all the answers. And it did! he thought suddenly while he watched the aircar start toward it, ascending to cross the Tomorrow Mountains. It must! Realization struck him forcefully, bursting the bonds of his terror. Was not the computer complex the repository of all truth? In the City he was free to ask the computers anything he wished, and though he had not previously framed such queries as were now torturing him, there was no bar to his doing so. His fellow Scholars had perhaps done it long ago. Neither they nor the Founders could have closed their eyes completely; yet they could scarcely be at peace with themselves—and even, at times, laugh about things—unless they had information that he did not. To get the information, he had merely to go back, as he'd been advised.

But he could not go so soon. That would look as if he had decided to seek Stefred's help; it would be an admis-

146

sion that he felt unfit to finish the job at the outpost. He was unwilling to concede anything of the sort, and not only because of what others would think, for he knew that without proving his capability he could not live with himself. He could never rely on himself again.

So in the weeks that followed, he went on working; he went on studying; he went on tutoring Brek; and though these pursuits gave him no pleasure, neither did he find them intolerable. From time to time he was struck with amazement at his ability to follow them while doubting their real significance, but for the most part, he kept doubt from his thoughts. He no longer let himself worry, nor did he have spells of unaccountable fear. Life in camp was simply neutral—gray, like the surrounding wilderness of unquickened land. He was suspended from the world. He had not yet returned from space. Yet in the depths of his mind he knew there would be a re-entry, a resumption of the search for truth; and for that he began to plan. The planning was a light in the grayness.

He had come to understand, Noren felt, what Stefred had meant when they'd talked over the radiophone. The reminder about their last discussion had referred not to the ignored warnings, but to the final part. *You will need more than courage,* Stefred had told him the night he left the City. *The kind of knowledge that will help is one you must find for yourself. It exists, and you will have access to it.* That was typical of Stefred's subtle guidance. Though he couldn't have known what would happen in space, Stefred might well have guessed that sooner or later certain questions would arise. He would not provide answers in advance. He would expect a person of intelligence to know where to look for the answers.

Eagerly, desperately, Noren planned his questions: the questions he would ask the computers when the opportunity came.

147

The final space flight was completed safely, with the shuttle bringing back the portion of starship that contained the weak and faltering beacon. Slowly the tower took shape, rising ever higher as level after level was added to it. The work was fantastically difficult, for without any materials with which to build scaffolding, the builders had to attach each section while standing on the one below, assisted only by ropes and lightweight plastic pulleys. Noren and the members of the space teams did the actual rejoining of the starship, but many Scholars helped get pieces into place, and one fell to his death from great height. There were several lesser accidents. Meanwhile, other men began the job of interior compartmentation, which was to be far less extensive than in the City's towers since relatively little plastic could be transported.

Noren found it hard to work high above the ground, not because he feared falling, but because it reminded him of the way he had clung helplessly to the starship in space. He suspected that others had the same thought; during supper of the evening before the attachment of the tower's top, Emet, one of the outpost administrators, sat down beside him. "I'm going for supplies tomorrow," he said, "and we thought you might like to come along. There's to be a conference in the City—"

"I have work to do," Noren said stubbornly.

"You can be spared for a day. We heard this afternoon that a conference is being held to discuss some results of the experimentation. You and Brek are the only people here specializing in nuclear physics, and one of you should attend. You will learn by listening."

Noren's spirits lifted. This was the chance he'd been waiting for! What Emet was proposing might not be a mere excuse; they might really think it of some value for him to go. Obviously, the experiments had not yet been completed successfully, for if they had, it would have been announced and everyone would be jubilant. However, there could well be new data of importance. The thought didn't excite him as it once would have, but he was elated for another cause: in the City he might have time to spare . . . enough time to consult the computers.

Since Derin's death an aircar had been kept in camp at night, so that in an emergency it could set out for the City at dawn. This also made it possible for people to go after supplies, take care of other necessary business, and return before dark the same day. It was not safe to cross the mountains after dark; carrying irreplaceable equipment over them was risky enough in broad daylight. The outpost had been located where it was only because the need to have it well separated from the City in case of future nuclear accident, yet at the same time within easy range of the aircars, outweighed the inherent danger of flying back and forth across a tall ridge. At times when vital metal things, such as components of the new power and water purification plants, were being brought, everybody was nervous lest there be a crash. Aircars were not hard to pilot, but they had been used almost exclusively at low altitudes, and the mountain country was hazardous.

It was also strange and forbidding, Noren thought, as he looked down on it the next morning. Little grew there, and many of the rocks were a garish yellow instead of gray or white like most stone of the lowlands. No one knew much about the mountains; they had not been explored except through occasional aerial surveys that had added nothing to the data obtained by the Founders from orbit, other than to verify that the mutant "savages" did exist there. Expeditions on foot were, of course, impossible, since not enough pure water could be carried.

Noren had never been in an aircar before. As a small boy he had once touched one that had come to his father's

149

farm, and ever since, he had longed to fly in one; now, like so many things, it had come to him too late. There was no thrill left. He had lost the capacity to feel. Emet looked at him worriedly, and Noren sensed that the camp's leaders had hoped attendance at the conference might cheer him up. He knew they were still deeply concerned about him, although they concealed it just as he concealed his own feelings. Determined to forestall any suggestion that his free time in the City might well be spent in a visit to Stefred, Noren asked quickly, "Could I try the controls, Emet?"

The man nodded. "Yes, as soon as we're past the mountains." He seemed to relax a little, and Noren found that although he himself was becoming more and more tense, it was not the tenseness of despair. Rather, expectancy was rising in him. He was about to obtain answers! The computers had answers to everything except the research problems yet to be solved. He was not so naive as to suppose that the answers would be easy to comprehend; but tonight, at least, he would have facts to ponder.

Above the rolling land between mountains and City, he took over the aircar's direction lever, which could be used from either of the two front seats, and Emet showed him how to maintain level flight. There was nothing difficult about it; Noren was almost sorry when Emet resumed control for the descent into the open top of the huge entrance dome. But his eagerness to gain access to the City's repository of truth outweighed all other thoughts. He shivered with anticipation as he stepped onto the landing deck.

"The conference is set for an hour past noon," Emet told him, "and I'll meet you here afterward." He smiled. "Until it starts, you're free do do as you like."

Walking down the stairs and into the main corridor, Noren realized why Emet had not inquired into his plans. He'd assumed he would look for Talyra! Yet the last thing he wanted was to encounter her at this point. Perhaps later, if what he learned proved heartening. . . . He went swiftly to the computer room, hoping fervently that he would not have to wait for a free console; after weeks of waiting, he did not believe he could endure even a quarter-hour more.

He needn't have worried; the computer room was strangely deserted. Its dim bluish light seemed somehow eerie when not a single person was in sight. Luck was with him, Noren thought thankfully. Even his privacy was assured; no one would be watching over his shoulder, wanting him to hurry. He settled himself in the booth farthest from the door and with trembling hands prepared to key in the first of his carefully planned queries.

Noren had conversed with the computer complex often enough to know better than to make the questions too general. He knew that to ask, "What is the meaning of life?" would very likely produce the same result as Brek's initial request for a full description of the mother world's history: the computer would offer more information than could be presented in a reasonable length of time. He had planned ahead because he'd been aware that the issue must be approached systematically, logically, if he was not to waste any of the precious moments available to him. Computers, he'd learned, gave one precisely what one asked for—that much, and no more. He had found that it paid to be equally precise.

Nevertheless, his fingers were shaking so that on the very first sentence he miskeyed. WHY DID AN UNPREVENTABLE TRAGDEY STRIKE THE HUMAN RACE? he asked, and the computer responded, NO REFERENT. His heart contracted; then he saw that he had spelled it "TRAGDEY" and tried again, telling himself that this nervousness was foolish. The question might involve deep feelings on his part, but the computer, which had none, would treat it just like any other inquiry. The answer would appear as quickly and as clearly as if he had requested a mathematical formula.

151

But it did not. Noren watched the screen expectantly and although the spelling of "TRAGEDY" changed, NO REFERENT remained there.

He scowled, wondering what error he was overlooking. Computers, once properly programmed, did not make errors; operators did. That was something he had discovered his first week in the City. No referent? Surely "tragedy" must be in the computers' vocabulary; it was a perfectly ordinary word. He had no time to lose, however, so he would come back to it after trying another approach.

The specific matter of why the Six Worlds had been destroyed was hard to lead up to, and after devoting a good deal of thought to the problem of how to do it, Noren had decided that the direct way would be best. Although he could predict the first few responses, it would in the end be quicker than attempting to tell the computer what information he already had. WHY WERE THE SIX WORLDS DESTROYED? he began; and, as expected, the answer was, BECAUSE THEIR SUN BECAME A NOVA. At that point he had merely to ask WHY? again, so that when the astrophysical data concerning elements, temperatures and pressures started to appear, he could press INTERRUPT. Then, with the computer on the right subject and waiting for clarification, it was time to ask what he really wanted to know: WHY DID THESE CONDITIONS OCCUR IN THAT STAR AND NOT SOME OTHER OF THE SAME TYPE?

The computer did not hesitate; its internal processes were, in terms of human time-perception, instantaneous. Flatly, finally, it responded, THAT IS NOT KNOWN.

Noren was momentarily dismayed, but then he cursed himself for his own stupidity. Of course it was not known. If it had been, the Founders would have had more than a few weeks' warning. He still wasn't touching the heart of the issue. WHY IS IT THAT INHABITED WORLDS ARE EVER DESTROYED? he persisted.

152

PLEASE REPHRASE, replied the computer.

Frowning, Noren sought another way to put it. This would be even more difficult than he'd anticipated, he saw, and he could not afford the time to fumble. WHY DID MANKIND EVOLVE ONLY TO BE NEARLY WIPED OUT? he ventured.

The computer responded tersely, INSUFFICIENT DATA.

HAS THIS HAPPENED TO OTHER HUMAN RACES ELSEWHERE?

THAT IS NOT KNOWN.

Well, he'd again queried foolishly; the computer, after all, knew nothing more than what had been entered into it by the Founders and by Scholars since. His plan of attack was already so upset that he could not get back to it. In desperation Noren asked the thing he'd originally thought would yield too much information: WHAT IS THE MEANING OF LIFE?

PLEASE REPHRASE.

FOR WHAT PURPOSE DO HUMAN BEINGS LIVE?

INSUFFICIENT DATA.

Not so much as a clue to suggest what questions might be more fruitful, Noren thought irritably. That was surprising; it did not work that way with science, where one's inadequate phrasing usually produced a reply from which one could deduce the correct approach. With an apprehensive glance at the console clock he tried frantically, FOR WHAT PURPOSE IS MANKIND IN DANGER?

INSUFFICIENT DATA.

IS THERE ANY PURPOSE AT ALL IN THE UNIVERSE?

INSUFFICIENT DATA.

Noren fought down the panic that was growing with his frustration. It was evident that he was not going to get what he'd expected. He simply did not know how to communicate with the computer on a subject of this kind, for it must certainly have more data than it had given out. He was beaten. Yet before he left for the conference, he would make one final try.

He looked around him, seeing that the room was still empty, and he was too overwrought to think about how peculiar that was; he was conscious only of relief. The last question, the one he had scarcely dared hope he might ask, knowing that he would never do so if there were a possibility of anyone's coming before he could clear the screen. . . . He drew in his breath and, rapidly, keyed: WHAT HAPPENS TO THE MIND AFTER DEATH?

Without delay, data appeared on the screen, detailed data about the cessation of brain waves. Impatiently, Noren stabbed INTERRUPT again. OMIT THE BRAIN, he instructed. OMIT ALL PHYSIOLOGICAL CONSIDERATIONS; DISCUSS THE CONSCIOUS MIND.

The screen went blank, and remained blank—except for the simple statement, THERE IS NO NON-PHYSIOLOGICAL DATA ABOUT DEATH.

Noren stared, incredulous. This was the cause and summation of his failure to elicit answers to his other questions; the problems were all closely tied. If the computer did not know anything about death, then it could not know why the thirty billion inhabitants of the Six Worlds had died in a single instant. If it did not know what death was, it could not know what life was either; no skill in questioning could make it explain why planets full of people should exist or cease to exist. Yet with these basic issues unresolved, on what could one's knowledge of the universe be founded? What meaning was there to "truth" that did not encompass the whole?

That is a mystery, his mother had said when Noren had first asked such things. *Only the Scholars know that.* But the Scholars did not know, and the shock of that left him wondering whether the search for knowledge might not be entirely futile.

154

VI

LEAVING THE COMPUTERS, NOREN FOUND HIS WAY TO THE
assembly room without conscious thought. It was not
crowded, and in fact even Stefred was absent; apparently
only the specialists in nuclear physics had been invited to
attend. Noren was so dazed that he scarcely noticed that
others also looked troubled, or that none of his acquaintances tried to talk to him. He sat in a sort of stupor, void
of all feeling, waiting for the conference to begin. *There are
no answers,* his mind kept repeating. *The City does not
contain all truth, and if it does not, is there any real truth
to be found? How can there be sense to such a universe?
How can these others live in it?*

He had assumed that the older Scholars must know
something he did not; now he felt that such questions as
he'd framed must never have occurred to them. They had
discussed the limits of their scientific knowledge often
enough, and surprising though it had been to find that even
apart from the problem of how to synthesize metal, the

155

Founders had not been omniscient about material things, he had accepted the fact. He had seen how knowledge of that kind increased gradually, through observation and experimentation. Yet never had anyone mentioned a general ignorance of other important matters—deep matters that, having once been thought about, could not possibly be ignored. If people had been perplexed, they would surely have said so! Why had he been singled out to endure this burden? Noren wondered despairingly. The rest had once seemed so much like him in their concern for truth. . . .

At the front of the room a Scholar was speaking quietly. "Grenald cannot be with us," he said, "although as I'm sure you all realize, he would not stay away by choice. Two hours ago he collapsed and has been taken to the infirmary. For more than a year the doctors have warned him about overwork, yet he drove himself until there was nothing left to be done. May the Star's spirit now restore the strength. . . ."

As the eyes of the people turned upward toward the overhead sunburst, Noren saw that many glistened with tears, and bafflement penetrated his numbness. Grenald was greatly respected, but he was a reserved and distant man for whom few felt warm affection. ". . . that he spent in our behalf," the speaker continued, "for while he cannot live to see the day he strove for, the darkness of this one will nevertheless diminish. We who go on would have him see that we are not vanquished."

Several of the women were by this time crying openly, and Noren perceived that some unexpectedly serious failure had been encountered in the work. Terror spread in a cold wave through his body. He felt paralyzed, unreal, as he had on the morning after the space flight. The voice of Grenald's chief assistant, who had taken the floor, seemed dim and far away.

"Those of you who've worked with Grenald during the

156

past few weeks already know the worst," the man declared soberly, "but to the rest it will come as a shock. I cannot soften it. You must understand that the obstacle these experiments uncovered is not in our technique, but in our basic theory. The results have been entered into the computers a thousand times in different forms; always the output is the same. The ultimate equations yield no solution. Last night Grenald and I ran them through again, and at dawn, when we turned off the console, NO SOLUTION had been there so long that it did not quickly fade. That is a portent, so to speak, of the significance of this failure. It will not fade; it will not be quickly overcome. The creation of metallic elements by nuclear fusion has been proven impossible at the theoretical level—"

Horrified, Noren focused his mind abruptly. *Proven* impossible? For all his doubts, he had not anticipated a defeat so final. "Impossible at the theoretical level" was quite different from "impossible by present methods." The latter said merely that other methods must be sought. The former included such impossibilities as rocks falling up instead of down, direct communication between people's minds, and the rising of the sun in the west.

"At the theoretical level," the physicist repeated, "and you're all aware of what that means."

Death, thought Noren with bitterness. The death of the human race. NO SOLUTION . . . NO REFERENT . . . INSUFFICIENT DATA. There were no answers. . . .

"It means we must find a new theory. It means we must expand our most fundamental ideas of natural law, as the science of the Six Worlds did over and over again during the course of its history. The pressure was not so great then, but with hindsight we see that the stakes were equally high. Let us not forget that. Let us not be dismayed by the years of groping we must face before further experiments can begin."

157

"A new theory?" someone protested. "We have no grounds for discarding the present one, or even for modifying it! It has not been invalidated; on the contrary, every aspect of it checks out. The fact that it tells us we cannot do what we would like to do is not the theory's fault. It would be nice if men could fly without the aid of machines, but the law of gravitation tells us they can't—and synthesization of metal has now been placed in the same category."

"We must have faith that this theory is merely a special case of some larger, more comprehensive principle," Grenald's assistant said gravely. "There was a time when the law of gravitation told men that they could not fly by any means."

Yes, but there nevertheless remained things that were beyond the realm of possibility, Noren thought; and there was no good reason for supposing that transmutation of elements wasn't one of them. Confidence that a verified theory would be overridden was unfounded. Cold logic told him that it was no less an illusion than the villagers' trust that "the spirit of the Mother Star" could protect people from danger. Words Stefred had once said suddenly came back to him: *Men have always looked toward something above and beyond them; they always will. They've called it by different names. You, I think, would call it Truth.* Sick at heart, he realized that this too must have been a warning. Everybody clung to illusions, even himself. He'd perceived that the whole universe might be illusory, yet he had not really given up hope until the computers had drained all vestiges of it from him. Now he saw the hopelessness of his lifelong search. That which he had named Truth did not exist.

He sat motionless, benumbed, as the scientists went over the results of their work, analyzed the inexorable equations, explained the unforeseen implications of the theory that had

158

shown that the research was in vain. He was split in two: with half his mind he grasped what was being said clearly, while with the other he reflected that details no longer mattered. The mathematics proved conclusively that success could never be achieved. Despite his preoccupation Noren followed the math without effort; one did not need to be an advanced physicist to understand what had already been formulated, not if one's mathematical aptitude was high. To Noren, math was far more telling than words. Certain parameters yielded by the experimentation, when inserted into the equations, made those equations insoluble. One could no more get around that than one could deny that two and two would never equal five.

The physicists did not try to deny it; yet astonishingly few seemed willing to accept its full import. "Tonight there will be a general meeting," the conference chairman said. "Our fellow Scholars will ask what this discovery means in terms of the Prophecy's fulfillment, and as scientists we must say that there now appears to be no chance. We can mitigate that statement only by pointing out that the apparent certainties of past eras often proved to be naive misconceptions—"

"But there is no time to wait for a new era!" one of the men interrupted. "We have ample cause for certainty that ours will be the last, that the Star will be the herald not of renaissance, but of extinction. In the meantime, we cannot in good conscience continue to affirm the Prophecy, nor can we maintain a caste system that has lost its justification."

"We must maintain it. To do otherwise would destroy all hope of a future breakthrough by our successors."

"How could it destroy what does not exist? You yourself just admitted that as scientists, we see no reasonable hope of breakthrough."

Slowly the chairman replied, "Though we are scientists,

we are also priests. And as priests we see that man cannot rely solely on reason. Reason deals with data we already possess, whereas a breakthrough involves concepts we don't possess and have no way of predicting."

"I can no longer serve as High Priest, knowing what I now know of the odds," persisted the objector. "I'll declare myself a relapsed heretic before I'll say again to the people that their descendants will have what we're withholding from this generation."

Noren flushed; the room was so hot, suddenly, that he could not breathe. Trembling, he got to his feet and somehow reached the door. He dared not stay. He lacked strength to face the test he sensed was coming. If someone made formal declaration of relapse. . . .

It was an extreme step, although not without precedent. Unlike the Inner City Technicians who had once been heretics and who had recanted under pressure, a Scholar could not be charged with relapse by anyone but himself. An unenlightened person, if he regretted his submission, was treated like others "guilty" of heresy; his candidacy for Scholar rank was restored. The trials of steadfastness were more stringent, but the basic issue remained the same. Relapse on the part of a Scholar was a very different matter. In effect, it was an announcement that he could not be trusted to keep the secrets, and he was thereafter isolated from all contact with non-Scholars. He was confined not merely to the Inner City, but to the Hall of Scholars itself. Since the time of the Founding only a very few people had chosen that course, and while their right to do so was respected, on the whole they were considered rather eccentric. Most Scholars felt that relapse was an unforgivable evasion of responsibility.

Would the attitude change now? Noren asked himself, as he walked blindly toward the dome where he was to meet Emet. Would many agree that it was wrong to keep

160

things from the villagers when there was no real expectation of saving mankind by it? No . . . it was inconceivable that those who thought like the conference chairman would disclaim the Prophecy, and the majority did think that way. Having recanted in honesty, they had become trapped in fraud. That was one circumstance for which the First Scholar's wisdom had not provided.

Emet was waiting by the aircar. "Noren," he said awkwardly, "we had no idea—we knew nothing about the conference beyond what I told you, and though I came today for an emergency meeting of the executive council as well as for supplies, there was no advance notice of the subject."

"You wouldn't have brought me along if you'd known?"

"Of course not. Do you think us heartless?"

"Do you think I'm not strong enough to hear bad news?" Noren retorted.

"I didn't mean that. For the Star's sake, Noren, can't you see—" Emet broke off, sighing. "We'll all need our strength; let's not waste it fighting each other. I know you don't want help. Things would be easier if you could accept friendship, though."

Noren did not trust himself to speak. After studying him intently for a moment, Emet continued, "You have more friends than you realize, friends who—well, who'll go to great lengths on your behalf. If I asked you, as a favor to your friends, to find Stefred right now and tell him that you prefer not to return to the outpost—"

"I can't, Emet."

They got into the aircar and took it up in silence. As they rose above the City's shining towers, Noren bit down hard on his tongue to keep the pain inside him from exploding. Those towers would never again look the same. As far back as he could remember, they had been the focus of all he valued, but there was no beauty left in them. The patchwork of farmland, villages, and unquickened wilderness blurred beneath him; he blinked his eyes and stared straight ahead at the barren mountains.

"Noren," Emet began when they cleared the last range and plunged swiftly toward the stark new spire of the outpost, "I won't say that you shouldn't be discouraged; we're all discouraged. The significance of what's happened can't be minimized. But just remember that some things in life aren't expressible in terms of mathematics. You're a gifted mathematician, and so far you've studied little else, but there is more."

With difficulty, Noren restrained a mad impulse to laugh. Emet did not know how much more he'd expected to find that morning.

"You're young," Emet reflected. "For you there is a chance. The Transition Period may yet come in your lifetime. From what I've heard of you, it's possible that you'll lead the way. Don't let yourself be daunted by the gloom we feel, we who've learned today that we will not live to see it."

At the camp, to which word had preceded them by radiophone, Noren's stricken appearance was attributed to the despair shared by everybody. He did not mention that there was anything else involved. He scarcely spoke at all. Brek asked for details of the failure, and Noren rebuffed him irritably; after that he was left alone. But he found himself obliged to go to Orison, for he knew he would be conspicuous if he did not. Although normally the ritual wasn't attended by everyone, on this night all gathered as if drawn by some invisible force.

It was very informal in camp, held as it was outdoors, around a fire; usually not even the presiding Scholars wore robes. Few had robes with them, since nothing extra had been transported, and when no villagers or Technicians were present, the symbol of priesthood was indispensable

162

only at services for the dead. *We are all dead,* Noren mused, as he saw that the available robes were in evidence, *but for a while we live on, knowing.*

Yet those conducting the service did not speak of death. And stunned though people were by the unanticipated blow, their spirits seemed somehow lifted as the liturgy progressed. *". . . We are strong in the faith that as those of the past were sustained, so shall we be also . . . and though our peril be great even unto the last generation of our endurance, in the end man shall prevail. . . ."*

That was hypocrisy! thought Noren in dismay. How could anyone who knew the facts say those things and mean them? He certainly could not. He was indeed a relapsed heretic, despite having fled from the conference to avoid declaring himself. He was not sure why he had fled; he was puzzled as well as mortified to learn that he'd lost the courage of his convictions. By the Star, he must regain it soon, he told himself grimly; for he could no longer accept a Scholar's role in the system he'd condoned only for the sake of man's survival.

*

As time passed, however, Noren found that he played the role, went through the motions, just as he had kept going after the space flight: he did what he'd been accustomed to doing simply because there was no way to stop.

He had work, for one thing—not only Scholar's work, but the farm work he'd done as a boy. It would soon be harvest season. Before the tower was finished, land-clearing and soil-treatment equipment had been brought in, for the raising of a crop had high priority. Relatively few people had been needed to clear the ring of fields that was to enclose the living area, to "quicken" it by inactivating the soil's poisons, and to perform the initial enrichment with metallic trace elements from the dwindling store brought long ago by the starfleet; these were mechanized functions,

163

the basic ones for which preservation of off-world equipment was essential. But when it came to planting, refertilizing and cultivating, everybody pitched in for a few hours each day. It was back-breaking work, since there were neither metal tools nor even handles for the stone ones.

Planting season had been determined solely by the availability of the land-treatment machines; the unchanging climate had no more to do with it than with the various villages' seasons, which, though by now traditional, had been scheduled for most efficient rotation of equipment. On most of the Six Worlds, Noren knew, seasons had had a physical basis: people had planted in mild weather, harvested in the heat, and then, during a long period of inconceivable cold, had actually allowed the land to lie dormant. "They let *quickened* land go to waste?" Brek protested unbelievingly. "No wonder they started to run out of food."

"All their land was quickened," Noren pointed out. "It stayed that way naturally. Besides, the seed wouldn't sprout when it was too cold."

"What made it colder at some times than at others?"

Noren explained how the axis of a planet was frequently tilted to the plane of its orbit, a mathematical concept that was far clearer to him than the thought of weather being so cold that people could not go outdoors without heavy clothing. Science had taught him that water solidified and formed crystals at low temperatures, just as it had taught him countless other facts about the behavior of chemical elements; but though he'd been exposed to intense cold in a laboratory once, it was hard to imagine such a state prevailing throughout large areas.

Harvest time ended the outpost's dependence on grain brought by aircar, but with harvest came not larger rations but more people. There had been a vote to decide whether the founding of another city should continue and the project had been approved by a large majority. Its advocates included not only Scholars who believed that any future experimentation was more likely than ever to be hazardous, but those who felt that an optimistic defiance of fate was more fitting under the circumstances than a perhaps-futile attempt to husband the City's reserves. So expansion proceeded, and the policy of scant meals remained in effect. Hunger was less noticeable than at first; the original group had become inured to it, and moreover, enough fowl had been raised to provide eggs for eating as well as hatching. Before, there had been nothing but bread and water.

Water, of course, had been—and still was—the most difficult problem. At first it had all been imported from the City. Even to wash one's hands in impure water was an unwarranted risk, since the element causing chromosome damage would, over a period of time, be absorbed through the skin. Not one drop of the precious cistern supply could be spilled. What rainfall there was increased it, but only twice had there been rain. Both storms had been in the evening, and everyone had marveled to see water come from the sky at any hour but the pre-noon one, when it fell four days out of six in the region of controlled weather. It had been exciting, for the unpredicted deluge seemed a gift from above; men had stripped off most of their clothes to revel in it. But not enough free water could be counted on to provide for crops, and before planting had begun it had been necessary to complete both a purification plant and the power plant on which it depended, as well as the purified clay pipes of the irrigation system.

The water-processing and power plants were much smaller than their City counterparts, and had been put together from barely adequate materials obtained by sacrificing reserves. The job had been tricky. At the time Noren had been working on the tower's upper levels and had not participated; but now, besides his shift of farm labor, he was on duty alternate nights at the fusion reactor, which was located in its original compartment within the former starship. Although not yet knowledgeable enough to deal with any emergency, he could call the Chief Engineer in case of problems, and it was vital that a continuous vigil be kept. Maintenance of nuclear power was one of the Scholars' most sacred duties, for without that power none of the other essentials could function. Once Noren would have considered his a post of honor, yet he found the long watch hours dark; they left all too much time for thinking.

Brek's non-farm job was the one he'd held as a Technician: the servicing of radiophone and other electronic equipment. In their spare time, he and Noren continued to study together. This had become a torment for Noren, since it seemed wholly futile, and in his private studies he ignored nuclear physics to concentrate on pure mathematics; still he could not turn Brek's questions aside. Wearily, he explained the vast difference between the kind of nuclear fusion that occurred in the power plant and the kind that would be needed to synthesize metal. Power generation involved fusion of hydrogen isotopes, the lightest atoms in existence. Because the repulsive force between elements was proportional to the product of their atomic numbers, the fusing of heavier elements would demand great amounts of energy: so great that in nature, such elements were created only in the interiors of stars, where there were temperatures and pressures beyond imagination. Metal-rich stars and planets formed in regions of space where other stars had previously exploded.

As he said this to Brek, Noren faltered and broke off, overwhelmed suddenly by the implications of a thing he'd originally learned by rote. An exploding star was a nova. Were some types of novas necessary to the evolution of habitable planets? Brek, looking at him, grasped the point and quickly switched the subject. That was the difference between other Scholars and himself, Noren thought rue-

166

fully. The others could turn from such enigmas; he could not . . . but neither could he solve them.

*

Every aircar now brought passengers as well as supplies, and many of the passengers were women. The wives of the original staff members came first, then more couples and a few unmarried girls: either Scholars or Technicians betrothed to the Scholars who were already in camp. Noren assumed that this was arranged by mutual consent until one afternoon when, without warning, he was called in from the grain fields to meet Talyra.

In the first surge of astonished joy he ran to her and held her tight, not thinking past the loosed emotions that almost overcame him. That did not last, however. "Noren, what's the matter?" Talyra protested, sensing his deliberate effort to check his feelings.

"It—it's just that life's hard here," he declared, "and I don't want you to know hardship." That was true enough, though the main difficulty was that he did not see how he could bear to be near her, knowing as he did that he could not take the step that was prerequisite to their marriage. He knew too that although to allow her to hope would be cruel, he could no more be frank in that regard than with respect to his ignominious failure to complete the task with which he'd told her he had been honored. Talyra had been proud, happy; what would she think if she knew that he'd succumbed to panic?

"You said City life would be hard for me," she reminded gently, "and it wasn't. I was content there except for missing you. When they announced that those who served in secret had gone to build a new City and that their loved ones could follow, of course I chose to come."

"But Talyra," Noren said, "since the day of my arrest we've not been formally betrothed; how is it that they let you?"

167

"The Scholar Stefred sent for me," she explained. "He asked whether it was by my choice that there has been no formal renewal of our betrothal. I told him that you did not wish to bind me since you weren't sure when you could marry, but that I consider myself bound anyway and accept no other suitors. And oh, Noren, he said that in that case, the betrothal is fact! He wouldn't have if he did not plan to bless our marriage, surely—"

"Permission for our marriage does not depend on the Scholar Stefred alone," Noren replied, thinking that Stefred, in sending Talyra without consulting him, had employed unfair tactics. But he saw that she could not be discouraged and that if he argued further, she might doubt his love and be hurt; so that evening he stood up with her at vespers and made again the promises of fidelity they'd exchanged before the village council, which were not really lies because he certainly didn't intend to marry anybody else.

Since the Technicians had begun to arrive, the Inner City's custom had been adopted: Orison was held in the tower, and the outdoor service, now called vespers, became formal. The committed Scholars took turns conducting it, wearing borrowed robes if they had not brought their own. Talyra, as usual, attended regularly; her implicit faith in the promises of the Prophecy nearly broke Noren's heart. "Darling," he said to her, "you've met many Scholars now; you know that they're human. Hasn't it occurred to you that they might mislead us without meaning to, simply by being mistaken?"

"In little things, of course," she agreed. "In big things like the Prophecy—how could they? They're *guided*, Noren."

"How do you know that?"

"I just *do*. Anyway, they said so, just a little while before I left the City. It was the night they all came to vespers

168

wearing their robes."

Noren frowned; he had heard of no such occasion. "We'd known for several days that something must be the matter," Talyra continued. "The Scholars had been looking terribly solemn, and they'd stayed inside their special tower most of the time. A girl I know who's married to one told me her husband cried in his sleep. Then at vespers, the Scholar Stefred spoke; he explained that new mysteries had been made manifest to them, mysteries that even they found frightening at first, but that the spirit of the Mother Star would guide them to understanding. And he said we must be patient if our friends and loved ones seemed troubled for a while. During the ritual, though, they didn't look troubled; they looked—well, *brave*." She added reflectively, "I didn't know before it was so hard to be a Scholar."

Brave? thought Noren. Was it brave to pretend that some mystical spirit, a mere symbol, would offer answers that rational effort could not uncover? It struck him as far more courageous to admit that one's life had been built upon delusion. Yet Stefred, who was the most honest man he'd ever met. . . .

He wondered what Stefred would say if he were to confront him with the issue. Remembering their talks, Noren longed sometimes to sit down in the study where despite demanding challenges, he had always felt capable and secure, and to go through the whole wretched series of problems; but there was now a greater obstacle than his pride. From Stefred he could hide nothing, and he still felt unable to declare his relapse openly. He was not strong enough to break the pattern through which his shaky balance was being maintained. He might despise himself for not stating aloud that there was no longer any excuse for maintaining the castes or for failing to share the City's contents with the villagers, but he could not bring himself to abjure his recantation. Several others had done so; they'd accepted vol-

169

untary isolation in protest against the majority's insistence that the system must be preserved. Something held Noren back. He could not understand it. Perhaps, he thought miserably, it was merely that having lost his self-assurance, he was not sure of anything else either; not even of his own conscience.

On the surface, at least, the majority opinion seemed sincere. As time passed it became increasingly evident that most Scholars really believed there was some remote chance of the system's fulfilling its purpose. They discussed it at length, of course; when away from the Technicians, either in the tower's restricted sections or beside one of the small mossfires around which friends met privately in the evenings, they talked of nothing else. Noren avoided these gatherings when possible, joining instead groups that included Talyra, but occasionally he was unable to escape.

"What we face is really the same dilemma that confronted our forebears more than once on the Six Worlds," the Chief Engineer said on one such night. "It's harder for us because we know what we're facing. The time span is shorter. Our personal responsibility is greater, and we've been forced by a unique emergency to use stopgap measures that would have been unjustifiable in the normal course of evolution. But otherwise, we are in an identical position: the exhaustion of our world's resources is predictable, no sure solution is apparent, and the survival of man depends on a breakthrough we can't foresee."

"That's a dangerous argument," someone observed. "Look at history that way, and you could make a case for half the schemes that were proposed by well-intentioned men who thought humanity couldn't survive without a controlled society."

"False analogy. In the first place, we don't have a controlled society here; we have control of resources, which is something else entirely. The people of the Six Worlds had

170

to control certain resources too, eventually, and they found ways to do it without abridging individual freedoms, just as we have. They had no moral grounds for controlling what we must control—machines and knowledge—because those weren't irreplaceable resources there. But what's more, the whole notion of a controlled society is founded on the supposition that man can foresee all the paths through which progress will come, and we are aware that he can't."

"I know that," Brek said thoughtfully, "but I don't understand the analogy you do want to draw. On the Six Worlds evolution was working as it's supposed to work; over the years people just naturally went on learning and developing and solving problems as they arose—whereas here, since resources are so limited that they can't, we're dealing with reversion. If it weren't that the Prophecy makes them look ahead, I'm told, the villagers would be worshiping their ancestors—or maybe even idols—as well as Scholars! So how is there any comparison between the situations now and before the nova?"

"Human nature hasn't changed," explained Emet. "Yes, there's been reversion here, because progress is inextricably tied to technological innovation, which is not possible in the villages. The backward movement of village culture has been held in check only by the outlook the Prophecy fosters. Without that, people would have become wholly superstitious about machines, for instance, just as primitive tribes once venerated forces of nature they could neither understand nor control. If there were no High Priests, there would be witch doctors. If there were no public recantations, there would be ritualized blood sacrifice. And if it weren't for the adoption of Scholars' children, banishing all heretics would cause the villagers to revert genetically as well. But when we speak of humanity as a whole, we're including ourselves, through whom it is still evolving, and we're as helpless and blind as the men of the past: we have no choice but to learn what we can and then gamble."

"Gamble?" questioned Noren. "At the conference in the City, Grenald's assistant said that whenever the Six Worlds' scientists had to expand their ideas of natural law, the stakes were as high as they are here, though without hindsight they didn't know it. I don't see that. When has there been a case in which gambling accomplished anything?"

"Well, take population growth," suggested the Chief Engineer, "since that issue is directly parallel. When the people of the mother world first realized that their world's resources weren't inexhaustible, some believed population growth ought to stop entirely. The idea had a good many fallacies, not the least of which was that it would merely have postponed the problem until it was too late to get enough of a head start on space exploration. Fortunately man's instinct, his inborn will to survive, saw to it that growth slowed down without halting. But you can't blame people of that age for being fearful. They *knew* the resources couldn't last, and they didn't know what was going to save them; it was too far ahead of their time."

"Couldn't they foresee rapid interstellar travel?" inquired Brek.

"Not with any degree of certainty. For a great many years the wisest men of the Six Worlds believed that to travel faster than light was theoretically impossible. It was contrary to some basic principles of their science; the very mathematics of that science proved that no invention could ever circumvent the limitation, just as our mathematics now indicates that we can't synthesize metal. Only when additional principles were discovered did the way open—and at the last minute, too."

"We're going to have to make a comparable breakthrough," Brek agreed. "Basic scientific theory, not mere technology."

172

"Yes, and our population situation is also comparable. Obviously our resources would last longer if the High Law did not encourage large families. But we're still very few on this planet, too few to limit growth if we're to survive plagues or other disasters and to reestablish widespread technology at the Time of the Prophecy; and furthermore, if the Founders hadn't decided to foster rapid expansion, there would have been less chance of having the men and women with the creative genius needed to produce the breakthrough."

"How could they have limited growth if they'd wanted to?" Noren asked. "I thought the antifertility drug used on the Six Worlds couldn't be made here, and surely they wouldn't have put anything into the High Law restricting love."

"There are other means of lowering the birth rate, which the High Law forbids, though there's no longer much need for it to do so. After all, you and Talyra wouldn't want *not* to have children, would you, even though you can't keep them?"

"To make love, and not wish for our love to be fruitful?" Repelled, Noren declared, "The idea's unthinkable."

"Yes, in our culture. On a crowded world it would not be. The Founders came from planets that were running out of food; they'd grown up feeling it was unthinkable for a couple to bring more than two children into the world. It wasn't tradition that made them frame the High Law as they did; they had to alter their own fundamental attitude, although they knew they were deliberately cutting short the time the survival equipment and the chemicals for initial land treatment could last. With mankind so nearly wiped out, that was the lesser risk—but it was a risk all the same. There's always risk in human affairs. Man never knows exactly what the future will bring; he knows only that things cannot and will not remain the same."

173

"They've stayed the same here for a long time," Noren contended.

"Unnaturally long, after the initial abrupt reversion of the villagers. That couldn't happen if there were the resources to make normal innovation possible, and without the Prophecy, which makes even the villagers *want* change, we couldn't survive it. If people can't go forward they go backward; they don't stand still."

Quite true, thought Noren, but also quite irrelevant. The men—Emet, the Chief Engineer, all of them—spoke as if there were just two alternatives. They were ignoring what happened when the promise proved false: when people could not go forward, and were thereby doomed to inevitable, though belated, extinction.

*

Talyra adjusted to the camp just as she had to the Inner City: with serenity. There was need for a nurse, since although there were few illnesses minor injuries occurred frequently; she was kept busy tending them. She also took her turn at meal preparation as cheerfully as the men accepted the farm work, though cooking was not a task she enjoyed. Hunger, which she had never known before, did not faze her. "We were warned before we came that it would not be comfortable here," she declared, "but Noren, what does that matter when we're actually helping to fulfill the Prophecy?" She gazed up at the towering spire and added, "When I was a schoolgirl I used to look at the mountains and wish I could live till the Cities rose beyond them. I never thought such wishes could come true."

"And I always supposed you liked things as they were in the village," Noren said, realizing how little he'd actually known her then.

"Nobody who believes the Prophecy could be content with things as they are!" she protested. "Oh, I know there are some who only pretend to be devout, and want life to stay the same forever; but it's as much a sacred duty to prepare for the Time of the Prophecy as to obey the High Law. I was silly once; I imagined all the changes were going to come on the day the Star appears. I didn't stop to think of how much work it would take."

They were sitting alone by their own small fire, while dozens of other fires, stone-encircled, made glowing dots in the mossland that surrounded the moonlit tower. "Talyra," Noren began hesitantly, "do you ever want to know more about the work than you've been told? Where the Scholars got the tower, for instance?"

"Of course I do," she admitted, "but there's much, after all, that's beyond knowing."

"I mean . . . do you still believe it's right for the Scholars to have mysteries they don't share?"

Talyra regarded him seriously, her face illumined by firelight. "Yes," she declared. "The world is full of mysteries we can't expect to understand. You still do expect it, darling, and I think that's why you're not happy—though I know it's not a thing you should be blamed for."

Stefred had been right about her, Noren saw. Talyra did not have the sort of mind for heresy. She was brave; she was intelligent; but though she would never want arbitrary power for herself, she perceived no evils in its being given to others, and that made her unfit to exercise the responsibility of a Scholar. If he'd wanted to assume the robe, there'd have been no need to postpone commitment longer for her sake; she would lose nothing by becoming technically ineligible for a status she'd neither seek nor earn. Yet he was still pretending that no final decision could be made about their marriage. . . .

The fire had burned down to smoldering ashes; Noren made no move to rekindle it. Drawing Talyra close, he kissed her, and for a little while his mind was far from the dark reaches of that which he could not know. The warmth

175

of the moment was all that mattered. . . . And then, abruptly, she pulled away, and he saw that she was crying.

"Talyra, what is it? What did I do?" he demanded.

"You—you haven't done anything," she faltered.

"Then what happened?"

"Nothing, except I realized that you don't really want to be betrothed to me."

Astonished, he burst out, "I've always wanted to be betrothed to you! Why should you question that now?"

She flushed and did not answer. "Darling," Noren persisted, "haven't I told you over and over again—"

Not facing him, Talyra murmured, "If you wanted me, you'd do more than talk about it."

"But you know I'm not yet free to marry."

"Are you also forbidden to love?" she demanded fiercely.

He sat up, not trusting himself to touch her, much less to admit how often his thoughts had turned in that direction. "That wouldn't be fair to you," he declared with pain.

"Why wouldn't it? It isn't the same now as in the village; when an Inner City woman has a child, she must give it up for adoption whether she's married or not. I would not be dishonored, for our betrothal is public and everyone knows that I let no one else pay court to me. What more would marriage be except sharing quarters?"

"It would be permanent," replied Noren.

"Are you suggesting that someday you'll want some other girl?"

"Of course not! But suppose I can never marry you, Talyra?" He dropped his head, adding wretchedly, "There may come a time . . . soon . . . when I will know positively that I cannot; and you must then forget me, Talyra . . . and choose some other suitor."

"I couldn't! I never could! Do you think I won't love you forever because I've not yet sworn it by the Mother Star in

176

a marriage ceremony?"

"I haven't the right to bind you, Talyra—that's why the ceremony can't be held. And I—I can't bind myself either, in certain ways."

"How can you say such things?" She began to cry again, quietly. "If you loved me, you couldn't say them."

"I say what I must," Noren replied brusquely, knowing that he dared not let himself go further. So many of his once-firm principles had crumbled; already he'd delayed declaration of renewed heresy despite knowledge that the Prophecy was false; he could not count on himself to stand fast about anything. What Talyra had said was true; there was no real reason why a betrothed couple should not make love, not when the rearing of families was impossible in any case, and when the bearing of offspring for adoption was, under the High Law, a virtue. In the villages it was shameful to father a child one was not willing to support, but among Inner City people that did not apply. Yet he could not love Talyra casually; his feeling for her went too deep. Once she was wholly his he would be unable to endure the thought of her marrying someone else. Might not priesthood then seem merely one more step in the path of hypocrisy he had taken, and might he not assume the robe for the sake of freedom to seal their union?

In the days that followed, such thoughts worried him more and more. Maybe Talrya was the cause of his reluctance to speak out, he reflected; after all, once he announced formally that he was no longer willing to uphold the system, he would be isolated from the Technicians and would never see her again. Originally, in the village, he had not been stopped by that, but perhaps he was incapable of making the sacrifice a second time. As far as he knew there was no other reason for hesitancy.

The pressure within him built up. He was guilt-ridden by the rankling memory of the space flight, and equally

177

so by his conflicting impulses. He could not trust his judgment any more. At times he hated himself because he had ceased to live by the code of honesty that had once meant everything to him; at others he thought honesty meaningless in a world devoid of ultimate truth; and it was hard to tell which torment was the worst. Inaction became unbearable—and so, with bitterness that masked his shame, he spoke at last to the one person in whom it was possible to confide: he confessed his hypocrisy to Brek.

Brek listened to the whole story, from the source of the panic in space to the facts presented at the conference, and he did not dispute Noren's assertions, though it was apparent that he did not share the terror Noren had felt on discovering areas the computers could not deal with. It was not in Brek to probe the universe that deeply. What he did share was hot anger at the betrayal, at the idea that he'd been led to endorse a system that could not deliver what it promised. He too had recanted solely on the basis of that promise, and Noren's statements about the scientific impossibility of fulfilling it were persuasive.

"I wasn't sure," Brek admitted. "Everyone goes on hoping, and I don't have the math background yet to judge. But if *you* say the proof's conclusive—"

"Absolutely conclusive," Noren told him. "I—I've been weak, Brek, and I'm confused about a lot of things, but not about math. Mathematical truth does exist. It's the only kind that's really definite."

"You think that good and evil are definite, don't you?"

"Yes," Noren agreed. "And all of us—all the heretics who've ever become Scholars—believe that this system is evil! We accepted it only because extinction of the human race would be a worse evil, and we thought it could prevent extinction."

"If it can't—" Brek paused, torn by indecision. Finally he said, "Noren, if it can't, it should be abolished; there's

178

no question about that. But declaring ourselves relapsed heretics wouldn't abolish it, any more than the work we're doing now sustains it. We're not priests, and here, we live much as the villagers do. We haven't any City comforts. We don't have access to the computers or to dreams. Actually, we've got fewer privileges than we'd have if we were confined to the Hall of Scholars."

Noren's heart lightened; he had not looked at it that way. "The only privilege for us here is study," he said slowly, "and that, we can give up."

"Even the math?" inquired Brek, scrutinizing Noren closely. "Are you positive that when you're so gifted—"

"The advanced fields would not be open to me if it weren't for my rank," Noren said firmly. It was a small price to pay for peace of conscience, though math was the one pursuit that had offered him temporary mental distraction.

Week followed week. The Day of the Prophecy, observed annually on the date of the Mother Star's predicted appearance, came and went; Noren was appalled to find that the Scholars went right ahead with the usual celebration. In the villages this was the most joyous festival of the year, surpassing even Founding Day, and in the Inner City it was also customary to make merry; yet it seemed monstrous to do so under these circumstances. All the same, people followed the traditions. Though no one had green holiday clothes in camp, the women baked Festival Buns for supper instead of ordinary bread, and after an exceptionally solemn and elaborate vesper service, there was dancing. Noren was obliged to participate for Talyra's sake, but he loathed such pretense.

Upon abandoning his studies he had volunteered for an additional shift in the grain fields, where he labored far more industriously than he ever had in his father's. The work was still hateful to him, a fact that brought him satis-

179

faction of sorts. Crawling on his hands and knees along a furrow, stone cultivating tool in hand, he could almost forget that he had ever recanted. He could almost forget that he had become a Scholar, thereby implicating himself in fraud that was none the less real for being unintentional.

Almost, but not quite. He *was* a Scholar, and moreover, his fellow Scholars' attitude toward him seemed to be changing. Although at the time of his disastrous space flight, they'd shown no signs of the contempt he was sure they must feel, he now noticed that their friendliness had cooled. Why? Noren wondered. No Scholar looked down on farm work. It had always been emphasized that one was free to do whatever available work one chose, though one could hardly expect to receive one's living if one did none at all. Could it be that the others despised themselves too, underneath, for not having the honesty to acknowledge the pointlessness of research even to the extent that he had acknowledged it?

He mentioned this to Brek one evening; but surprisingly, Brek was dubious. "I don't think it's that," he said slowly. "No one was upset when *I* stopped studying. But you— you've too much talent to waste; people feel that you're letting them down by quitting. They'd all hoped the foundation for a new theory might come from you, that you'd develop into some kind of a genius."

"It was a vain hope," Noren declared fiercely. "I wouldn't quit if I thought I had any chance of helping matters; you know that! Years of study and research that can't lead anywhere, though . . . that's something else. It's self-delusion, and it's deluding others." His throat tightened painfully, for still, inside, he ached at the thought of the scientific career that had once seemed so exciting. It was the only kind of life he'd ever wanted; it would always be, if it were not so meaningless. . . .

All knowledge was meaningless. That was what hurt the

most. Knowledge was the one thing he had cared deeply about, and the discovery that its very roots weren't secure was even more disillusioning than the insurmountable problem in the research. When Truth was not to be found, the harsh pronouncement of the physicists' mathematics was reassuring, in a sense; grim certainty was easier to bear than no certainty at all.

A few at a time, the Scholars who had worked with Grenald in the City began arriving at the outpost, where their main task—in addition to the hours of farm labor that were shortened when shared among more people—was the outfitting of the tower. They were subdued, in some cases obviously crushed, but that did not seem to alter their diligence in readying lab facilities for the future. The equipment brought by the aircars was even less adequate than that used in the City; men devoted endless days to designing schemes whereby portions of it could be made to serve purposes for which they had never been intended. A way to hook up two machines with a featherweight's less wire than had previously been required was cause for major jubilation. These men were, Noren thought, like children playing a game where the winning of pebbles *mattered.*

Life in camp had settled into a routine: a mode of existence that to people of any other time and place would have seemed wholly incredible. The single tower, built of the most remarkable substance ever created by man, rose out of gray wasteland, bordered, at a short distance, by a narrow ring of green. Inside the tower were sophisticated laboratories, a small satellite computer linked by radio to the City, an air-conditioning system built to sustain life in interstellar space—but no plumbing. There were electronic devices but no electric lights; people carried battery-powered lanterns from room to room because there was no wire for installing permanent fixtures. They sat on the floor

181

because as yet no one had had time to weave wicker furniture. Around the tower were low primitive structures of uncut stone that housed not people, but a nuclear-powered water-processing plant and similar equipment. The people were still sleeping on the open ground.

To be sure, the ground was comfortable, since it was covered with thick, spongy moss; the cubbyholes most had chosen amid the undulating hillocks were private; and the weather was such that sleeping outside was preferable to confinement in a stuffy building. Everybody was too busy to bother with houses. Houses would have been superfluous. In the villages their value lay in permanence, but the camp's inhabitants felt none. They could not make homes outside the City; they could rear no families. They had more hardships than villagers with fewer compensations. They cooked on open campfires, ate from unglazed pottery bowls, and washed infrequently because in the absence of rain, the watering of crops had priority. Yet looking at the tower, they envisioned the new city it might someday grace; and irrational though their optimism seemed, most looked with lifted hearts.

Noren did not enter the laboratories. Except when on duty at the power plant, he kept away from the tower itself, avoiding with bitter determination all contact with memories that had become too great a hurt. But at length, just before supper one evening, he was summoned inside. The Scholar Grenald had come and wanted to talk with him.

*

Grenald had looked old on the night of the decision to build the outpost; now he looked aged, older even than the doddering graybeard who had sold pots in the village of Noren's birth. He had been ill for some weeks after the unhappy finish of his research, and it was common knowledge that he had little time to live. It had been his wish to see the place where his successors would carry on after him.

182

The wish had been respected, though everyone feared that the strain of leaving the City might prove fatal.

He and Noren faced each other in a cool, cavernous compartment of the unfurnished tower, Noren wondering what Grenald would say. It would be disapproving, no doubt. There would be an attempt to talk him into continuing his studies. The disapproval was mutual, for he felt that Grenald, of all people, should have accepted the finality of the verdict, considering that it was the result of a theory he himself had proven. Still, the old man had been an inspiring tutor, and Noren hoped that it would be possible to reply honestly without revealing that in him, all inspiration was dead. *You are his heir,* Stefred had said. . . .

"You are not what I once thought," Grenald declared, after appraising Noren for some time in silence. In a harsh voice, as if each word was forced out by effort, he added, "It's been the worst blow of all, Noren, to learn that you are a coward."

Despite his stunned surprise, Noren kept his face impassive. At last it had been stated openly. He had supposed that at the time of the space flight Grenald had been too absorbed by the research to pay much attention, but no doubt he'd been talking to people since.

Grenald seemed somewhat taken aback by Noren's failure to respond with hot denial; he continued less brusquely, "I did not expect you to take that from me. I hoped simply to jar you; I assumed you yourself didn't realize—"

"How could I not?" Noren mumbled.

"People deceive themselves sometimes."

True, thought Noren, but Grenald was hardly the man to talk. "You once expected to die for your heresy," Grenald went on, "and you were willing. Has a year so changed you that you now refuse a lesser risk? Perhaps it's for the girl's sake; I warned Stefred that you shouldn't be allowed to become involved."

"Wait a minute," protested Noren, puzzled. "I've re-

183

fused no risk! Maybe they didn't tell you, but I volunteered—"

"For extra farm work, yes, but you will not be kept here long on that account. You and Talyra will return to the City years before any experimentation is resumed. If this outpost blows up you'll remain quite safe."

"You thought . . . that I've given up science because I was afraid of being killed in the *experiments?*" For the moment Noren was too astonished to be angry.

"What else can one think when a boy of your gifts suddenly decides not to use them for mankind's benefit?" demanded Grenald. "It's not as if you disliked study; if that were so, I would not speak as I do, whatever I might think privately about your lack of responsibility. But I know you too well to believe you'd ever tire of it. I also know that if you were totally without faith in the power of science to save us, you would have opted for dissent long ago; you've never been one to hide your convictions. That's why I'm sure you have fears you're not aware of. Though you may say I'm not qualified to judge, since the physicists of my generation did not face the perils those of yours will, I cannot believe you'd consciously abandon research for that reason."

Noren met the penetrating eyes that seemed too clear for the thin, wrinkled face before him. "You're right," he said stonily. "I would not."

He turned his back on Grenald and strode out of the dim tower into sunlight, heading for the fields automatically because there was nowhere else to go. Was that what everyone thought—that he'd quit from fear? he asked himself. Was that the real cause behind people's growing scorn of him? Enraged though he was, he could scarcely blame them; a man who had panicked in space might logically be expected to panic at the idea of working under constant threat of thermonuclear disaster. . . .

Sickness came over him; he knelt by a freshly fertilized

184

row of grain shoots, pretending to cultivate, and his face burned crimson although he was alone. Was it *true?* No . . . no, he could honestly say that such a fear had never so much as occurred to him. His preoccupation with death had not taken concrete form. Yet cowardice was the root of the trouble, all the same. He had indeed abandoned both his responsibility and his most cherished personal convictions. He had held back from declaring the truth others refused to recognize: people were alone in a cold, vast universe that had capriciously destroyed their predecessors and would offer no better chance to their descendants—yet if there was any meaning at all to life, then there was meaning to the dictates of conscience, and conscience decreed that men who were doomed anyway must die free. Since the Scholars' supremacy could not save the human race, all must have equal voice in the affairs of the last era.

Grenald had been right, Noren thought, in spite of the way he'd misinterpeted things. He, Noren, was a coward; and though he'd known that, he had not faced the full extent of it. He had not realized what was keeping him from expressing his belief that the system should no longer stand. Now, as if the idea were entirely new, he guessed why he had hesitated. He guessed that all along he must have perceived the one real path of redemption.

But it was a path he could not take alone. He could not leave camp alone in an aircar he did not know how to fly. Noren frowned, considering it. Brek . . . Brek was a pilot, and in Brek he had already confided. Brek shared his view and would share the action it demanded.

That evening he ate no supper, for he had no appetite and he did not want to confront Talyra. She would not seek him at his private sleeping place, though she had made plain she would welcome him to hers. Nor would others intrude on a night when he wasn't on duty. Brek, however, would be concerned if he didn't appear, and would search everywhere.

He was lying face down, as had been his habit since he'd come to fear the sky, when he heard Brek approach. Scrambling to his feet, he announced without preamble, "Refusing to become priests, or even scientists, isn't enough, Brek. That's passive—and if we don't believe that people should be kept in ignorance, we've got to demonstrate how we feel."

"I don't see that there's anything we can do," Brek said.

"There's one thing," replied Noren grimly.

"Didn't we decide that to abjure our recantation would be pointless? Our being isolated from non-Scholars wouldn't abolish the system; we could do no good by it."

"Brek," Noren maintained, "it's the principle that counts. We recanted on false grounds; we affirmed a Prophecy that can't come true and a caste system that the Founders themselves would no longer consider justified! We ought to speak out to the Scholars whether we could do any good or not . . . but that's not exactly what I have in mind."

Brek studied him. "You wouldn't speak to the Technicians!"

"Here? No, there are too few, and they wouldn't listen; they'd just think we were crazy. But villagers will know us for City dwellers. They may not believe we're Scholars since we'll have to go unrobed, and we haven't Technicians' uniforms either; still, our clothes aren't like any obtainable in the villages. Besides, we know enough to speak in a way no village heretic could. We'll be heard."

Brek sat down, pondering the idea. "Just what will be heard?" he asked slowly. "A proclamation that the end of the world is coming, that the Time of the Prophecy will be a day of doom instead of rejoicing? Somehow, Noren, that doesn't strike me as very constructive."

"Perhaps not, but it's *true*."

"I suppose it is."

"Think, Brek!" Noren persisted. "The villagers and Technicians are being deceived. Does it make any difference whether the Scholars are maintaining the deception to stay in power, the way we once thought, or because they themselves are deluded?" He paced back and forth, treading the moss to a hard mat. "No!" he exclaimed in answer to his own question. "Truth is truth, and people have a *right* to it! I've always believed that truth is more important than anything else. If human survival could be made possible by hiding it from all but those who care enough to prove themselves, that would be tolerable, but since it can't, everyone ought to know the facts. They ought to know that there's no use in their being denied the tools and machines we're safeguarding for posterity, that the villagers alive now could live better if the City were thrown open—"

"I'm not sure we know all the facts ourselves," Brek interrupted.

"I studied more than you did," Noren said. "I may not know all the details, but I know enough of the basic theory to be sure that creation of metal will always be contrary to it."

"Everybody concedes that; if basic theory weren't involved we'd have no need for a major breakthrough."

" 'Breakthrough' is just another word for 'miracle.' It's what you call an event that doesn't fit natural laws, that goes against logic." Groping for a way to express the thing that had confused him since long before his disillusionment, Noren continued, "Actually, an idea like that underlies all the symbolism that's grown up around the Mother Star. People expect something more of it than fulfillment of the Prophecy would give them even if every promise could be kept. You know they do, Brek—sometimes I think you do yourself."

Brek didn't look up. "I used to," he admitted in a low voice.

Slowly, another thought took form in Noren's mind. Brek,

187

who had believed in the Mother Star, had been more cruelly deceived than heretics like himself, he saw; and as for people like Talyra. . . . "For the machines and the knowledge to be sealed away to no good purpose is wrong," he said soberly. "But there's something even worse." The words came with difficulty; he did not know how to describe what he was feeling. "Do you remember how in the dream, when the First Scholar proposed that his successors should become High Priests, his friends protested . . . and how he reassured them?"

"Of course. They were shocked because they thought he was suggesting the establishment of a false religion, and he had to explain that he didn't mean them to—" Brek stopped, suddenly overcome by indignation. "But the way it's turned out, they *did*—and if we keep silent we're party to it."

"I don't understand religion," Noren said. "I never have. I didn't understand all the First Scholar's thoughts even while I was sharing them. But they involved something . . . sacred, Brek. I don't know what he called it; maybe you do, since according to Stefred, each person experiences the dreams differently, depending on what comes from his own mind. Anyway, whatever it was, I do know the First Scholar wouldn't have used it to fool people. He wouldn't have employed that kind of falsehood for *any* purpose, not even for saving humanity . . . and if he'd lived to know that the Prophecy isn't as true as he believed it was, he would have repudiated it, just as we've got to."

Brek nodded. "It's a—a perversion of all he stood for to let the Mother Star represent something false," he agreed painfully. "How can any Scholar not realize that? Noren, I—I think I'm more of a heretic now than I was in the first place."

Noren sat beside him, searching his face; it was too dark by this time to see it clearly. "There's an aircar in camp,"

188

he said cautiously, "and someone's got to go for supplies. You're a pilot—"

"Yes, but—"

"If we leave just at dawn, nobody will see us; they won't suspect until it's too late. There'll be nothing they can do once we're gone. The villages in the third season zone harvested this week, and tomorrow people will gather in the squares to celebrate. We can land in the largest one, and coming by aircar, we'll draw a big crowd."

"We'll do that, all right," Brek declared. "Crowds can turn into mobs, Noren, and somehow I don't think people are going to like what we say to them. Village heretics have the nominal protection of village law, but City dwellers who dispute the Prophecy while claiming to be Scholars—well, there's no telling what'll happen."

"They'll kill us," Noren stated calmly. "Did you think I didn't know that?"

Brek himself had known, obviously, and had accepted it as he had the apparent death sentence he'd incurred at his original arrest. "I—I wasn't sure whether you'd thought that far," he said.

"Oh? You assumed that if I had I'd be afraid?" Noren strove to control himself, realizing that he was being unfair to Brek, and added quietly, "I saw my best friend murdered by a mob when I was small."

"You never told me."

"I've never talked about it to anyone. He was a lot older than I was, and the first heretic I ever knew. They arrested him . . . and then later that night they burned the jail. With us it will be over faster; once they grasp what we're saying, they'll probably stone us." Noren's voice was hard, bitter. "They'll tell themselves they're destroying wicked ideas, but underneath, at least some of them will believe—and the ones who do will throw the most stones."

"You don't have much faith in anything," Brek observed,

189

"not even in people benefiting from what we offer them."

"I'm a realist. As I told Talyra once, faith is nothing more than being content with ignorance."

"What are you going to tell Talyra now?"

"Nothing," muttered Noren. "What could I?" He would have no chance anyway, he knew. Even if he was not killed, he would be isolated in the City; he would spend what remained of his life inside the Hall of Scholars.

Brek looked uncomfortable. "It—it doesn't seem quite right to do this by stealth," he maintained. "I mean—well, they trust us. There's no rule against my flying the aircar without telling anyone; they'll think it odd, but they won't object. No Scholar would misuse equipment, so they'll assume we've gone for the supplies and that we left early because we wanted a few extra hours in the City."

"I know," Noren said, equally distressed. That was the aspect of it he liked least. "We won't try to escape the consequences," he declared. "If for some reason the crowd's not violent—if Technicians are there, for instance—we'll go back to the City afterward and confess. Besides, it's not as if we were endangering the aircar! Villagers won't damage it no matter what they do to us; it's sacred to them."

"Yet if they all believed us and overthrew the system, a lot of equipment would be damaged. We'd have hastened the end."

"As long as there's going to be an end, what difference does it make how soon it comes?" Noren argued. But underneath he was aware that his concern for the fate of the aircar did seem inconsistent.

*

Noren did not sleep. What point was there in sleeping the night before one died? Lying still in the dark, he closed his eyes to the stars while the endless, futile questions circled in his mind: why were worlds formed . . . why were

190

worlds destroyed . . . what *was* life, and what was death? At that last one, terror spread through him again, but he mastered it grimly. He would not yield to terror; he was through with that! Truth was the only important thing, and though the kind he'd once sought might be non-existent, he was determined to stand by the principles that were firm.

There was no point in eating or drinking either, he decided when dawn approached, silhouetting the Tomorrow Mountains against pale yellow. Food and water were in short supply and should not be wasted. He was not hungry anyway. His mouth was dry, but he knew that was partly the result of fear and therefore he paid no attention. In any case, to go to the cistern might attract notice.

The camp was quiet; no one was yet awake. No guard was kept in a settlement founded on mutual trust. On his way to the aircar Noren passed the low hillock behind which he knew Talyra's chosen hollow lay. Picturing her there asleep, untouched by any premonition of the grief he could not spare her, he knew he could not leave without seeing her once more.

His feet, sinking into the spongy moss, made no sound. He did not plan to wake her, only to look; she slept fully clothed on a lightweight sheet of brown cloth, as did everyone. Standing there, Noren cried silently, *Oh, Talyra, if only we were back in the village . . . if only I'd not been a heretic at all. . . .* But he knew he did not mean it. He could not have been other than what he was.

Talyra stirred and then sat up, roused not by noise but by his mere presence. She smiled joyously. Too late, Noren realized what he had done. If he simply walked away, she would be hurt and bewildered; she would suppose he had come, only to decide that he did not want what she was clearly willing to offer. She'd remain forever convinced that he had reaffirmed their betrothal more from duty than from love.

191

"Darling," he whispered, "there's no time . . . but I had to see you. I'm—leaving. Brek's waiting in the aircar—"

"Leaving? For how many days, Noren?"

"For good."

Talyra, stunned, gasped, "But *why?* Even yesterday you said nothing of going back—"

"I didn't know yesterday."

Rapidly she began to fold her belongings into the sheet. "I'll be sent back too, in a few days," she declared. "Do you think if I spoke to the Scholars, they'd let me come now?"

"No!" Noren exclaimed, too loudly, and then, whispering again, "No, you mustn't!"

His tone of voice gave him away; Talyra was too keen not to sense the desperation in it. "You don't have permission either!" she asserted. "The aircar never leaves till after breakfast; and anyway, if the Scholars had told you last night, you'd have said goodbye then."

He could not say that he did not need permission; she supposed him a Technician like herself. Noren pulled her to him, kissing her, but she wrenched away. "You never kiss me like that," she said, "not as if it was . . . the last time. What's wrong, Noren?"

It was hard for him to keep back the tears. "We . . . we won't see each other in the City. By the Star, Talyra, I never wanted things to turn out this way—"

He expected her to be hysterical, but she was not. Very calmly she announced, "If we can't see each other in the City, then we'll at least have the trip. Either you let me come, or I'll wake the Scholars and ask."

"No, darling, it's wrong for you—"

"For me more than for you? I don't think so. No Scholar has forbidden me; I break no provision of the Law. They are good and just and sometimes more human than you are! *They* would not expect me to say goodbye like this."

Noren was in no shape to think rationally; he knew only that though any Scholar she might wake would tell him to go and her to stay, he could not face a Scholar with so bald a deceit, nor could he watch her sorrow. Incapable of reply, he started for the aircar, with Talyra walking beside him. He avoided Brek's eyes when they climbed in, and there was nothing Brek dared say in her presence. He did not know how much Noren had revealed to her. "Let's get going," Noren urged, and the aircar lifted. Only as the outpost fell away beneath did he realize that he could not possibly reveal anything.

It was of course unthinkable that Talyra should witness what was likely to take place in the village; but more than that, he could not bear that she should know of his relapse. She would grieve over that even without guessing his peril. There was nothing to do but go on into the City, get supplies, and land in the village on their way back.

They climbed into the brightening sky and leveled off over the mountains. "Take over for a few minutes," Brek said. "I didn't check much, leaving the way we did." He turned to the dials on the control panel.

Noren held the direction lever as he had done when flying with Emet, but his mind whirled so that he could not keep it steady. Brek's face was tense, drawn; plainly the change of plan dismayed him. Talyra, who sat behind, was silent. How were they to endure the hours of delay? Noren thought. To leave the City before late afternoon might arouse suspicion; they would have to occupy themselves, perhaps talk to people, all day long. They might even encounter Stefred!

He stared down at the mountains, deeply shadowed in the early light, and it was as if they were no part of the earth. A touch of the same paralyzing detachment he'd felt in space hit him, whereupon his fear burst into panic. He must *move*. . . . Without conscious intent he gripped the lever and pressed it forward till the ridges swung closer, tipping at odd angles like things viewed while one was weightless. Their bulk was appalling, yet still they seemed flat, not solid. . . .

"Noren!" Brek shouted. "Noren, what are you trying to do? We're losing altitude—"

Noren came to himself and in horror jerked the lever back. The aircar rose abruptly—too abruptly. It began to lose power. In flat country that would not have been serious, for even a disabled car sank relatively slowly, drawing on reserves; but the terrain below was not flat, and Noren had no experience with air currents. In the effort to regain control, he veered off course and the rising sun shone full into his eyes through the domed canopy, blinding him; it was the nova once more. . . .

Brek made a grab for the lever. But it was too late; even before the jagged peaks closed in and he heard Talyra's scream, Noren knew that they were going to crash.

VII

NOREN OPENED HIS EYES TO SUNLIGHT AND A SKY THAT WAS abnormally blue. He was lying amid the wreckage of the aircar; there was a sharp yellow rock within a hand's span of his body, driven through what had once been floor, but he did not seem to be injured. The padded seat had cushioned the jolt of falling. As for the others. . . .

"Talyra!" he shouted, struggling to free himself from the straps. "Talyra, where are you?"

"Here," she answered from behind him. "I think I'm all right; I don't hurt anywhere. But I can't get loose."

Part of the aircar's domed top had collapsed on her, pinning her to her seat. It was not heavy enough to have caused injury, but because of its bulk Noren could not lift it alone; he scrambled back to where he had left Brek, who, although also apparently unhurt, was not yet conscious. "Pour some water on his face," Talyra suggested.

"There isn't any water," Noren replied, noticing that the front section of the aircar, which contained the small

195

emergency supply tank, had been smashed into rubble against the outcropping of rock into which they had plowed. Not until he stood up, surveying the landscape around them, did he realize the implications of what he had said.

They were somewhere in the higher reaches of the Tomorrow Mountains; tall crags closed them in on every side. Beyond those crags, should there be a passage through, would be only more rock, interspersed with gravelly patches containing occasional clumps of wholly inedible vegetation. He did not know if there would be any water, but if there was, it would be impure water, and they could not drink it.

Or perhaps they could. It would not really matter whether they did or not, since they would not live long enough to have children.

There was not the slightest possibility that they could survive; he knew that. The radiophone had been in the smashed portion of the aircar, and it did not take Brek's knowledge of radiophones to see that this one was beyond repair. Nor was there any possibility of repairing the propulsive mechanism, pieces of which were strewn here and there among the rocks. It was pure luck that the force of the crash had been absorbed by the impact of that section, thus sparing the cabin . . . though on second thought, Noren decided, the luck was bad rather than good. A quick death would have been easier than what lay ahead of them.

He crouched beside Brek, first feeling his pulse and checking for broken bones, and then, when he was reasonably sure that there were no serious injuries, shaking him into consciousness. Brek sat up painfully, holding his hand to his side. "Have you contacted anyone?" he gasped.

Noren shook his head silently. "We'll do that later," he said. "Let's get Talyra out first."

Brek glanced at the wreckage, stifled his cry of dismay, and with Noren's aid got to his feet. Together they moved the pieces of canopy under which Talyra was pinned and unfastened her seat straps so that she too could rise. All three of them were dazed, bruised and shaken, but they could walk; supporting each other, they made their way to a level piece of ground and stared back at the shattered aircar.

"It—it's not going to fly again," Talyra stated unnecessarily.

"No."

"Can we talk to the City by radiophone? Or to the outpost?"

"Noren and I will go and see," Brek told her. "You stay here."

"Wait," Talyra said, seeing him wince as he drew breath. "You're hurt, Brek."

"It's nothing."

"It's a broken rib," she declared, investigating with a nurse's practiced skill. She looked around her, searching for something that could be used to cut bandages; the fabric of their clothing was too strong to tear. "If only I were a doctor and knew the words that ease pain—"

She had come a long way since the days when she had considered an aspiration to be a Technician blasphemous, Noren thought; village nurses did not dream that those words—sacred ones reserved for the induction of hypnotic anesthesia—could be learned, much less pronounced, by an ordinary person. "I'll hunt for a piece of sharp metal," he said, "so you can make bandages when we get back. Come on, Brek."

They returned to the aircar, the search for a cutting tool giving them an excuse to remain there while they discussed the situation out of Talyra's hearing. Brek had no need to examine the radiophone; there wasn't that much left of it. "I couldn't salvage enough to transmit any signal, let alone a voice," he said sadly. "What are we going to tell her?"

"The truth."

197

"Are you sure—" He broke off. "That's a stupid question; I know you too well to ask it. But Noren, we've got to offer some kind of plan."

"A plan for what? For walking out of the mountains? It would take weeks even if we had provisions."

"For signaling, then."

"Brek," Noren protested, "you know as well as I do that they haven't enough aircars for a search. If we could contact them, they'd come, but otherwise they'll simply fly the regular route."

"We're not far off it. Maybe we can attract their attention. We could start a fire, for instance."

"In the first place, it wouldn't show except at night, and they won't fly at night; in the second place, there isn't anything here that will burn." That was all too true; there was no moss in the area, and certainly not straw or tallow. The components of the aircar were incombustible, though its batteries could perhaps be used to provide a spark.

Wretchedly, Noren confronted cold fact. For himself he did not care, but by his actions Brek and Talyra had been doomed. He looked back over the long chain of events that had led to this moment, thinking that there could be no more fitting retribution for his earlier weaknesses. The aircar destroyed; his own death wasted; Talyra's meaningless and unnecessary. . . .

And painful. It was not quite as hot in the mountains as in the low country, but there was heat enough to make thirst a torment past bearing. Starvation, if they should find water enough to last until they starved, would be still slower. Then too, Brek's injuries might be less trivial than he was making them out to be. Watching him, Noren said quietly, "I think I could induce anesthesia if you want me to try. You've had practice in going under."

"No," said Brek. "Hypnosis wouldn't be a very good idea; I'll need my wits, and you couldn't make it selective enough."

What good would wits do? Noren thought. In some cases, one's wits merely confirmed the futility of further effort. Brek went on, "I'll be all right once Talyra bandages my ribs. Look, Noren—if you're going to tell her how things stand, you'd better do it privately. Go back to her now, while I find something that will cut cloth."

Reluctantly, Noren headed back to the place where Talyra waited, sitting down beside her on the sun-warmed pebbles. "The radiophone's smashed," he said frankly, "and we can't fix it."

"Then we can't call for help?"

"There isn't any way to."

Talyra met his eyes. "I'm not scared, Noren," she said in a not-quite-steady voice.

Not scared? Then she was closing her mind to the obvious, Noren thought; he himself was terrified. He had, to be sure, started out that morning in the belief that he would not live till sundown; but death had somehow seemed a less real and immediate prospect than it did now, when it was to be slow, certain, and shared by the only person he had ever loved deeply. Of course, he was not going to let Talyra see how afraid he was, and perhaps she felt the same way. She too had pride.

"We mustn't panic," he agreed, putting his arm around her.

"What are we going to do first—after I fix the bandages, I mean?"

"There's not anything we can do, Talyra."

She stared at him, shocked. "You mean we're just going to sit here and wait to be rescued? I don't think that will work! Without the radiophone they can't possibly find us in all this wilderness."

His first impression had been correct, then; she did not realize that it was hopeless. With sorrow, a more stirring sorrow than he had felt during the past weeks of lethargy and bitterness, he admitted, "No, darling, they can't."

"You're talking as if you're ready to *give up*."

Noren faced her, knowing that decency demanded it, whatever the cost in personal anguish. "Talyra," he began, "it's my fault this is happening; you're here because of me, and I was even flying the aircar—"

"Don't blame yourself," Talyra said gently. "It was an accident, and after all, you didn't ask me to come. I was the one who insisted."

"That doesn't change the fact that I'll be responsible when we die."

"You mustn't say that!" she burst out. "We may be in danger, but that doesn't mean we can't live through it. The spirit of the Mother Star will protect us."

Horrified, Noren realized that this reaction was what he should have expected; it was entirely consistent with Talyra's whole outlook. Yet it was based on a delusion. She must not cling to any such false hope. "You've said yourself no one can find us," he pointed out, "and there's no food, Talyra. We can't escape from the mountains without food; it's much too far to the nearest village."

"I—I know. I don't see a way out either . . . but it's *wrong* not to search for one! It's wrong to assume we're going to die when we're not sure."

"If I weren't sure—if there could be any means at all of saving you—do you think I wouldn't try it?" Noren demanded.

"No one can be sure of such things," insisted Talyra. "There are mysteries beyond our imagining; the Star's spirit is more powerful than we guess. Doesn't the Prophecy say, '*We affirm life in the face of annihilation; we shall reaffirm it though death be in view; and the affirmation will be our strength*'? It's heresy to deny that, and to give up is a denial."

Yes, thought Noren, and he was again a heretic; had it

200

not been for the crash, within hours he would have pro-claimed himself a relapsed heretic before the people. He was unwilling to hurt Talyra by telling her that, but he should at least enlighten her about the Mother Star. To believe literally in symbols of an underlying truth might be all right, but he could not bear that she, like his mother, should die trusting in something that did not exist.

"I've been told more of the mysteries than you have," he said slowly, "and they are not as you think. The Mother Star can't change the laws of nature."

"Of course it can't," she agreed. "But we don't know all the laws of nature, do we? Sometimes . . . sometimes, lately, I've wondered whether even the Scholars do."

"They do not," declared Noren grimly.

In a confident tone Talyra proclaimed, "Then the Schol-ars themselves could not say that nothing can save us."

"The Scholars," Noren continued with pain, "know much about the Mother Star that is not in the Prophecy. They know, for instance, that it has killed more people than it will ever save."

She reached for his hand, saying soberly, "Noren, don't speak of this now. It's not that I can't bear it; it's just that you've suffered over it too long, and here we've got enough else to worry about." At his astonished stare she went on, "Do you suppose I can't guess what sorts of things have been torturing you all this time? You needn't answer; I know you're not free to tell—but I'm not stupid, darling. In the beginning I thought they were punishing you, but when you swore they weren't, I began to figure it out."

"Figure what out?" he asked, wondering how much he had given away.

"Not any deep secrets," she assured him. "But you said at your trial that you preferred truth to comfort, and I don't doubt that the Scholars took you at your word. There really isn't any other way they could have persuaded you

201

to recant, is there? They showed you mysteries, and naturally not all the mysteries are pleasant ones. People *do* die. Everybody dies sooner or later, and the Mother Star doesn't prevent it; we all know that. Only we don't think about it very much. The Scholars must have to, and someone like you, who starts out by thinking, has to, too."

At a loss for words, Noren turned aside. It was uncanny how close Talyra could come to facts she lacked the background to interpret. Yet in spite of that she still believed what she wanted to believe! She was still convinced that some miraculous force could deliver her from danger! Would it really hurt anything for her to go on believing a while longer? he thought suddenly. It would be days before they died, and hope, even groundless hope, would make the waiting less dreadful. With weariness, he confessed to himself that he had not the heart to destroy her illusions.

"We won't talk about it," he said; then, because he saw that she expected it, he took her into his arms. And when they kissed, he realized that although he should be strong, he should give comfort, it was she who was comforting him.

*

Later, when a portion of Brek's tunic had been cut into bandages with a fragment of metal he'd found in the wreck and Talyra had bound his ribs securely, they decided to climb out of the canyon. "We've a much better chance of being seen from higher ground," Brek insisted; and Noren, knowing that only action could maintain Talyra's optimism, concurred without argument. If they were to go, they must do so at once, for they'd neither eaten nor drunk that day and their stamina would not last.

They were hardened to some degree, of course, by the weeks of camp life; the self-discipline of voluntary rationing had inured them to hunger and thirst. But by the same token, that discipline had taught them to recognize and meet their bodies' needs. Fasting to the point of malnutrition

202

was not permitted in camp, and dehydration was even more closely watched. One learned to know the warnings; to pay no heed would be harder than to ignore what might be dismissed as mere discomfort. Moreover, having no excess reserves, they would face starvation sooner than well-fed villagers would have—that is, if they did not succumb to thirst before finding a stream.

The question of drinking stream water was discussed before they set out; Talyra raised it herself by observing matter-of-factly that rescue would be of little benefit unless it came soon, and Noren seized the opportunity to introduce what was bound to be a difficult topic. "Talyra," he said bluntly, "do you remember how at my trial I admitted having drunk impure water?"

Nodding, she protested, "But it's a sin against the High Law to do that!"

"Yes. Still, there is no other water in the mountains, and the High Law does not demand that we die for lack of it."

"We'd be transformed into idiots—" She stopped, realizing that the villagers' tale that had come automatically to her lips must be untrue; though originally she'd told herself that others were right in thinking Noren's admission an idle boast, she knew him better now. In horror she whispered, "The other story . . . the one mentioned in the courtroom—"

"About a man who drinks impure water fathering idiot children?"

His face confirmed its truth; for the first time since the crash she was moved to tears. "That's the reason you can't marry," she faltered miserably, "and you—you couldn't bear to tell me. Oh, Noren—"

"It's not the reason. One can drink a limited amount, and I didn't exceed my limit; the Scholar Stefred has assured me of that." There had also been confirming medical tests. He had been warned, however, that he could drink very little more.

Taking him aside, Brek protested, "Are you really going to run the risk, Noren?"

"What risk? There won't be any child, that's certain."

Reddening, Brek glanced at Talyra and muttered, "I thought—well, anyway, someday—"

"There won't be any 'someday,' not for any of us."

"Oh. But what if something unforeseen happens; what if we get out?"

"You, too, Brek?" Noren snapped. "I'm keeping up the pretense for her sake, not yours. You're scientist enough to be realistic."

"I suppose so."

There'd be no idiot child anyway, Noren thought; the doctors would see to that if further medical tests showed any chromosome damage, for in such cases the High Law permitted sterilization. He would, of course, break off the betrothal at once if he alone was affected, since Talyra would feel disgraced if she bore no babies, and she should marry someone who could give them to her. But what point was there in considering that? Reason told him that under no circumstances could either of them stay alive.

Before leaving the wreckage they combed it thoroughly for materials that might somehow be of use. Though none were found, not even anything shiny enough to reflect sunlight upward as a signal, both Talyra and Brek were adamant about taking along all the metal they possibly could. "It would be sacrilege to leave it!" exclaimed Talyra when Noren objected to the idea of loading themselves down unnecessarily. In this Brek supported her, despite the fact that whatever he carried would add to his pain. Metal was sacred, and to sacrifice any was unthinkable; Noren could produce no argument other than the one he had decided not to use. It would make no difference in the end whether that irreplaceable metal was lost at the site of the crash or elsewhere, but to say so would be defeatism in Talyra's eyes, and moreover, she seemed to look upon it as a sort of talisman. Once, as a village girl, she had possessed a silver wristband—a holy thing passed down to her by an aunt to whom she had been kind. She had sold it for money to aid in his escape and had never expected to touch a metal object again; although as a Technician she'd often done so, she still treated such objects with reverence. Perhaps, Noren thought ruefully, she felt that the spirit of the Mother Star was more likely to protect people who were guarding metal than those who were not.

By the time they were ready, with all detachable wire and other metal parts tied in makeshift packs devised from the material of the seat cusions, it was almost noon and the heat was increasing rapidly. Their thirst was already intense, and as Noren looked up at the whitish cliff to the east that seemed to offer their only chance of ascent, he decided that perhaps the effort, arduous though it would be, would prove wise in that it would hasten the inevitable finish. They would be more likely to find water if they circled the canyon, searching for passages between the cliffs, but they could not be seen from the air there; even Talyra realized that such a course would serve merely to prolong their suffering. He was glad that a more rapid end was in view.

The cliff's surface was rough and steep, and it was hard to find footholds. Their shoes were not designed for traversing country like this, although they were the kind worn by villagers, made from the thicker parts of work-beast hides and bound together with heavy thongs. Again and again Talyra almost slipped and fell, and Noren too had trouble keeping his balance, so that the hand he held out to her was not always firm.

They spoke little, for their dry mouths burned with a fire greater than the scorching sun that struck their shoulders. Brek, forced by the exertion to breathe deeply, swayed and clutched his ribs, his face contorted with agony. It would not be possible to reach the top, Noren felt, not if there were many places where progress required one to cling to protruding rocks; their strength would give out. He found himself moving not by will, but automatically, simply because to stop would demand a decision he lacked the energy to make.

At last, after five or six hours, they stumbled up the final stretch of sun-baked slope onto a wide plateau, blocked on one side by still higher cliffs but otherwise surrounded by a gaping abyss. Talyra, daunted by its barrenness despite her courage, began to tremble, both with physical fatigue and with the fear she had earlier suppressed. "I—I don't know what I expected to see," she murmured.

There was nothing to be seen: nothing but more rocks, more dead ground, and stretching everywhere into the visible distance, more jagged mountains. The pleateau was infinitesimal compared to all that wasteland. If a low-flying aircar were to pass directly over it, they might be spotted, but aircars did not fly low over such terrain, not if their pilots' minds were on the job. Already the City had lost one; to risk another would be to risk the sustenance of villagers yet unborn. No car would come without an unmistakable signal, a signal that could not be sent.

Noren dropped his pack and sprawled on the stony ground, heedless of the heat that scorched his skin, not noticing that his feet were raw and blistered and that what remained of his left shoe was stained with blood. After a moment or two the others did likewise. For a long time they lay there, and though in the back of his mind he knew that if he did not rouse himself soon, he might never do so, it did not seem to matter.

The air was very still. It was thinner at this altitude than in the settled lands; that was why the sky was so blue, he thought idly. Blue . . . and still farther up, it was black. At

206

night it would be black here. He feared the blackness still, and the bright stars, and the other darkness that was death: he feared them because they were past all understanding. Yet he could no longer hope to understand. He was too weary even to try. *No,* something inside him kept protesting, *no, that's a betrayal of truth . . . truth's the one thing I'll never abandon. . . .* And suddenly it did matter. He was going to die; he could not expect to understand it beforehand—but whatever it was, was *true.* It was wrong to fear the truth, whether one understood it or not. And it was wrong not to care whether one lived. . . .

"Noren!" Talyra was shaking him urgently. "Noren, listen! Don't you hear something?"

He sat up, dazed, analyzing the stillness; and then, as from a long distance, he heard his own voice ask, "Water?"

"Yes! Yes, I'm sure it is—somewhere behind us. . . ."

She clutched his hand and he went with her, not stopping to reason, not questioning the instinctive impulses of his body. Brek followed. Instinct led them to the tall cliff behind, where from a small cleft a thin, swift stream cascaded; instinct made them thrust their faces into the cool foam and gulp enough to damp the fire that was consuming them. But something more than instinct made Talyra stop.

"You said there's a limit," she declared, backing away. "We can't drink more than we need; it's sinful—and besides, we don't know how many days we'll be here."

Noren, his thirst far from quenched, drew back also, revived by the moisture and by its extraordinary coldness. He saw no real value in stopping, but he could hardly indulge himself while she remained thirsty, and Talyra still had her irrepressible hope.

"The spirit of the Mother Star is with us," she reflected, tilting her head to gaze up into the deep sky that for her held no terrors. "We have been led to this place; shall we not receive further blessings? It would be a sin to drink impure water without believing that we're doing it to preserve our lives."

He watched her, the love he'd restrained so long suddenly overwhelming him. Deluded, foolish, unreasonable . . . she might be all those things; but she was untouched by the grim fate awaiting her. The life in her was strong, and he was stirred by it in a way he had not been during the past weeks when so many problems and questions had weighed him down. Those worries were far away now, the burden of them dissolved. Life was what mattered . . . life, and truth, which were one and the same . . . and they need not be understood to remain valid. Could love be understood, and was not love a form of truth? He had loved Talyra through all the time when he'd considered truth the only thing of importance to him; yet he'd been blind.

We are soon to die, he thought, *but now we are alive. As long as we're alive, life will go on.* "Darling," he began, holding out his arms to her. "Talyra, darling—"

They embraced, and he kissed her with more ardor than he'd previously dared to release; but the sun, hovering over the western crags, was glaring down, and though Brek had walked away, the plateau was bare of outcroppings or shrubs. It did not seem decent. Noren and Talyra followed the rivulet that trickled along the base of the cliff from the place where the cascade splashed, seeking shelter.

There was an archway, an opening in the rock wider than the stream, leading through into a shallow canyon. They stooped under, well shaded from sunlight although the sky was bright beyond. Noren's arms tightened around Talyra—and to his dismay the joy in her face gave way to stark terror.

She was looking through the arch, where, some distance down the slope, the stream joined a larger one bordered by clumps of reeds. "Noren," she gasped, "there are *people* there!"

208

He glanced over his shoulder, disbelieving; then cold terror struck him also. What he saw was no less horrifying because he had greater knowledge of it than she. It was in fact a good deal worse than anyone but a Scholar could realize. "No, darling," he whispered, motioning her to be still. "Those aren't people. Those are savages."

*

Eight or nine of the creatures squatted by the stream, though they did not appear to have ever washed themselves in it. They were, of course, completely naked. That in itself did not seem shocking, for although they had human form, their brains were not human; Noren knew that they were incapable of speech, much less rational thought. Their ancestry was of the Six Worlds, but they were as drastically changed as the work-beasts, and they were not much brighter.

Talyra knew their origin, for the basic facts were taught in every village school: how at the time of the Founding a few people had defied the High Law, drunk too much impure water, and then fled in fear to the mountains, thereby losing all trace of their heritage. They (in reality their offspring) had become idiots that lived like beasts. These and other gruesome details, such as a story about savages eating slithery things that swam in streams, were commonly used to frighten disobedient children, as was quite necessary if a repetition of the incident was to be avoided. "Were it not for man's adherence to the High Law we would be as they are, Talyra," Noren murmured.

"Yes," she agreed soberly. "But once you wouldn't have thought so, though—" She stopped, remembering that it was not proper to speak of his past heresies; and Noren flushed with the recollection of the night he'd tried to convince her that their own remote ancestors had been like the savages. He'd had it backwards. On the mother world human beings had indeed evolved from savagery, but these were not "savages" of that sort. These were mutants, the product of damaged genes rather than evolution, and had no future potential. In them no vestige of human spirit remained.

He cringed as the largest mutant, a male, stood half-erect, revealing the filthiness of its body and the absense of mind behind its vacant stare. If the Founders had not controlled the City—if the Scholars did not continue to do so—all mankind would be like that . . . and it would be "mankind" no longer. It was as justifiable to prevent such degradation as for a starship captain to take full command of his ship to safeguard its passengers' lives. Yet if there could be no prevention? If control of people's inheritance was useless because in spite of it, their descendants would inevitably become mutants like these that crouched and gibbered beside the stream? Such futility should not be hidden, for it made guardianship of the City indefensible.

Talyra pressed close to him; the big male and two smaller ones had snatched up something and moved toward them, upstream. Noren's stomach lurched; they were now close enough for him to see what they carried. "Talyra," he said firmly, "go back to the plateau—"

"Without *you?*"

"Go back and tell Brek to come here; he won't hunt for us, and I don't dare shout. Tell him to come, but don't come with him."

"I won't leave you, Noren!"

"You must," he insisted. If he retreated from the archway, the mutants might follow, whether or not he and Talyra had been seen; only from that vantage point could he hope to defend the plateau. But he could not do it alone, and Brek, unaware, would not approach until morning.

Talyra sensed his desperation, knowing nothing of its cause, and slipped away. Noren gripped the largest rock he could find and held it in readiness, knowing the gesture a feeble one. If the mutants came before Brek did, he had no chance. Still, there were only the three males—the fe-

210

males probably were not dangerous—and at the moment all were well occupied. It would be twilight soon; perhaps they'd sleep. . . .

He could not take his eyes from the loathsome scene before him. *Not this,* he pleaded inwardly. Death he could face, but not this death, certainly not for Talyra. A lingering one, however painful, would be better; it might even be better if they jumped from the cliff.

At a sound behind him, he froze, but it was Brek. Talyra had returned too, as Noren had known she would. "What are they doing?" she asked in a low voice.

There was no point in evading a fact that was clearly evident. "Eating," Noren replied tersely.

Talyra peered ahead into the dusk. "Noren," she exclaimed, "they're eating *flesh!* It's not fowl's flesh; the bones are too big—it must be a work-beast's—"

He had wondered, briefly, that she could be so composed; now he realized that she hadn't noticed the shape of the bones, nor was she aware that there were no work-beasts in the mountains. She had no way of guessing what all Scholars knew about the ghastlier habits of these creatures. "They are animals," he reminded her, "without intelligence or speech. The High Law does not apply to them."

"Impure flesh will make them sick, though."

"No sicker than they already are," said Brek grimly. He was pale, on the verge of getting sick himself.

One of the smaller mutants looked up from the meager portion of raw meat it held and its eyes focused abruptly, not with hostility, but in the manner of a carnivore sighting prey. Giving a loud grunt, it lurched forward.

"It's seen us!" Talyra whispered. "It's coming toward us; it—it looks as if it might want to hurt us. Why, Noren?"

"I don't know," Noren lied, struggling to remain steady.

In strength, he and Brek were no match for the attackers; they wouldn't have been even if Brek had not been crippled

211

by his broken rib. Besides lacking comparable weight, they were weakened by thirst and exhaustion, and the mature male—which was now advancing behind the younger ones —was a huge brute with years of experience in making kills. The mere fact that it had lived past maturity proved that, since among its kind only the victors survived. The mutants had turned to cannibalism because they had no other source of meat, and the eating of meat was deeply ingrained in their biological inheritance; but grown males would have fought to the death in any case. They'd have fought for band dominance and, Noren recalled in dismay, for possession of females, as most animals had done on the Six Worlds; for Talyra, slaughter was not the chief peril. He and Brek had been told these things. They had not, however, been told how to defend themselves, since the possibility that they might have to had never occurred to anyone. Intelligence was their sole armor.

"We can't let them approach," Brek said quietly. "Once they grapple with us we're finished." He seized a rock, preparing to aim it at the oncoming "savage."

"Wait," Noren told him. "They'll not be frightened off, and if you miss his head you'll merely enrage them. We've got to know more about their ways." Though the mutants did not use tools, they might throw rocks themselves, and as to whether they could do it purposefully he was not sure. "Wait, Brek," he said again, "and be ready to aim when they're nearer; with your injury, you may not get many chances. I'm going to try something."

Behind him, Talyra stood shaking, recognizing the immediate danger if not its potential aftermath. "Keep back," Noren ordered, "but gather all the stones you can. Pile them at my feet." Picking up a small rock, he hurled it as far as he could, aiming not for the mutants but well beyond them.

All three of the creatures turned instantly; what they

lacked in wit was partially made up for by keen hearing and fast reactions. Quickly Noren grabbed more stones and threw out a barrage. The mutants remained facing the direction in which it landed, and shortly, they too began flinging one rock after another—but theirs were tossed aimlessly and fell wide of the mark, some even landing in the stream.

"It's a good diversion," Brek observed, "but you can't keep it up forever. If we don't kill them now, they'll simply attack again later."

"I know. This was just a test." Stopping, Noren outlined the only strategy that seemed feasible. "We draw their attention back to us. Then we stand fast and let them get close, very close. When we're sure we can't miss, we make them turn again, and while they're facing the other way we aim to hit."

"What's to say they'll keep on facing the other way?" protested Brek. "Two of us can't hit three of them simultaneously."

"No, but we can each disable a small one, then deal with that big one together."

"I can throw rocks too, at least I—I think I can," Talyra ventured, her voice quavering only a little.

Noren frowned. That would add to their chances of success, certainly. She could not throw with sufficient force and accuracy to kill, but she could toss the stones to make the attackers turn, thus allowing him to act faster. "All right," he agreed reluctantly, "but don't do it till I give the word—and aim a long way past them." He drew a deep breath and flung another stone, deliberately directing it to a point only a short distance away. Then he grasped a larger, heavier rock like the one Brek held, and with pounding heart, he waited.

The mutants, confused, advanced slowly. There was ample time to absorb an unforgettable picture of their slouching gait, the filth of their long matted hair, and worst of all, the mindlessness of their faces. This travesty of human life—this housing of animal mentality in men's bodies—was more hideous than anything Noren had ever encountered. He had seen men behave like brutes; some of the ones who'd abused him at his arrest and recantation had been of a low sort. Some would have killed without hesitation when sufficiently inflamed. But they had not revolted him as these mutants did, for despite their faults they'd been human beings still.

He and Brek stood in full view, calculating how long it would be before one lunged at them, knowing that to move too soon—or too late—would mean sure defeat. Finally, when their taut nerves could endure no more, Noren breathed, "Now, Talyra!" and as the mutants whirled toward the sound of a new hail of stones, he heaved his rock with all the force that was in him. It struck the foremost one's skull, felling the creature, but Brek's first throw only grazed its target. Though his second hit true, the largest savage turned and charged before he and Noren could act in unison; not till it was within instants of seizing Brek were they able to bring it down.

The two of them walked forward, shaking with released tension. The stench of the bodies was overpowering. Noren stared for a moment, realizing that the horror was not quite over, then returned to Talyra. They clung together, her body quivering with sobs. "Darling," he said gently, "go now. Go to the plateau and wait for me."

"No—"

"You mustn't watch the finish, Talyra."

Grasping his meaning, she obeyed. Noren and Brek, suppressing their sickness, went to the felled mutants, two of which were merely unconscious, and did what had to be done. Afterward they dragged the carcasses some distance downstream and dumped them beside the foul and bloody

214

half-consumed one, covering them with reeds. The females had fled. It was unlikely that there would be another band nearby, for the vegetation that was the mainstay of their diet was more plentiful at lower elevations; and in any case revenge was beyond their conception.

"I'll sleep here," Brek said as they returned to the archway, "and guard it, though I doubt that any more will come. There's no need for you to worry, Noren."

It was nearly dark by this time. Noren washed in the clear shallow water, letting none touch his lips, and went back through the arch onto the barren plateau. The dead stony landscape was softened by the glow of three crescent moons; it looked unearthly and yet less unreal than most things had been since the space flight. The inertia he'd fought against was gone.

Talyra was waiting near the cascade. At night, the emptiness of the plateau gave a sense of privacy, not desolation, and indeed it did not seem that any place could be desolate when she was there. He knelt on the still-warm pebbles, smoothing a hollow with his hands. "There should be moss, at least," he mumbled. "This is not fit for you, Talyra. I've never brought you anything but hardship—"

She flung herself down beside him, chiding softly, "Oh, Noren—as if I cared about *that!* We were almost killed, and now we're alive; haven't we cause for joy?"

We cannot stay alive, his mind told him, but the thought was remote; it was a time for feeling, not thinking. Curiously, the imminence of death freed him to feel. There was a point past which one could not reason, could not analyze, perhaps; maybe Talyra's refusal to despair was not so foolish after all. Her joy enveloped him; he knew fierce joy of his own, and surrendered to it as they joined in the ultimate affirmation of survival.

In the morning, when they woke to brilliant sunlight and bathed briefly in the perilous water of the cascade, Talyra

215

drank a very little; but Noren, being far closer to the safe limit than she, carefully rinsed his parched mouth and did not swallow.

*

The days that followed were the strangest Noren had ever known. Suspended between life and death, he felt a peculiar lightness, not only from fasting but because burdens were lifted that had been too heavy for him to handle. The whole universe no longer seemed his concern.

Most of the daylight hours they spent at the cliff's archway, for it provided the only nearby shade and their thirst was too great to permit much movement. At night Brek continued to sleep there while Noren and Talyra returned to the plateau. Their joy in each other overrode all fears, all discomforts; it seemed ample compensation for the painful things. Noren stopped worrying about what was past and what was to come, and lived one moment at a time. Though the moments brought suffering, they brought elation, too; he was free for elation, since there were no grave decisions left to be made.

They felt no hunger after the first; although they were weak from it, their stomachs did not torment them. The plants the mutants ate were nò temptation. To taste that vegetation was out of the question, for while they might escape poisoning and eventually adapt, as the mutants' ancestors had done, the chance of rescue was too small to warrant such a course. None of them even considered living on indefinitely in the mountains. There was an unspoken agreement between them that death would be preferable: not only because of the subhuman offspring that might come with the years, but because if Noren and Brek should be poisoned or killed, Talyra might be left at the mercy of the bestial creatures that would sooner or later reappear. At her insistence Noren had explained their ways, and she was aware that for a woman there was more to be feared

216

than cannibalism.

So hunger was accepted, then ignored. It was thirst that brought anguish, all the more so because they were within sight and sound of the tantalizing stream. With calm realism, they estimated the maximum length of time it would be possible to survive without food and calculated the amount of water that could be safely consumed each day if one's entire limit were spread over that time; Brek and Talyra had to endure nothing worse than a continuous craving that they were obliged to deny. Noren's quota was considerably less, and he suffered intensely, drinking only as much as was essential to prevent high fever. Although moistening his skin provided some relief, it could not be done too often. During the worst hours, the long hot afternoons when he waited with burning forehead and throat afire for the shadow of the crag beyond the arch to tell him that it was time to permit himself a few more drops, he wondered why he had changed his mind about the pointlessness of restraint. To his amazement, he could find no answer. He knew only that something inside him would not let him go to Talyra if the limit were to be passed. The fact that their present situation made this irrational did not seem to alter it.

Brek's injury was increasingly painful; the attack on the mutants had been a strain. Talyra redid the bandages and also bandaged their raw, blistered feet, using the carefully saved metal scrap to cut strips from her own tunic and Noren's. All the metal they'd salvaged was piled neatly near the cliff where, Noren felt privately, it would remain until the light of the Mother Star touched it—by which time, one way or another, its loss would have ceased to count.

He no longer dwelt on such speculations; but while he was turning away from abstract thought, Brek was thinking more deeply than in the past. "Noren," he said the fifth evening, when Talyra had gone on ahead, "we—we were wrong . . . what we planned, I mean. This may sound crazy

217

to you, but if it weren't for Talyra and for the aircar being destroyed . . . I'd almost be glad we crashed. We were going to die anyway, and it's better like this. We aren't harming people by it."

"The truth wouldn't have harmed people," Noren protested indignantly. "Truth *doesn't*."

"No, not if it doesn't destroy their faith in a greater truth. I agree it's no kindness to deceive people about important things, not even to spare them unhappiness. That's why I let you persuade me. Only now—well, now I'm not sure that what we were going to say is true."

"You're afraid to acknowledge it?" Feverish and irritable from the searing thirst that made speech an effort, Noren replied with rancor. "You know as well as I do that there's no more chance of the human race surviving on this planet than there is of our staying alive here in the mountains."

"We've managed to hold on so far."

"What's that got to do with it? We've had certain resources, resources that won't last indefinitely. That's *fact*, Brek! When they're gone, we'll die. I'm afraid, too, but not so afraid I can't face up to it."

Brek looked at him strangely. "Is that what you set out to prove, Noren?"

With a rage he did not wholly understand, Noren turned his back and started toward the plateau; but Brek was not ready to drop the issue. "I should have seen it sooner," he declared. "I'm sorry for you, Noren, if what you said that last night in camp is what you believe! But I don't really think it is."

"I do believe it," Noren said doggedly. "I've learned too much to believe anything else. There won't be a magical, miraculous breakthrough 'in the last generation of our endurance,' as ritual has it, any more than there'll be a magic rescue for us now. What do you expect, some unpredictable solution that we're led to by the spirit of the Mother Star,

218

the way Talyra does?"

Brek leaned back against the cliff wall, looking up at the section of fading sky framed by the arch. Then, slowly, he asserted, "It's not impossible."

"You're no more honest with yourself than the rest," accused Noren bitterly. "When the going gets rough, the ideas you grew up with come back. You could study all that the Six Worlds knew and still believe that there's some mysterious force in the universe that provides for people's welfare."

"Yes."

Appalled, Noren perceived that Brek meant what he was saying. Against all logic, he had returned to the teachings of the religion in which he'd been reared—not only those the Scholars had planned to substantiate, but the ones that had never had any scientific basis at all. "You wouldn't have gone through with it, would you?" he demanded. "At the last minute you'd have backed out and left me to reveal the facts alone."

"I wouldn't have abandoned you to the mob, Noren."

"Would you have left me in the City? Turned me over to Stefred maybe, to keep me from betraying the sacred trust?" He laughed grimly at the irony of it: Brek, who had once risked himself to save him from the Chief Inquisitor. . . .

"I—I don't quite know," Brek confessed. "I think I'd have gone to the village with you and argued against what you said."

"That would have been dangerous," Noren retorted, "for someone who's decided he wants to live at the price of deception. People wouldn't have stopped to notice which of us they were stoning."

Brek's rigid control gave way, and he too lashed out in anger. "Are you admitting you wanted to die?"

"*Wanted* to? You don't understand much—"

"I understand more than you think. *You* talk to *me* about

219

self-delusion? You've hated yourself ever since that space flight because you've been afraid you were a coward, so afraid that a time came when you had to disprove it—at any cost. Even suicide! What we set out to do was suicidal; I knew that. I was willing to die. But not for as many reasons as you were. You were trying to show yourself and everybody else how heroic you could be."

Noren stumbled forward, fury amplifying his depleted strength, and seized Brek's shoulders; but Brek was past the point of restraint. "What's more, it wasn't a very big sacrifice, was it?" he went on, his voice harsh and unpitying. "Your life wasn't worth much to you or to anyone, the way you were sulking—"

Outraged, unable to control the conflicting feelings the suggestion aroused, Noren swung on Brek and struck his face. Both of them were in bad shape; both fell, Brek letting out an involuntary cry as his injured rib hit stony ground.

In dismay, Noren bent over him, overwhelmed by remorse. *Brek,* he thought, *oh, Brek, I don't blame you for despising me; everything I do ends in disaster. . . .* Aloud he said, "I'm sorry. You look at things differently, but you're entitled to, I guess. Maybe you're even right. I don't know myself any more; I don't understand half of what I think. Yet I can see facts. I can still reason, and reason says there's no hope for us on this planet—"

"Go tell *her* that," Brek said, glancing toward the plateau where Talyra waited. "Tell her that whether she lives to bear your child or not makes no difference."

Noren bowed his head. "I can't, Brek. I can't, and I don't know why; I still believe that truth's the most important thing there is—I'll never deny that—so if I love her, don't I owe her honesty? She doesn't want to be shielded. She's stronger than I used to think."

Brek did not reply. After a while Noren pulled himself to his feet and left the archway. But he saw no beauty in

220

the plateau that night, and though Talyra slept in his arms, he felt no peace.

The next day his fever was worse, yet he drank barely enough to keep it below the danger level. Talyra helped him to the shade and sat silently beside him; none of them wasted energy on talking. The world was unreal again to Noren, this time as the result of near-delirium; he felt the heat, and the air seemed full of bursting suns.

"The spirit of this Star shall abide with us, and with our children, and our children's children. . . ." Neither Talyra nor Brek whispered it aloud, but he knew that both believed it, and were the stronger for their belief; he knew that if they had not believed, all three of them would now lie dead in the canyon where they had crashed. *He* had not insisted that they make the effort to move on. He had not found the water that had staved off death this long. Yet he did not want to die any more; he wanted, desperately, to live! He wanted mankind to live. Though it was hopeless, he wanted to work with all his strength toward the future so many believed in. He wanted his child—the child that might already be conceived—to continue after him, whether as villager or as Scholar. Why had he begun to feel this way only when it was too late?

If he had believed as Talyra and Brek did, there would have been no crash. But what good did it do to realize that? Wanting to believe was not the same as believing; he could no more force faith on himself than those who'd condemned his heresy could have forced it upon him. He was what he was, and he could not discount the facts he knew.

"Noren," Talyra said softly, "are you awake?"

He nodded, for his mouth was too dry for him to force out words. "I see something up there," Talyra continued, pointing to a portion of cliff wall that was visible beyond the arch. "I was looking, thinking how bare it is, and then the sun struck something shiny. I—I think it's *metal*."

221

"Metal . . . there? But that's not possible," Brek declared, getting painfully to his feet. "No other aircar has ever come down in the mountains." He walked through the arch and shaded his eyes, staring upward.

"Are you sure?" asked Talyra. "Maybe the Scholars once landed here."

Brek frowned; he knew, as did Noren, that the Scholars had not. If the small object glinting in the midday sun was indeed metal, it could only be that one of the people from whom the mutants were descended had penetrated farther into the wilderness than had been supposed; first-generation villagers had possessed whatever articles they'd had with them when they were locked out of the City.

"A Scholar would not have left any metal behind," said Brek, answering Talyra's suggestion without touching on unrevealed secrets.

"That's true," she agreed. "And we must not leave it unprotected, either! However it got there, it is sacred and should be guarded."

How futile, Noren thought miserably. The piece of metal didn't look big enough to make a real difference in the resources of mankind; still every scrap was precious, and if they had been going to get back he'd have been the first to say that it should be recovered. But they weren't. What benefit could there be in retrieving it to eventually corrode in company with the salvage from the aircar?

Corrode . . . that was odd; if it had lain in a niche in the cliff wall since shortly after the Founding, it should have corroded long ago. Even equipment that did not have to be stored in air-conditioned buildings required occasional protective treatment, for the planet's atmosphere was hard on the alloys that had met the Six Worlds' needs. To be sure, some metals did not corrode at all, but they were rarer than those that did, and far less likely to have been among the personal belongings of the mutants' ancestors. This object

222

shone like silver, yet had too much bulk for any sort of jewelry. His curiosity aroused, he pulled himself up from the half-reclining position in which he'd been resting, but he was too weak to rise and join Brek.

The question of retrieval was academic, he realized. None of them would be able to climb that cliff; it would be dangerous to try it without ropes even if they had their normal strength. As it was, besides being debilitated by hunger and thirst, Talyra had neither the skill nor a long enough reach, Brek was incapacitated by the broken rib, and he himself was giddy with fever. "We can't do anything," he asserted through cracked lips.

"Darling, we must!" insisted Talyra. "It's a sin to let a holy thing like that be lost in the wilderness."

"We're lost ourselves."

"No!" she burst out. "I won't let you give up, Noren! If we die expecting to live, we'll be none the worse for it; but if we stop living because we expect to die, we'll have thrown away our own lives."

Noren looked at her, seeing a confidence that her growing recognition of their doom could not shake, and he knew that for the sake of their love he must make her believe he shared that confidence. Through some flamboyant, mad gesture he must offer proof that he did; for otherwise, in her view, he would be throwing away not only his life and hers, but very possibly that of an unborn child.

A child who belonged to the future . . . the future that wasn't going to come. . . . He was no longer thinking coherently. Somehow, what he was about to do seemed no less a defiance of wrong than the gesture he'd planned to make in the village.

*

Crawling to the stream, Noren thrust his face into it and drank deeply, then splashed water over the rest of his body. He lay there, letting the moisture cool him, realizing that

223

this gave him but two more days' leeway and that after that, during the remaining time before they starved, he would stop rationing himself and sleep alone. At length, when he was somewhat restored, he got shakily to his feet and approached the cliff.

Brek accompanied him. "I wish I could help," he said quietly.

"You don't consider this—suicidal?"

"Not in quite the same way."

It was not the same. Surveying the rock wall above him, Noren did not doubt that he would succeed in scaling it, and somehow he did not expect to fall to his death. Strength surged through him, as if he had tapped a resource to which he'd previously had no access, and with cautious movements he began to climb.

There were handholds and footholds, but they were widely spaced and hard to judge. He could not judge them accurately, Noren knew; he must simply make the best estimates he could and then gamble. Surprisingly, he was unafraid, despite the handicaps of faintness and pain from his bandaged feet. He saw everything very clearly: the shades of rock color; the shapes of the crevices; and, over his head, the gleaming piece of metal. It beckoned him, and the closer he got the more peculiar its appearance seemed. It was round! He had never seen a spherical metal object of that size—about as large as his fist—and he could not imagine why it had been placed in such a niche.

Balancing precariously with one foot well supported and the other braced by a mere toehold, Noren clung to an orange-yellow crag and stretched his free arm to grasp the strange ball. "Push it out," called Brek. "There's no need to *carry* it down." Noren ignored the advice; for some reason he felt that he should not risk smashing the thing. It was more than scrap metal, though what its function had been might remain obscure. He inserted it carefully into the open neck of his tunic.

224

Climbing down was harder than climbing up, since the footholds below could not be seen. Gingerly Noren probed for them, assisted by Brek's guidance from the ground. Fatigue made his muscles tremble. He was sustained only by the touch of the smooth metal sphere against his chest; near the bottom, when at last he slipped, he instinctively clasped his hands over it as he fell.

Talyra rushed to him, Brek at her side. Noren's burst of unnatural energy had faded; he was bruised, one foot was twisted, and even with help he could not stand. He wanted to lie where he'd fallen and never move again. Yet the sphere's fascination was too great for that. Sitting up, he drew it out and examined it thoughtfully. It wasn't uniformly smooth; there were oddly arranged indentations, some of which were almost translucent.

"That isn't just metal," Talyra observed. "It's a Machine."

"Yes, I'm sure it is," Noren agreed. He pressed his finger into the deepest indentation, feeling its texture. Abruptly, to his amazement, one of the translucent ones gave forth a greenish glow.

For a long time he stared, while Brek and Talyra looked on with the respectful awe any unknown machine merited. Then he tried pressing other hollows, obtaining other variations of light, memorizing the scheme whereby the number of glowing points could be increased or decreased. Finally, with the sphere wholly dark again, he raised his eyes. He could not comprehend the thing; he could not be sure that he wasn't taking a terrible risk; yet to reject any potential opportunity. . . .

"Talyra," he asked slowly, "does this machine frighten you?"

"No, Noren."

"It should be put with the other metal on the plateau, but I can't walk, and Brek shouldn't. Will you take it?"

"Of course; I'm not hurt. Do you mean right now?"

"Yes." He placed the sphere into her hands, adding,

225

"Just before you leave it, Talyra, press *here* and *here* and *here*—so that all the lights will glow."

Brek started to speak, but Noren shook his head. "All right, Noren," Talyra said, puzzled, but trusting him and perceiving that he did not want to be questioned. She walked swiftly through the archway and disappeared.

"I suppose you had to send her away," Brek said, "so that we could talk about it. But I'd have liked to look at it more. What was it? I've never heard of any equipment like that."

"I don't think anyone has," Noren declared, "here, or on the Six Worlds either. It's not the product of our technology, Brek. I—I think it must have been left by the Visitors."

"An alien artifact?" demanded Brek incredulously. "How do you know?"

"Well, I can't be positive, but it just doesn't follow the principles of Six Worlds' engineering. And those holes were made for fingers . . . but not ours; they aren't placed right."

"Noren," Brek objected, "if that's the case, why did you want it taken up to the plateau where we can't study it? And why, for the Star's sake, did you tell her to turn it on? We've no idea what it'll do."

"I think it may give out some kind of radiation."

"That could be dangerous."

"It could also be detectable—from a distance."

"From the City," Brek breathed excitedly.

"There's a chance. Don't say anything to her; it may not reach that far, and even if it does it may be lethal as far as we're concerned. It could even explode, though I don't think it will while she's activating it, since it didn't when I was experimenting." Noren lay back, gazing at the wild and inhospitable peaks of the Tomorrow Mountains. "We have nothing to lose," he murmured. "If we don't try this, we're dead, so isn't *any* attempt—even one we're not sure of —better than none at all?"

226

VIII

THE AIRCAR CAME JUST BEFORE SUNSET, DROPPING OUT OF
the eastern sky to hover above the plateau. Brek heard it
first, and in that instant Noren—who had not really dared
to hope—knew from his face that the gamble had paid off.

Raising his head from Talyra's lap, he cried, "Run, darling! Wave, make them see you!" She'd heard it too and
scrambled to her feet, racing back through the arch toward
the faint but unmistakable humming sound. She did not
connect the aircar's arrival with the mysterious metal
sphere, yet she showed little surprise; she had felt all along
that in the end the spirit of the Mother Star would bring
help.

Noren was unable to walk; the two Scholars from the
rescue car had to carry him to the flat place where they'd
landed. Brek, with assistance, got there on his own. He explained about the sphere while Talyra stayed beside Noren.
It was indeed alien, the Scholars agreed. They had not
known what to expect, for the radiation was powerful and

227

unlike any the computer complex had monitored before, although it was not of a hazardous sort. No one had seen how it could be coming from the lost aircar, yet because its source was in the region where the crash was presumed to have occurred, a team had been sent at once. Now, with reluctance, it was decided that the sphere must be left where it was until more could be learned about it; to take it into the City would be an unjustified risk. It could be found again, and indeed would serve to mark the pile of metal that the rescue car, which was already overloaded with passengers, could not carry. After that it would be studied at the outpost.

Hearing that, Noren was stricken with disappointment. For a few minutes he had held with wonder a thing from another solar system . . . a thing made by a human race unlike his own. He wanted to see it once more, to share in the unraveling of its mysteries. But he could not expect that he'd be allowed to leave the City again. His confinement this time would be final and complete; he had forfeited the trust of those who were guarding the secrets.

It was nearly dark when they reached the City. Looking down from the air as they approached its cluster of lights, he remembered the first time he'd seen it so, driving a trader's sledge up the final hill and halting at the crest to gaze with unbearable longing at the stronghold of all hidden truth. How naive he'd been. Even while he lived in the City he had not thought it a prison; he'd assumed that everything he sought was there. . . .

Talyra squeezed his hand and smiled. Wan, emaciated, clothed in the tattered remnants of a tunic cut away for bandages, she was nonetheless radiant. To Talyra it had all worked out as it was meant to work. And perhaps, Noren thought sadly, she had again glimpsed the truth more clearly than he had; she'd seen through some window that to him would be forever obscure. They would surely have died if he had not carried through the masquerade for her sake. Still, he could not do that indefinitely. He'd once feared that he might accept priesthood rather than give her up, but when it came to the point of choice, he knew he would never be as great a hypocrite as that. Those who became High Priests were not hypocrites either, yet much as he might wish to believe as they did, he could not alter what he felt.

So, having had her love, he must once again sacrifice it. Since their marriage could never be authorized, he must free her from the betrothal. It would be best if there proved to be no child, for she would be hurt less that way; still he could not regret their brief hours of happiness. Little more lay in store for him, for though he knew that insofar as he was permitted, he would devote his remaining years to the work that had come to seem worthwhile despite its hopelessness, he was aware that neither love nor work would be enough to satisfy him. He would always be searching for something that was not to be found.

He turned to Brek, who did not meet his glance. Like himself, Brek had refused the hypnotic sleep offered by the rescue team; they had assuaged their thirst and hunger and had submitted to preliminary treatment of their injuries, but they had not wished to evade what awaited them on entrance to the City. Or rather, they hadn't been willing to admit that they wished it. They were answerable both for the loss of an irreplaceable aircar and for their unfulfilled intent to betray secrets; neither could be easily dismissed. Perhaps they would be considered relapsed heretics and denied all contact with non-Scholars, Noren realized. Perhaps he would not even see Talyra after he had confessed. To his shame, he was thankful that her presence made immediate confession impossible.

The lights loomed brighter, then vanished as the aircar dropped into the open top of the entrance dome and settled gently. A crowd of faces appeared at the door: solicitous

229

faces, faces that showed not reproof, but relief and welcome. One, Noren saw, was Stefred's, and he looked away, lacking words, while he was carried down from the landing platform and through the maze of corridors leading to the Inner City's courtyard. People didn't yet know the whole story. Curious though they must be, they did not press for details; but they stayed with him until he was laid on a couch in a small private cubicle of the infirmary.

"You must have rest," the doctor said. "If you will not consent to hypnotic sedation, I'll have to use drugs—"

The pride that had kept Noren adamant made him yield. Drugs were scarce; it was not fitting for any to be consumed by a Scholar. He accepted the hypnosis, slipping resignedly, almost gratefully, into oblivion.

When he awoke, he found himself physically recovered, though still quite weak, and realized that days had passed while his body was nourished intravenously. As remembrance hit him, he was overwhelmed by remorse and despair. He no longer knew what was true and what was not; but he was certain that, not knowing, he could have done nothing but harm by destroying the villagers' belief in the Prophecy. To be sure, deceiving people was wrong and they should be given the chance to claim their entire birthright if their descendants were already doomed . . . but what if mankind was not doomed? If a chance of a scientific breakthrough did exist—a chance as remote and unlikely as his discovery of the alien sphere—his proclamation could have ruined it.

Reason, mathematics, told him that there was no such chance. He still could not feel any hope. But as Talyra had said, if one stopped living because one expected to die, one threw away one's own life. Had he thrown away the significance of his? he wondered. Could he, untrusted, share fully in the research? He knew that he would not be punished for what he had done. Even if he was isolated as a precautionary measure, Stefred and the others would be all too compassionate. Something else Talyra had once said echoed in his mind: *The Scholars don't punish, that's not their way; you simply have to live with the consequences of what you are.*

The doctor entered and examined Noren briefly, pronouncing him fit to have visitors. "Stefred has asked to see you," he said. "Will you receive him, Noren?"

"It's not my place to refuse."

The man regarded him, disturbed. "You are a Scholar," he said, "and Stefred's equal; he would not presume to command except in matters concerning his official duties. Like your other friends, he merely wants to know whether he is welcome."

"I—I'd rather not see anyone," Noren asserted. It was true; he could not bear the thought of talking, not even to Talyra, and least of all to Stefred, whose trust he had betrayed. Besides, he reminded himself, Stefred had deceived him. He'd promised him access to knowledge that would help. . . .

But later, when he was released from the infirmary, it was to Stefred's office that he went; for he owed Brek that, at least. He knew Brek would not denounce him, and would not be able to speak freely until he, Noren, had denounced himself.

*

Mustering all his poise, he stood erect before Stefred's desk and declared forthrightly what his intentions had been at the time of the crash. Stefred remained impassive, but Noren knew him too well not to recognize that mask; he wondered whether the Chief Inquisitor was concealing contempt, pity, or a mixture of both. Very likely he would never be allowed to find out.

"Brek admitted something similar," Stefred told him, "though he implied that he hadn't discussed his plan with you."

Noren, who had also tried to imply that the plan had

231

been a private one, dropped the formality of guarding his words. "Brek isn't to blame," he said. "It was all my idea, and though he listened to me at first, he regretted it later. He would never have gone through with a public revelation. He—he doesn't deserve to be barred from going back to the outpost, much less to be confined to the Hall of Scholars."

"Do you?"

Wretchedly Noren murmured, "I'm unworthy of trust."

"It's unlike you to feel that way."

"I haven't felt like myself for a long time, Stefred."

"Since the space flight?"

"I guess that's obvious. But there's more to it than you can imagine, and I—well, I'd better give you all the details."

Stefred nodded. "There are ways I could make it easier," he said. "Hypnosis, for instance, or a shot of the drug I used during your initial inquisition."

Noren looked up, tempted. That would certainly be less painful. "Whether I give you such aid is up to you," Stefred added quietly.

"I—I've got to tell it straight, then."

"Do you understand why?"

"Because it's not just what I did or how I felt; I have to make sense of it. Consciously."

"Yes. But it will take more than confession to accomplish that, Noren."

"I have to try."

Pushing buttons on his desk to ensure that they'd be uninterrupted, Stefred said soberly, "We'll try together. I'm more closely involved than you realize; still, I can't offer any simple solution."

"I don't expect you to." Sitting down in the chair near the window where so often in the past he had faced difficult things, Noren started at the beginning, at the moment of searing terror that had paralyzed him in space. He went on to describe it all: all the fears, the doubts, the unan-

232

swerable questions that had led to his final disillusionment; all the rage that had followed; all the decisions he had reached. Stefred spared him nothing; whenever Noren faltered, he was led on with astute, searching inquiries that left no room for equivocation. At first it was agonizing, but as the discussion proceeded, he found himself rising to the challenge and even welcoming it. He was heartened by Stefred's very ruthlessness. To his surprise, though he was confessing to weakness, to cowardice, to failure, the Chief Inquisitor showed him no mercy; rather, he acted as if these self-accusations were untrue.

By the time he had explained the strange reversal of feelings he'd experienced in the mountains, Noren had regained much of his normal composure. How was it possible? he wondered as he spoke. How could he be talking naturally, confidently, as if life could indeed make sense, when he'd seen what a senseless place the universe was? "You can't know what I really felt," he concluded ruefully. "I've told all I can put into words, but—"

"But there were things for which no words exist. I do know about them, Noren." Stefred met his eyes unflinchingly. "I knew beforehand; that was the information I withheld. The responsibility is as much mine as it is yours."

Incredulously Noren burst out, "You knew what would happen to me in space?"

"I feared it. Noren, on the Six Worlds no competent psychiatrist would have let you become an astronaut; you are too introspective, too imaginative, too prone to think deeply instead of concentrating on the task at hand. But most people who become heretics are like that. The risk applied to nearly all the eligible Scholars." He sighed, continuing, "Brek and one or two of the others were less vulnerable; I assigned pairs accordingly. And I did what I could to prepare you: I gave you so much else to worry about that I hoped you'd be distracted—by your love for Talyra, by the physical danger, and finally, in case that wasn't enough, by anger at my admission that I was not telling you everything. I dared not warn you of your real peril because that would only have turned your mind into the wrong channel."

Indignation rose in Noren, but he curbed it, sensing that Stefred too must have suffered during the past weeks, that the decision he'd made had been difficult and costly. "You warned me that there were hazards I wasn't aware of," he said, "and I chose freely. I wouldn't have chosen to evade them even if I had known."

"No. That was your strength, Noren. That was why I believed that if the worst happened, in the end you'd come through."

"But I didn't," Noren said miserably. "I failed you, and if it hadn't been for the crash, I'd have done even worse damage."

There was a short silence; Stefred, on the verge of a reply, seemed to think better of it. Steeling himself to the inevitable, Noren asked, "What's to become of me now? I can't ever make amends—"

"For the loss of the aircar? No, all you can do is work toward a time when the building of more aircars will become possible."

A gesture, reflected Noren—yet a more positive one than his attempted martyrdom, which would not have accomplished its purpose either. Stefred had undoubtedly realized that no act of his could endanger the system; otherwise he'd have taken steps to confine him sooner. "Will I be isolated from the Technicians?" he inquired, wondering whether the chance of their believing a renegade would be thought great enough to matter.

"Certainly not, not unless you choose now to formally retract your recantation. And I don't think that can solve your problem."

"Can anything?"

234

"It depends on how much courage you have."

Bending his head, Noren mumbled, "Not as much as you gave me credit for; we've proved *that,* anyway."

"Really?" Levelly, as if control of his own feelings required effort, Stefred said, "The day you disappeared, Grenald spoke to me with more self-reproach than I have ever heard from anyone. He hadn't known you had cause to take his accusation seriously; he thought it so preposterous that you'd recognize it for what it was: a calculated challenge to your pride."

Astonished, Noren looked up as Stefred continued, "This may surprise you, but I think you've displayed a good deal of courage all the way along. I think you have enough to go on with what's been started. It will mean confronting some things that frighten you, but you've never wanted to escape that."

"Yes, I have," protested Noren shamefacedly. "I volunteered for another space flight, but when they turned me down I was—relieved. And besides, the space work is finished. We can hardly send the shuttle out again just on my account."

"Of course not. That isn't what I'm talking about."

Noren's skin prickled as he ventured, "There is one way, isn't there? A—a dream—" He found himself shaking, though he kept the tremor from his voice. "You could make it like that test one, without letting me share the recorder's thoughts."

"I could," Stefred agreed, "but I'm not sure it would be wise."

"You were lying, then. You don't think I'd be equal to it."

"I think you would be. As a matter of fact, you'd probably find it an anticlimax; you'd feel worse than ever about having once let space bother you. Controlled dreaming is a very useful technique, Noren, but it's not a substitute for

235

life, and in real life one can't go back. One must come to terms with the past without reliving it."

"You mean I've got to learn to trust myself . . . without proof."

"Yourself—and other things." Stefred smiled. "Since you're perceptive enough to see that, you don't need my help. Sometimes psychiatrists do use dreams as therapy, but in your case no therapy is called for. You're not mentally ill and you never have been. You simply have a mind daring enough to explore questions many people never face up to."

"Have you ever heard of anyone else being panicked by them?" Noren inquired grimly.

"If I say no," Stefred observed slowly, "you'll have the satisfaction of considering yourself a martyr to a unique concern for ultimate truth; and if I say yes, you may find comfort in the thought that you are not alone. Which way do you want it?"

"I want the facts, just as I always have," Noren asserted, caught off balance. "Are you asking whether I'd rather have you lie?"

"I'm suggesting that you think the situation through a little more objectively, Noren. Do you really suppose you're the only one of us to whom such questions have occurred?"

With startled chagrin, Noren read the facts from Stefred's face. "I can't be," he admitted in a low voice. "You knew; you must have been tormented by them yourself! Oh, Stefred, how could I have been so weak as to be thrown by it, and then to—to feel that the martyrdom of a public relapse would absolve me?"

"Think deeper," said Stefred relentlessly. "You couldn't control your feelings; to reproach yourself for them now is self-abasement. That's no solution either, and it doesn't become you, Noren."

After a long pause, Noren declared, "You're telling me that panic isn't uncommon. I was justifiably afraid, and

236

trying to cover it up was false pride."

Nodding, Stefred agreed, "The questions you framed are unanswerable, and to be terrified by that is a sign not of weakness but of strength. A weak person wouldn't have opened his mind to such terror. It hit you young, and hard, under circumstances in which you had nothing to hold to—that's the only difference between your experience and the one most Scholars eventually undergo."

"But then why—"

"Why didn't I enlighten you earlier? I couldn't have, Noren. It wouldn't have done any good; in this particular adventure one has to proceed at one's own risk, at one's own pace."

A trace of uncontrollable fear brushed Noren's mind again as he grasped what he was being asked to confront. "Questions that have no answers . . . Stefred, I don't see how I can ever face that! Before this happened—well, it was hard not knowing all I wanted to know, but I expected to learn it all in time; at least I thought the answers existed *somewhere*—"

"They do," Stefred said gently. "The fact that neither you nor any other human being can obtain all the answers doesn't mean they don't exist, any more than the fact that we can't see all the stars in the universe means those stars aren't there."

"And someday I'll just get used to being condemned to ignorance?" Noren demanded bitterly.

"Yes, one way or another. The easy way is to stop searching."

"I can't," retorted Noren with growing anger. "I—well, I still care about truth; I always have, and I'm not going to change."

"I'm glad to hear it," said Stefred dryly. "For a while the reports I was getting from the outpost had me worried."

Noren flushed, knowing he should have spotted the trap

before falling into it. "We know more than the people of the mother world once did," he mused, "yet if they'd just quit— Did they wonder about the sorts of things I do, too?" Even as he spoke, he realized that it was a foolish question. Of course they had. They must have, if they'd been intelligent enough to discover as much knowledge as they'd accumulated.

"The wisest had thoughts worth preserving about those things," Stefred told him, "thoughts you can study if you query the computers properly." Regretfully he admitted, "If I'd known that you visited the computers the day of the conference, I would not have let you go away unsatisfied. I was negligent there, Noren."

"You had enough to worry about that day without keeping track of me," Noren said. "Besides, the computers weren't telling me anything."

"That was because they are programmed to teach lessons that can't be learned in one short session," replied Stefred, "lessons that in your case proved more painful than was intended." He went on to explain, "The Founders knew that young Scholars would think of the computer complex as the repository of all truth, and must sooner or later be made aware of the distinction between *truth* and *fact*. They also knew that since the beginning of time the key to advancement of man's knowledge has lain not in discovering the right answers, but in discovering the right questions to ask. So in certain areas of inquiry—areas that a person doesn't explore until he is mature enough to grasp such ideas —they deliberately refrained from programming leading responses. They didn't expect any Scholar to leave the City, of course; and given time, you would have persisted until you caught on."

"Is that what you meant when you said I'd have access to a kind of knowledge that would help?"

"No," Stefred declared. "I wasn't referring to the com-

238

puters then. You won't understand what I meant until you attain such knowledge for yourself."

*

Noren went to the computer room; he sat at a console and calmly, carefully, phrased his questions: not WHAT IS LIFE'S MEANING? but WHAT HAVE MEN THOUGHT ABOUT LIFE'S MEANING? . . . not WHY WERE THE SIX WORLDS DESTROYED? but TO WHAT CAUSE DID MEN OF THE PAST ATTRIBUTE UNPREVENTABLE DESTRUCTION? He stayed there until long past the hour of Orison, and by then he realized that the study of what men had written on these subjects would absorb not mere days, but years. Yet he had seen enough to know certain things.

He knew that others had suffered as he had, and that there was no way to escape it except by giving up the search.

He knew that there were two paths one could follow if one were willing to give up: one could decide it was all too futile to bother with, or one could fool oneself into thinking that one had already found the answers. Some men had done that. Some, in fact, had felt such a great need to convince themselves of what they'd found that whenever anybody appeared whose answers were different, they'd fought over it. If they'd been powerful men with many followers, the fights had, at times, turned into wars.

But Noren also knew that there'd been men who had not given up. They had recognized mysteries that they could not resolve and had borne it; they'd gone on gathering the bits and pieces of truth available, in full knowledge that they would fail to assemble the whole pattern.

And he knew that these men had been sustained only by faith.

Their faith hadn't always been called a religion. Sometimes it had; but many, particularly the later ones, had simply trusted that there *was* a pattern without using any symbols for the elements beyond their grasp. For the most

239

part, such people had not been in a predicament as difficult as the Scholars'. Those facing adversity had tended to find symbols indispensable.

Noren thought back to the dreams in which he had become the First Scholar, remembering the painful yet triumphant time while he lay dying. For years the First Scholar had sought symbols; he had, Noren realized abruptly, sought them not only for his people's comfort but for his own. WHAT WAS THE FIRST SCHOLAR'S PERSONAL RELIGION? he keyed in, perplexed.

THE FIRST SCHOLAR WROTE NOTHING ABOUT THAT, responded the computer. IT IS BEST UNDERSTOOD FROM HIS RECORDED MEMORIES.

But aside from the idea for the Prophecy, the recordings had contained nothing of this, at least not unless one counted the First Scholar's sureness that a way for mankind to survive permanently would be found. Noren perceived that this surety, which had been so puzzling in the light of his scientific knowledge, must indeed be counted as faith; yet that wasn't enough. If questions about *why* instead of *how* occurred to all wise and courageous men, they must certainly have occurred to the First Scholar. No such questions had troubled him during the dreams.

He returned to Stefred. "The dreams I had before my recantation were edited," he declared, "to conceal the First Scholar's plan for choosing successors. Later I experienced them in a more complete form. Was that edited, too? Is there a third version?"

"Yes," Stefred admitted, "for those who request it; and it's a more constructive thing to go through than another dream of space would be. But if I were you, Noren, I'd wait a while. Wait till you understand what happened to you more thoroughly, because something quite similar will happen in those dreams."

"You mean it happened to *him?*" There had been a gap

240

of many years in the dreams, Noren recalled, and he had never been told exactly what the First Scholar had undergone during the interim.

"I've said before that his mind was very like yours," Stefred replied simply, "and after all, he had witnessed the destruction of the worlds he knew."

"But he went on to create the Prophecy . . . and it—it meant more to him than a way to give people hope. It symbolized his whole attitude toward the universe! If anyone had faith in the future, he had."

"Did you suppose he was born with it? Some people are—people like Talyra, for instance—and their faith is entirely valid. Those who are born to question must find it through experience."

Noren swallowed. "Is there any chance, do you think, that I—" He broke off, embarrassed by the strange, compassionate look Stefred gave him. *There isn't,* he thought, *and he doesn't want to hurt me.* "Only you can be the judge of that," Stefred answered, and Noren left without asking whether one could live without faith indefinitely.

He found Brek waiting for him in their old room, and it was apparent that he wanted to talk. "I—I messed things up pretty thoroughly," Noren said after an awkward silence, knowing that any attempt at specific apology would be too weak. "I don't expect you to understand—"

"It's not that," Brek said quickly. "We've both done things we're sorry for, and they're past. Only there's something else." He paced nervously from one side of the cubicle to the other. "I wish we could go back to sharing the same ideas, but—well, there's something I've got to tell you, something *you* won't understand, and that you'll probably despise me for. I can't help it. In this I've got to make my own decision."

Puzzled, Noren stood patiently while Brek paused with his back turned and then, with quiet determination, an-

241

nounced straightforwardly, "I'm assuming the robe tomorrow."

Noren's initial amazement gave way to surprise at his obtuseness. Of course. Brek had not been born to question; though he'd defied injustice and had balked at accepting the seemingly privileged status of a Scholar, once those obstacles proved unreal, there was no barrier to his becoming a priest. He would be a good one. "I don't despise you," Noren declared. "I—I think I envy you, Brek."

"Envy me—you?" Brek burst out. "But Noren, that's crazy! If you no longer feel that commitment's wrong, why don't you wear the robe yourself?"

Why didn't he? Because there was more to it than right or wrong, Noren thought unhappily. Priesthood was not merely a matter of committing oneself to certain ethics and certain actions. A priest must know more than science could teach him. Brek could represent that other knowledge—the kind one must attain for oneself—without hypocrisy; he himself could not.

"I'm unfit," he said in a low voice, "and anyway, as a relapsed heretic, I've forfeited the right."

"Did Stefred tell you that?"

"He didn't have to."

"It's not true," Brek contended. "Commitment concerns only the future, and you're no more a relapsed heretic now than I am." He spoke with cool assurance, and for the first time, except during that one exchange made in anger, he'd contradicted Noren directly. Their roles had been reversed, Noren realized; Brek did not need his guidance any more.

"Noren," Brek went on slowly, "there's another thing I think you ought to know. It's none of my business what's passed between you and Stefred—"

"No," declared Noren firmly. "It isn't."

"But he risked a lot for you, and since he's not likely to mention it, I've got to. The man I heard it from must have had that in mind when he didn't pledge me to silence."

"Risked?" Noren inquired in bafflement. "How?"

"By not ordering you recalled from the outpost."

It was true, Noren thought, that except for the promise not to force him, such a move would have been natural; Stefred had known what was troubling him and must have had a fairly good idea of how he would react. "I suppose so," he admitted despondently. "I might not have gotten people to fight the system, but if I'd been killed trying, the scientific talent everyone's had such fine hopes for would have been lost."

"Don't belittle it. It's important to others if not to you, and he took a big gamble. But more than that, he staked his own career; the issue was raised in the executive council, and he told them that if they reversed his decision, he'd resign as department head."

"But *why?*" Noren gasped.

"That was his only recourse; he could see he was about to be outvoted."

"I mean why should he go to such lengths to keep his word? I'd have released him; I'd have come back voluntarily if I'd known." With chagrin, he remembered how Emet, just after an executive council meeting, had asked him to remain in the City for his friends' sake.

"I'm in no position to judge," Brek said, "but I think there was more to it than the fact that he'd promised. The others all wanted to help you, but Stefred felt you should be let alone. And he thought you were better off outside —that if you stayed, you'd redeem yourself."

Then he miscalculated, Noren reflected, and such a great miscalculation was scarcely to be believed of Stefred. Yet it was either that . . . or Stefred still knew more than he was telling.

*

He did not want to see Talyra, for he knew that when he did he must break their betrothal. He would not do so publicly until the child was born, if there was to to be a child;

243

but he could no longer let her think there was hope of their marrying. Nor could they go on as they had begun in the mountains; the joy of it could not last. His burdens had been set aside then; now they were back, and in time those burdens would crush their love, for he could not keep up a convincing pretense of happiness. Talyra had put up with his dark moods too long already, and she deserved better. He would not have her stay with him out of sympathy.

All the next day he avoided her by remaining inside the Hall of Scholars, but he had to attend vespers since Brek was to preside, as it was customary for the newly committed to do. There was little ceremony attached to commitment; one simply signed the official roll book and then, the same evening, donned the blue robe and appeared to Technicians as a priest. The service was no different than it was when conducted by a Scholar who had been doing it regularly for years. No special notice was taken except by one's friends.

Noren purposely delayed his arrival until the last moment, so that when he approached Talyra the hymn had started and she had no chance to speak. He did not intend to touch her, but as Brek mounted the platform he found himself reaching for her hand. She would be astonished, of course, and perhaps flustered; he must not add to her bewilderment by failing to greet her with affection, though his throat ached so that he could not sing.

The others' voices resounded through the courtyard; then, in the hush that followed, Brek began the invocation. ". . . *The Mother Star is our source and our destiny, the wellspring of our heritage. . . .*" Talyra's eyes were raised devoutly, so she had not noticed yet; but at the familiar voice she turned to look, lips parted in awe. Noren pressed her fingers. ". . . *It is our life's bulwark. . . .*" Brek spoke with utmost sincerity, and he was not talking about the Six Worlds' sun alone. He had seen life in a way that he himself could not, Noren thought wistfully. It would be nice to go on believing that he could not take that view because he

244

was too honest to accept false comfort, but real honesty told him that doing so would be a greater self-delusion. What Brek had attained was the result not of blindness, but of vision.

"I'm so glad for him," Talyra said when the service was over and they walked hand in hand across the dusky courtyard under three orange moons. "I sometimes wondered if he was a candidate—I mean, his having been a Technician outside and all. You must have suspected, too. Oh, I know we mustn't speak of people's backgrounds," she added hastily at Noren's frown. "But aren't you curious about how they chose him?"

Talyra did not know that Brek had been a heretic, of course; though everyone in the Inner City was aware that some of the Scholars were former heretics, the Technicians had no reason to suspect that they all were. Past lives were not mentioned, and she wouldn't even have known that he was a Technician by birth if she hadn't seen him at Noren's trial. Nor would she ever learn that he'd been a Scholar before he assumed the robe. "The choice does not lie with the Scholars alone," Noren told her. "The role of High Priest must be earned, but it must also be chosen by the candidate himself; that much is no secret."

"Did you know when we were in the mountains that he wanted it?"

"No," Noren declared, "I didn't."

They sat on a low stone bench in the shadowy triangle between three towers, and Talyra caressed his face fondly, expectantly. Noren kissed her, but he dared not do so with passion, and he knew that she was baffled. With sorrow he began, "Darling, I have to tell you . . . I've learned that permission for me to marry can't be granted. There was . . . well, the aircar, you see—"

"But that was an accident! Surely they wouldn't punish you for it!"

"No . . . but I shouldn't have been in that aircar at all, you

245

know. It's not a matter of punishment, but of—consequences. There's more to it that I can't explain—"

"You needn't," Talyra said reassuringly. "In time they'll absolve you, and meanwhile, we'll just go on being betrothed."

He should have known that it would not work, Noren thought. He must be cruel to spare her the greater hurt of seeing their love wither from his failure to find contentment. "Talyra," he said painfully, "we shouldn't have done what we did . . . those nights. Now that we have, you see, there's no stopping, no going back to the way we were before—"

She shrank away, wounded. "Do you want to stop?"

"Of course I don't, but you—well, you should, because you'd be better off with someone like Brek than with me."

"I'm not in love with Brek!" she exclaimed, shocked.

"I don't mean him specifically. He's not in love with you, either; do you think I'd give you up for his sake? What I'm trying to say is . . . he has the same outlook you do, and there are plenty of others who have. I'm not one of them. You've told me that yourself. I—I can't make you happy, Talyra."

"Can I make *you* happy?"

"If you can't, no girl ever can. But it's just the same now as when we said goodbye in the village. 'You are what you are,' you said, 'and our loving each other wouldn't make any difference.' "

She was silent; then, turning back to him and taking his hands between hers, she murmured, "I also said that someday you'd find the spirit of the Mother Star had been with you."

"Someday may be a long way off, Talyra."

"It's already here! Do you think I could watch you week after week, loving you, and not notice when it came?" At his confusion, she shook her head, laughing softly. "Darling, you're blind. You're still off in the sky somewhere, dreaming; you haven't looked at the world since it happened!"

246

"Since what happened?"

"Do you really not know that during those days in the mountains you stopped being afraid?"

"I resigned myself to dying, that's all."

"No," she told him. "Not to dying—to living! You were never afraid of death, and I think that when we crashed, you . . . you almost wanted to die. I won't ask why. That doesn't matter any more, because all of a sudden you were aware of the Mother Star's protection. You knew that however things turned out, it wouldn't fail us, and then, when you stopped worrying, you were at peace with the world. You were whole and free."

"I wish that were true," he said sincerely. "It's not, though. I didn't have any hope of our being saved, the way you and Brek did."

"But Noren," she protested, "you *did,* underneath. All along you did. Why else wouldn't you have drunk more water?"

He stared at her, his mind reeling. He'd asked himself why he should abstain and had obtained no answer. Nevertheless, he had refrained from exceeding the safe limit; could he have done so without any underlying purpose? The water would not have harmed him; it would have been damaging only to any children he might subsequently father. If he had been totally without hope—if he'd been sure that Talyra would not live long enough to bear a child, nor he to love again—he would have had no reason to suffer thirst. He would have had no more qualms about drinking than in the days when he had believed the High Law was groundless.

Yet he had known positively that there was no logical chance of survival. He had climbed the cliff where the sphere lay only to please Talyra; he'd not thought it could possibly be of any use. That it might lead to rescue had not occurred to any of them. If underneath he'd had knowledge not born of logic, knowledge that had driven him to struggle against such odds, wasn't it conceivable that the wish to continue his work rose from the same source? And wasn't it valid to hope that the research might also succeed against all logic?

Through experience, Stefred had said. Those who are born to question can attain faith only through experience.

Talyra sat looking at him, waiting; and all at once Noren knew that the gulf between them no longer existed. Perhaps it had never been as unbridgeable as he'd believed. "You saw what I lacked before I did," he whispered, "and you saw what I'd gained before I did, too." He took her in his arms and there was no need for either of them to say anything more.

*

"I'm still awfully confused," he admitted to Stefred the next morning, not yet able to acknowledge, even in his own mind, the reason he'd sought him out. "How could she have known something I didn't know about myself, when so much has been kept secret from her?"

"You've no doubt that she was right?"

"None."

"Then be thankful that she had the wit and the spirit to tell you what you would not have accepted from me." With warmth, Stefred went on, "I could have given you the key when we talked two days ago. You were so bewildered, so torn by problems you weren't able to resolve, that it was hard to remain silent. But a lecture wouldn't have helped. You needed to fit the pieces together—which you can do now, if you try."

There was a long pause; then Noren said thoughtfully, "All that time . . . when I held back from declaring myself a relapsed heretic . . . was it not cowardice after all? Was it that I still believed the Prophecy without knowing I did? How *could* I—"

248

"Noren," Stefred interrupted, "have you ever wondered why you and Talyra love each other?"

"Why—why we just *do!* A thing like that isn't something to be analyzed, Stefred."

"Certain feelings can't be," Stefred observed dryly. "A scientist's ability to analyze is a priceless gift, Noren, but it sometimes gets in the way. However, in this case my question wasn't meant as an object lesson."

Smiling, he continued, "You and Talyra share something deeper than a casual love affair. Why? Back in the village you were little more than children, and you didn't know each other any better than villagers usually do at the time of betrothal; it wasn't surprising that you were in love then. But when you parted, you considered yourselves unalterably opposed on an issue very basic to your view of life. You expected to be separated permanently, and you both had opportunity to meet others whose beliefs were more compatible. Isn't it rather strange that your love endured?"

"You mean how could she go on caring for someone who scorned what she values most? I—I don't know, Stefred."

"I'd have thought you'd be asking how you could go on caring for someone who valued what you scorned."

Noren contemplated it. "There's just one answer," he said wonderingly. "I didn't scorn it as much as I thought I did, and—and she sensed that. Perhaps I sensed it, too, underneath; perhaps I wanted it all along."

"You had it all along."

"Yet I was so sure I valued only the truth," Noren declared ruefully.

"And you were right. Not all truth can be expressed in scientific terms, Noren, not even by us; and from the beginning you valued the whole truth, including the parts unavailable to you. At your trial and inquisition you said so specifically."

"I assumed you could make it available if you chose,"

Noren reflected, "and then when you gave me access to your own sources of knowledge—" He broke off, realizing with chagrin that although as a boy he had questioned what he'd been taught about the Scholars' supernatural supremacy, he'd never doubted that they possessed the answers to all mysteries. To find that they did not—and could not—had shaken him in a way he hadn't thoroughly understood, for despite himself, he had clung to a naive picture in which they and their City symbolized the knowledge he craved. When the City's computers failed him, he had held all the harder to the one thing left that was sure: mathematics. He'd been afraid to believe the Prophecy after mathematics discredited it! That would have meant admitting that math itself was not absolute. . . .

"I couldn't give up my symbol any more than Talyra could give up hers," he concluded. "I needed one."

"So do we all," Stefred replied.

Startled, Noren stared at him, then turned slowly to survey the room, the tower's view, the far-off outline of the Tomorrow Mountains where for a time he had abandoned despair and fear. Countless things meshed into a previously invisible pattern, a pattern that made unexpected sense of them. "I—I think I see now," he said at last. "The Mother Star is a symbol of . . . the unknowable. Not just to villagers and Technicians who can't know our secret, but to us, too, because there's so much *we* can't know."

Stefred nodded. "There is no magical virtue in that particular symbol, and some Scholars prefer to adopt their own, or one of those used on the Six Worlds. But symbolism is most powerful when it is shared, and on the whole, those of us who have inherited that of the Prophecy find it more meaningful than anything else we could employ."

"And priesthood is more than receiving people's homage—"

"A High Priest does not receive. He gives. He gives hope

250

and faith to people who might otherwise have neither."

"But in order to do that," Noren mused, "he has to find those things himself. I never thought I would, but now . . . oh, Stefred, if it weren't that I set out to destroy them—"

"You wouldn't have destroyed anyone's faith, Noren."

"I suppose nobody would have listened, but if it hadn't been for the crash I'd have tried. At any rate, I'd have destroyed the prospect of my accomplishing something important in the research. Why should a chance accident like that determine the course of a person's life—perhaps even of . . . a world's history?"

"Look at it the other way around," Stefred suggested, "and ask yourself why the accident occurred."

Noren frowned. If anything was unanswerable, that was, yet he had been at the controls. . . . "You mean—I didn't really want to do what I was planning to?"

"That's one possibility. There are others, none of which depend upon chance. Neither of us will ever know what forces were operative, Noren. This much is certain, though: when brought to the test, you would not have chosen the destruction of hope over a gamble on the truth that lies beyond your vision."

"How can you be sure?"

"You had the power to destroy Talyra's," Stefred pointed out, "and you didn't use it."

Stunned once again, Noren sat motionless while the implications grew clear in his mind. He'd known he owed Talyra honesty, known she did not want false comfort, yet he hadn't been able to speak truth as he saw it. This too had been the result of inward knowledge! This too had been not a betrayal of truth, but an expression of his real belief.

He had not seen the analogy. He had not stopped to think that it was all or nothing: the affirmation of life, of survival, for the world of the future as well as for Talyra and himself —or a narrow view of "truth" that in permitting him to

251

repudiate the Prophecy publicly, would have crushed his buried hope for their lives and for that of their child.

"You were sure beforehand," he said in wonder.

"Of course. During your inquisition I studied your subconscious feelings; could I have done that without seeing your underlying faith? Would I have exposed you to emotional peril if I had not seen it? For that matter, I wouldn't have judged you a potentially gifted scientist if I hadn't believed that in due time you would plunge beyond our knowledge, just as you plunged beyond the villagers'—and to take such a plunge, one must sense that there's something ahead."

"You—you had faith in *me*. And you knew that sooner or later, as long as I was outside the City, some kind of test would arise; that's why you insisted on letting me stay."

"It was the only way for you to regain your self-trust," Stefred agreed. "Once you'd begun to doubt, the thing had to be carried through to the end."

All or nothing. . . . Very softly Noren declared, "Commitment's not something you decide on . . . you just find you're already committed. And when you put on the robe you're merely offering to share what you've found."

"Are you ready to offer that, Noren?"

"Yes," Noren replied, overcome by emotions for which no speech seemed adequate. "Yes, I guess I am."

*

Alone, he stood in the dim assembly room under the glittering sunburst, looking up with reverence he had not felt before; and the once-frightening words echoed in his mind as words of comfort. "*. . . There is no surety save in the light that sustained our forefathers; no hope but in that which lies beyond our sphere; and our future is vain except as we have faith. Yet we are strong in the faith that as those of the past were sustained, so shall we be also: what must be sought shall be found, what was lost shall be regained,*

252

what is needful to life will not be denied us. And though our peril be great even unto the last generation of our endurance, in the end man shall prevail; and the doors of the universe shall once again be thrown open to him. . . ."

Noren's eyes blurred with tears. He had never been so moved. There had been excitement and sometimes pleasure in things he had done during his first term in the City, but never this particular kind of happiness. Lately he had felt that for him no happiness was possible. How incredible, he thought, that in the space of a few hours he could be so changed.

The new peace of mind was not permanent, he knew. There would still be bad times. Yet there would be satisfactions, too—in his studies; his work; his growing comprehension of all he must absorb if he was to contribute significantly to the research upon his return to the outpost beyond the mountains; in the love he shared with Talyra; in the children they would give to a world that would someday be transformed. Wasn't that how it had always been, for everyone?

Man will survive, he thought, because men *do* survive: not all men, under all conditions, but some at least to carry forward the heritage that is ours. In our natural environment instinct ensures that—the instinct that enabled us to evolve from mere animals into human beings with the mind and spirit to advance—and in an alien world where evolution can't progress normally, our instinct guides us in different ways. We do what we must. Hating it, knowing it involves evil and injustice that ought not to exist, the human race lives on in the only way it can; but we who recognize the evils go on working to abolish them, just as our forebears did. It is all part of the same pattern.

Crossing the room to the small closed alcove he'd never before entered, he knelt at the low shelf where, beneath a miniature sunburst, a thick, well-worn book rested: the roll book of the committed. Noren leafed through it with awe, for on the first page, under the faded legend, "We the undersigned do hereby hold ourselves answerable for the preservation of human life on this alien planet and for the restoration of our people's birthright," was inscribed the seldom-pronounced name of the First Scholar himself; and below it, other strange names with even stranger dates: birthdates in four figures—Six Worlds' reckoning—with the Year One listed as date of commitment. That had been before the Prophecy was conceived; further on was written a formal pledge to work toward the keeping of its promises and to fulfill the solemn obligations of priesthood. And then came page after page of two- and three-digit dates opposite the names of those who had upheld the trust through all the years since the Founding.

At the last, on a still half-empty sheet, Brek's signature stood out, clear and fresh and decisive, showing no trace of hesitancy. Noren signed below it with a firm hand, wondering how many others would do so before the need for such commitment was past.

There would never be an end, he realized as he rose and left the alcove. The book would be filled and a new one begun; the Time of the Prophecy would come and go; but there would always be priests because no matter how much future Scholars might learn, some things would remain unknowable. It would not be the same once the Prophecy was brought to fulfillment. Scholar status would carry neither rank nor privilege, and heresy would cease to be regarded as a crime; people who wished to offer themselves would apply voluntarily for acceptance. They would no longer be the only ones engaged in scientific investigation. Yet the search for truth—all truth—being the proper function of a priest, such work would naturally remain one of their prime concerns. They would begin to look ahead to the time when interstellar travel must be resumed, for the world would

254

never have rich resources, and once people learned what their forebears of the Six Worlds had possessed, they would look to their religion for a new promise. And would not the Scholars give them one, one less specific than the Prophecy, yet just as sure in the sense that if it was not fulfilled, mankind would someday die? No race could endure forever confined to a single world; knowing that, the Scholars would be committed to the discovery and mastery of still another alien environment. Someday they themselves might man the exploratory starships. Someday, perhaps, they might meet face to face the Visitors who'd made the mysterious sphere. . . .

That evening, as the hour of vespers approached, Noren drew the blue robe from the storage compartment beneath his bunk and unfolded it, remembering the day it had been given to him, the day of his recantation; and he was suddenly conscious of the distance he'd come since then. He would stand before people now not as a despised rebel, a hero in his own eyes if not in theirs, but as an avowed representative of their most cherished traditions. It was odd, Noren thought, that he no longer seemed to mind.

Carrying the robe with him, he went back to the Hall of Scholars, for though he had neither time nor desire to eat anything, he hoped he might speak to Brek. He encountered him coming out of the refectory; they gripped hands wordlessly, and both were aware that the temporary rift between them need never be mentioned. "I'll find Talyra," Brek said, "and tell her you want to see her before the service."

Noren nodded gratefully. He was barred from disclosing his status before he appeared robed, which by tradition he must not do until vespers, and the sight of him so attired would stun Talyra; it would be best if they could exchange a few private words as he emerged from the Hall of Scholars. Returning to the tower's vestibule, he stood just inside its door till he saw her approaching. Then he flung the robe over his shoulders and, feeling its full weight for the first time, he walked forward to meet her.

She inclined her head in the automatic gesture of respect, not yet recognizing him; then as he drew near, she froze in startled disbelief. Noren waited, stricken by fear that this revelation would turn her love to deference. But the face she raised to him was radiant, and when he opened his arms she came unhesitatingly.

"Talyra," he said, "I'm free now! The waiting's over—" His heart lifted at the thought that soon, perhaps within a few days, she would come to him in the festive red skirts of a bride.

Nestling close to him, enveloped by the blue folds of the robe, she whispered, "It was this all the time? Not the heresy, but—this?"

"It was both," he admitted, saying all he would ever be able to say. "They were—well, mixed up."

"And the things you suffered, the ones you couldn't tell me about, were . . . preparation?"

"You might put it that way."

"I should have guessed," Talyra murmured. "I should have guessed when I first heard that villagers could become Scholars; you wanted so much to learn everything they knew, I should have known that once they saw what kind of person you are, they'd let you."

"You had no cause, since I wasn't permitted to reveal any of it. There will always be secrets I can't reveal. That's why our wedding had to be postponed: it wouldn't be fair for a girl to suddenly find herself married to someone who is bound by such great secrecy."

"Did you think I'd object, darling?"

"Not really. But it was your right to be warned before choosing."

"As if I'd choose to leave you! But that you've chosen

256

me . . . I'm honored. After the way I doubted your faith—"

"I doubted it, too," he told her. "If it weren't for you, Talyra, I'd still be doubting. They taught me secrets; they are teaching me to do a Scholar's work; to that I was sealed long ago. But I wasn't ready for priesthood until you opened my eyes."

They embraced quickly; then she walked by his side to the semicircular platform around which Technicians and Scholars were gathering. The dusk was clear, and the stars that sparkled overhead seemed uncommonly bright. He could gaze at them undismayed, Noren realized with gladness. Their image would not haunt him any more.

Around him, the assembled people had begun the vesper hymn. Just before he released her hand Talyra asked softly, "Will you bless me, Noren?"

"The blessing is our heritage from the Mother Star," he replied gravely, "and is not mine to bestow. It falls upon all of us; I merely proclaim what I've found to be true."

Mounting the steps, Noren looked out at familiar upturned faces: Brek's, Stefred's, those of many whom he could always count as friends. To his surprise he felt no nervousness; and though he held the Book of the Prophecy, he had no need to consult it, for the words came readily to his lips. ". . . *So long as we believe in it, no force can destroy us, though the heavens themselves be consumed.* . . ." He glanced up at the surrounding towers, envisioning the starships that would someday be rebuilt, as he extended his hands to pronounce the sacerdotal blessing: *"May the spirit of the Mother Star abide with you.* . . ." And with me, he thought reverently. May I hold fast to that upon which we all must draw. Talyra smiled at him, glowing with love and pride; and Noren knew joy that his faith was no less genuine than hers.

Sylvia Louise Engdahl has been fascinated by the idea of space exploration and life on other planets since she was twelve. But junior high school, high school, working for an AB degree at the University of California at Santa Barbara, teaching school for a year, and then developing and testing programs for air defense computers kept her from writing about space for many years. Now, however, Miss Engdahl is settled in Portland, Oregon, where she is able to devote full time to her books and her ideas about space. She is the author of *Enchantress from the Stars, Journey Between Worlds, The Far Side of Evil,* and *This Star Shall Abide,* for which *Beyond the Tomorrow Mountains* is a completion and a second half.